HER

A NOVEL

BY

CHERRY MUHANJI

AFTERWORD
MATTIE U. RICHARDSON

aunt lute books — san francisco

Aunt Lute Books
P.O. Box 410687
San Francisco, CA 94141
www.auntlute.com

Cover and text design: Amy Woloszyn
Cover photograph: Haruko, San Francisco
Cover photograph makeup: Kathleen Bifulco
DeeAnne Davis' tuxedo donated by La Rosa Formalwear

Senior Editor: Joan Pinkvoss
Copyeditors: Martha Davis and DeeAnne Davis (1st edition)
Production: Eileen Anderson, Elizabeth Brodersen, Claire Drucker, Nancy Fishman, Kathleen Wilkinson (1st Edition);   Chelsea Adewunmi, Shay Brawn, Marisa Crawford, Andrea de Brito, Gina Gemello, Anisha Gidvani, Shahara Godfrey, Andrea Blythe (2nd edition)

This book was funded in part by a grant from the National Endowment for the Arts.

This is a work of fiction. Names, characters, places, and incidents are either the product of the author's imagination or are used fictitiously, and any resemblance to actual persons, living or dead, business establishment, events, or locales is entirely coincidental.

Library of Congress Cataloging-in-Publication Data

Muhanji, Cherry.
   Her : a novel / by Cherry Muhanji ; afterword by Mattie U.
Richardson. -- 2nd ed.
      p. cm.
   ISBN-13: 978-1-879960-72-5 (pbk. : alk. paper)
   ISBN-10: 1-879960-72-9 (pbk. : alk. paper)
   1. African American women--Fiction. 2. Detroit (Mich.)--Fiction.
   3. Nineteen sixties--Fiction. 4. Lesbians--Fiction.   I. Title.
   PS3563.U367H4 2006
   813'.54--dc22

                                                    2006028449

Printed in the U.S.A. on acid-free paper
Second Edition 10-9-8-7-6-5-4-3-2-1

ACKNOWLEDGEMENTS

To all the women at the Women's Resource and Action Center in Iowa City who, rain or shine, came faithfully to hear me read portions of this manuscript every Black History Month for three years; to Arkela Revels for language; to Bobbi Barlow who gave me permission to fictionalize an account in her life; to MariAnna Sierra.

Special acknowledgement to Ilene Alexander; my son, Tracy Cherry; Cheryl Clarke; Mae Henderson; Egyirba High; Jasmine Love; Papusa Molina; Peter Nazareth; Joan Pinkvoss; and David Williams.

To Jonathan Walton

who,
if he had lived,
would find this book more than interesting

ONE

⁓⌘⁓

Houses collect things: old newspapers, junk mail–Her. She had come under cover of night, a stowaway with Brother's child tucked in the bottom of her belly. He had stuck his Alabama dirt farmer finger in her Dee-troit urban-ghetto Ford Motor Company hi-yellah hole and she had went from *somewhere* to nowhere, somehow. She understood somewhere. It had been up against her house, inside the 1959 DeSoto with the fluid drive, under a blanket at Belle Isle, even at the foot of the Ambassador Bridge that spanned the Detroit River. But it was being nowhere somehow that was confusing.

Brother's house grew people: real cousins, arthritic aunts, nervous uncles, and Aunt Marian's boy, the one with the ti-tongue. They had moved North, each trailing a dream from behind, like a peacock in mating season, in full color, from plantation to plant in one easy step. The house collected its inhabitants in bundles, separating them into rooms where the women moaned at midnight–not from the men jacking off inside them, but from the remembered dirt between their toes, from the smell of honeysuckle that fondles the nose, sending sweet orgasms into the mind. "Sweet Jee-sus," the women said, while the men smiled and grunted in their sleep, and they sat behind the glow of cigarettes way past the midnight hour.

The young man stood before his mother. He was tall–angular–and not completely out of his boyishness. He had an overkept butter, one that he had to touch up every two weeks, and the unmistakable beginnings of a moustache. His arms dangled from his body and his legs seemed to grow out of his waist. Everything about him was disproportioned—even his manner, which was what disturbed his mother when he announced much too proudly, "This her, Momma."

"I know who she is, but what she wont?"

Brother hadn't expected the question and the young girl didn't understand it. She heard it roll toward her, enter the stream flowing in and filtering out through her mind, but she wouldn't undress and bathe. Best to ignore it. She knew she wanted sweet potato pie, red velvet furniture, and Brother's finger in her hole. But his mother didn't ask "what she wont?" like she was gonna run out and get the pie and buy the furniture and special order Brother's finger. Miss Charlotte suspected her of something. No, "what she wont?" lifted her skirt, like Bobby Jenkins did in the first grade, intent on enjoying the mystery, if not the meaning.

Her—the golden child, all fuzz and peach blossom. She sensed, as she stood before the height, weight, and breadth of this dark and richly black woman, that she had better find the open door, move through it, and leave *this* reign uninterrupted.

Brother knew, as Miss Charlotte said all the time, "the hi-yellahs ain't worth much." That was why he wanted one. He also knew he would be king of the mountain he humped because he'd own the mountain.

"The hi-yellahs," Miss Charlotte would rage on, "plumes and fumes over the toilet water, but not over the toilet."

When he told her he was gonna do the good and right thing and give the baby his name, Miss Charlotte declared, "Damn that, how ya know it yo's? Why ya gon' pay such a price fo' bein' a man?" she asked, suspecting, but never really understanding this shifting and weighted son of hers. "Ain't no man ever cared 'bout my black ass, not even King Solomon."

Brother knew that was simply not true. His father's feelings were everywhere in the house. They were left on the mantel; they languished atop the doorsill and were finger-painted in every room in the old house—except the parlor. But his mother took no note and when she swept, sudded, and rinsed, they floated away, only to return later, huddled like frightened children at the entrance to the parlor door.

Every Saturday morning, his father surrendered up a new assortment of feelings, like hot air balloons pressing against the ceiling, as he recovered (and he was always recovering) from the slow death of Friday night. Saturday mornings he lay on the bed, head pounding, while Billie egged him on; her voice scratching lazily from the Victrola, *Ain't Nobody's Business if I Do.*

"Chile, come here."

The young girl moved forward, eyes down, and stood before the older woman sitting grandly in a wing-backed chair with lace doilies plastered starch-stiff against the arms and the top of the chair's back.

"Why, ya just a little shit!…What ya called?"

"Sunshine," Brother quickly interjected, irritated that his mother had not cared to remember her name. The girl moved to say something but thought better of it.

"What yo' Momma say 'bout this hurryin'-up marryin' ya'll done done, *Sun*shine?"

The young girl lifted a bright clear sunflower face, pierced by gray-green eyes that immediately entered into combat with Miss Charlotte's black black irises—ebony lanterns bent on destruction. Sunshine answered, "Momma's been quiet. Daddy does all the talking. He drove us downtown to face the judge."

"I be damn!"

Sunshine flushed red but remained mute. Her eyes watered but never wavered.

"What she say 'bout marryin' this sooty black boy of mine?" Miss Charlotte asked leaning forward, looking directly into those gray-green eyes, wedging the full size of her body between them, her own eyes glaring.

"Not much."

"Uh hum. Far as she concerned ya done misceg'nated." The word stung the air and Sunshine flinched. It had a bite—a snarling mouth. One she knew and had run from all her life—only to hear it again now in this unsuspecting place, growling out of the mouth of her brand-new mother-in-law, dissecting her like Milton Ware had done his frogs last semester in biology class.

"Who ya take after?"

"My daddy."

"Uh hum. Where yo' peoples from?"

"Detroit," Sunshine replied, aware that the older woman was really asking another question.

"I mean they *real* home, girl."

"Georgia."

"Yeah," Miss Charlotte said, smacking her lips and rubbing her hands together and moving back in her chair. "I can tell one every time. Ya one of 'em almost-tis," she said with a laugh, delighted with herself. "I bet yo' Momma married one too. Prayin' all the while she weren't gon' git no telltale throwback."

Brother shifted his weight again as Miss Charlotte eyed him, not with disgust as he suspected, but with wonder. Actually, she really didn't know him. Brother had spent his childhood wrapped securely in the starched skirts of King Solomon's mother, Gert, who reigned supreme over the boy while she was alive. He would breeze right past his mother with his cut finger or a brand-new friend on his way to Gert's room, where he remained sometimes till bedtime. Other times, the boy played alone in some lonesome corner of the downstairs with an imaginary friend in a friendly world made up as he went along. Despite a house full of cousins and somebody's children visiting all the time, he preferred his world peopled by Gert and his imaginary friend Jolie, and by Bible-story picture books given to him by his grandmother.

Gert had raised two sons, King Solomon and Sweet Bubba. She had little concern for women, and eyed Charlotte with disdain, as well as the rest of Charlotte's sisters. Her job, as she saw it, had been to raise her boys to understand what it meant to be Black in a white world. In her mind, that meant to keep them tied up on the farm, too busy to notice what they were missing. Sweet Bubba was the first to run off. He ran to New York City and later went off to Paris, France, to fight the Kaiser. King Solomon hung on the longest "and was content," Gert said, "till he met that fancy woman of his, just back from New York herself, and she 'fixed' him—so help me God."

The next thing Gert knew he was moving her North to Detroit (something she never forgave him for)—leaving the land to make motorcars.

Since Gert's death, Brother had riveted his attention on his mother for the first time. His efforts to enter her life some five years ago were met with Charlotte's long stares, her impatience, and a long

series of indulgences that turned him from just plain bad to wicked—
so Lizzie, one of his aunts, was quick to say.

Brother's young wife continued to look inside the dark irises of
the older woman, who, unknown to the young girl, had dressed for
the occasion. Otherwise she would have worn her ever-present ban-
danna. Now she wore a nut-brown wig that framed her face in rust-
colored ringlets. Her face was covered by powder too light for her
complexion. And she had put on a rather uneventful dress, leaving
her house slippers on. But her voice, and especially her body movements, were rhythmic and synchronistic with the up and down movements of the black and gold dragon stenciled on the side of the porce-
lain coffee cup that moved from hand to mouth.

She looked over the rim of the coffee cup and asked, "So ya is in
trouble with yo' folks...especially yo' Momma, right?" She paused
briefly, waiting for a reaction, then busied herself pushing to one side
the lace doily on the mahogany end table just at her elbow. It gave
her some trouble as she tried more than once to safely land her
empty coffee cup on its smooth surface.

The daughter-in-law, having exceeded her level of interest,
slipped her hand inside Brother's, quietly directing him to go. Miss
Charlotte sat upright in her chair watching their exit, recognizing too
late that the child, in her calculated rudeness, had won this round.

She laughed, but just a little, as the pair of backs slipped through
the parlor door. Georgia niggahs beat Alabama's by a mile, she
thought. This boy done brought bad news into my house and brung
it right in my face. I bet her Momma (bless her heart) tried real hard
to make her into her own image. Now how come that ain't happened?

In the months to come, Miss Charlotte would reach into the
girl's "nowhere," toss her an easy rope, then let her drown, all in the
same breath, in the same sentence, and with the same sweet scorn.

"Let me rub yo' feets down with some camph'rated oil, chile."

"Thanks. I'm fine."

"Bettah gain you some weight, gal, that baby's gonna be po' as
Job's turkey."

"No need. I'm fine. Nobody eats for two anymore. It's not healthy for the mother or the baby."

"Men write them books ya read all the time, right? When one of 'um have a baby then they can write what a woman oughta do. Nothin' like a bone but a dog, chile. Meanwhile you need some meat on 'em bones. What ya wont, chile? A boy or a girl?"

Her move. Her chance. Like a flower waiting to be picked. The one planted among the mint and licorice roots. The one to draw through the nose. The special one, the one that women planted near the doorstep.

"I want what Brother wants."

Miss Charlotte, just for a moment, seemed wounded but recovered quickly and replied with bridled annoyance, "I smell yo' soup scorchin', chile."

The house unpeeled its face at night and quietly placed it on the nightstand—musing, uncertain, like a prostitute who, taking off one silk stocking at a time, wonders about the john who can't get it up, sitting transfixed in the corner. Like Beverly, the Easter-Egg-Man, who was always transfixed but seldom in a corner, who found himself that way as he watched the roll of her hips and the slit of yellow thigh exposing sunrise.

"Is Beverly your real name?" she asked Easter-Egg-Man. He nodded *yes* making no sound.

"We always called you B.J. in school. I bet Beverly got you in trouble."

"It's the name she gave me."

"Who?"

"My Mo-thah," he drawled in a mocking tone.

"Why'd she do that to you?"

"She was a yellah bitch, and took it out... She screamed a lot. Till this day if I catch a bitch screaming at me I..." He suddenly stopped, shrugged his shoulders, and moved his attention back to the can of paint sitting between them in the hallway. "It's a slave name no diff'rent than you," he said matter-of-factly.

"But I don't have a boy's name like you have a girl's."

"It's still a slave name!" he exploded, slamming the paintbrush back in the can, causing some to splatter on her leg. "Git you some history, baby, if you think you know! The Man took us from the Mo-thah—Africa! Ya dig? Spooned us into the bottom of boats and figured they done got ovah... Understand? We was a people, baby...an AFRICAN people!" he continued, stopping between out-bursts, then exploding again, sending out billows and billows, "AFRICA! AFRICA! AFRICA! Can ya feel it? Can ya dig it?" Exasperated, his attention settled back on her. "You gotta reach, baby."

This niggah's crazy! she thought. And who is he, anyway? And why did he bother her? "You gotta reach" didn't make any sense to her. She had never thought of Africa as a place to reach for.

"Git some history, baby," he hissed this time. His eyes narrowed and widened and narrowed again. She took a step back as he made swallowing sounds. Unexpectedly, he stooped to finger the yellow paint that had splattered on her leg. Nervously, she stepped back again and his eyes drew her up—like a zipper, stopping at her belly.

"When that baby due?" The question continued zipping up her body, slowly, till it touched the tip of her mind—and melted there, making her helpless to acknowledge it. But the change of subject altered the timbre in the hallway, and the weight of his anger lifted, hovered, then drifted away. Leaving her to answer in spite of herself, "The doctor said Feb'rary, Miss Charlotte said March."

"What'd *you* say?" he asked.

Her move again. But no open door. She moved back to a safe place. "Well, I'm not sure."

Suddenly he exploded again, "Ya'll Miss Annes all the same. Open a niggah up with a whip or a smile, dependin' on! And then actin' like you ain't held him open and planted row and row of pussy up and down his mind. And when he come to harvest," he said, changing his voice to falsetto, "You Ofays holler rape!" Then he dropped his voice back down an octave and asked, almost musically, "Ya dig?"

The house let out a muffled cough and sat forward, knees pressed together, hem neatly tucked in place. It remembered with slow excite-ment the rub of the Easter-Egg-Man placing the palm of the paint-brush against the wall—moving up and down, up and down. With the slap of many licks, the house felt the beginning of a shiver, slight at first, then an increasing shudder. Each slap of the brush against the wall was slow and lingering; swish, swish, the brush moved, the sound steady and low, making a slow guttural sound with each stroke. Long yellow strokes of paint (for Miss Charlotte loved yellow) that covered its face, arms, legs, and thighs.

"Ya sleepin' in there?" Miss Charlotte asked, rapping on the bedroom door.

"I was."

"Why ya always holed up in here?"

The question was as fair as it was unfair. True, she had barricaded herself in the bridal bedroom—not getting on with the women in the old house as women do. On occasion, when she was caught by them—away from the small hot prison of the nuptial bedroom, in some other part of the house, usually the kitchen—she offered nothing but bits of information they didn't care about. What they wanted was a small joke, a laugh, a shared trauma, a piece of her—anything but information dumped on them like they wadn't grown folks already. And this offended them. The others, including Charlotte's two sisters, Lizzie and Laphonya, gave the child the benefit of the doubt because she was from the North and had that northern way of showing off: looking grown folks straight in the eyes, calling them by their first names, and never staying around long enough for them to have their say. But Charlotte didn't feel that way.

"Ya need to git up and walk that baby 'round," Miss Charlotte said, opening the door and stepping across the threshold. "Brother's warmin' up the car. Make sho' he pick me up by three."

"Easter-Egg-Man'll be workin' in here today. He'll move yo' stuff," Miss Charlotte announced.

"You don't mean in this room, do you?"

"He's careful...and he'll cover the bed."

"Not *today*, Miss Charlotte. I can't stand the fumes."

"I thought ya was *always* doin' just *fine*," the older woman shot back. "Then when?" Miss Charlotte demanded, pressing the issue further, testing for signs of some serious backbone from this scrawny intruder.

"After the baby's born."

"Don't ya want a nice clean room for the..."

"No."

Miss Charlotte smiled to herself but continued to loom above the young girl, the nut-brown wig framing a face covered with ginger-brown powder that was closer now to her skin tone but didn't quite reach to the edges—leaving an oval circle, giving her the dusty face of a colored clown.

Everything about Miss Charlotte was "almost." She was almost big, but not quite—more big-boned. She was almost full-figured but not quite that either. The eye was in danger of being hypnotized as it followed her surprisingly long neck that flowed into her spine and rippled downstream toward the magnificent scoop of her lower back. Once there, it stopped short, paused, and drifted on like a piece of sandalwood bobbing in the undercurrent of the river that moved in her hips. There was a leanness about those hips that pricked the mind in a secret way. They were ripe, loose like a young girl's, almost. Her lips were full too, but not so full that one gazed fixedly on them. The eye lingered, then wandered on, unable to reconcile the ginger-powdered face with the rest of her.

The slim-shouldered girl was conscious of Miss Charlotte watching her. She placed her hands under her belly, cradling it as she struggled to sit up in bed.

"Wheee! He gon' have a time gettin' out of ya!... See you take him fo' a walk today, ya hear?"

She hated it when Miss Charlotte spoke to her as if the baby was already here. This was Charlotte's way, she knew, of throwing her a bone with a little meat on it. But the young girl had learned not to accept it, because the next day she would just as easily snatch it away.

"Did you know Easter-Egg-Man graduate with Brother?" Charlotte asked. Not sure where the question was going, Sunshine didn't answer. In fact, they had all graduated from Lincoln High together. At least, Easter-Egg-Man had been there, but never in the same classes as she and Brother. She didn't know what classes he had taken, except he had fallen from the top of the senior class, and, she had heard, had barely managed to graduate. Now he looked like a wild man. He had blown out his conk and had a mountain of hair on his head. And he refused to comb it. Just like he refused to shave, directing all his attention and everybody else's to AFRICA!

"He's one crazy jig-ga-boo, all right. Got no ambition. Wouldn't take no money fo' college."

Sunshine looked up, surprised.

"I hear tell he can speak that Latin stuff and count figures in his head fastah than you can call 'um." Suddenly distracted by Brother's shorts in a heap at the foot of the bed, Miss Charlotte stooped and lifted them with the tip end of the truck key.

"Is that from my icebox?"

Sunshine pretended she was still busy trying to sit up in bed. Under Brother's shorts was an ice tray with the ice turned to water and a half-burned blue candle.

"Hum" was the only remark Miss Charlotte made. Since she never imagined that Brother could make love so creatively, she figured it was Sunshine who was up to something.

Sunshine knew she was once again under suspicion. But that's not what angered the young girl this time. The heavier, older woman hadn't just stooped. She had squatted with a movement that both confused and enraged the daughter-in-law. The gesture was odd but graceful. Where did it come from? Especially from a woman who had to be, at least, three times her age. But there it was–a flash of something underneath the black skirt, the nylon blouse, the powdered face. And just as surprisingly, the woman stood up with equal ease, having gained whatever information the squat had revealed. Wherever the gesture came from, there was no mistaking that here was a body that liked what it could do.

She took a long look at the young girl who now sat upright with her legs dangling from the high mattress of the bridal bedroom.

"That mattress too high fo' you?" Not waiting for an answer she said, "I got one in the basement. Git the Easter-Egg-Man to bring it up."

The young wife shifted her weight, moving it unconsciously against yet another demand from Miss Charlotte.

"Any who, Easter-Egg-Man'll be comin' 'bout nine. Make sho' you let him in. Tell him he can start on the hallway. Cousin Lester's on his way North."

Sunshine stood on wobbly legs and reached for her robe. "I gotta pee" was all she could say.

Miss Charlotte went out closing the door hard.

TWO

She could see the slow curl of the tail, the weight of the rattle seeming to press the poisonous tongue forward. Jarred, she jumped from the dream. The doorbell! She pulled the weight of her body from the bed, too slow. It rang again. She was out of breath by the time she opened the door.

"Is Charles at home?"

"Charles?" It seemed only natural to add before clearing sleep from her mind, "Aunt Marian's boy, the one with the ti-tongue?"

Char-Lee, or Charles Lee. Before Brother was born, King Solomon had found Charles Lee and his family squatting on the back forty of Gert's farm. Marian, the child's mother, had begged King Solomon to take the boy North. Mindful that the boy was still running around in what looked like a long nightshirt, no underpants, no shoes, and speaking a language nobody could understand, King Solomon protested, "What'll ya tell his pappy?" Reaching down—in an unconscious gesture—testing for moisture in the soil, he waited for Marian to answer.

"I'll tell 'em he done run off," she said, standing barefoot, all swollen and milky and hung down with babies. There was a knee baby and a lap baby and a baby baby, ready to be born.

Thinking the boy just quiet and well-behaved, as southern children tend to be, King Solomon took him North to the family and to Charlotte, who discovered the boy couldn't find the exit door out of his own mind. Mostly he understood what went into it, and obeyed instruction, but never replied or initiated anything on his own. Every day at four o'clock, he would sit by the front door, waiting for King to come in from work. If King was on second shift, he could count on the boy lying asleep on the floor somewhere between the front door and King's bedroom. King came to love Char-Lee in ways that he would never love his own son. Nothing else (outside of King) seemed to interest the boy, except the wooden whistle that he had brought with him on the long trip North.

By the time Sunshine entered the old house, Char-Lee was a legend in it. One day, she had seen King with his arms full of sheets and blankets on his way to the third floor, because Char-Lee was coming home for a visit. It was then that Brother, in the quiet of their bedroom, had told her what he knew of Char-Lee's story.

One evening near dusk when the old house was full of purple shadows, Char-Lee, who sat for hours inspecting his whistle but never playing it, began to play. The music came drifting down from the third floor and startled everybody. It was like nothing that anybody had ever heard. Even Uncle Bubba, who lived in the old house at the time, and who had been as far away as Paris, France, during the Great War, hadn't heard anything like it. King Solomon followed the sound and found the boy alone, seated on the floor—knees crossed with his back to the door. He played facing the open window in one of the unoccupied rooms on the third floor, unaware of King Solomon dumbstruck in the doorway. The music he made was like a cantor's cry. A lament. A wail. But what Solomon heard was the boy's indescribable grief. The realization of what was inside that frail body nearly broke King. He could never get past the wound of Char-Lee, even when his own son was born.

Now grown, Char-Lee would often show up unexpectedly—bumping a steamer trunk up the stairs to his old room on the third floor. After about three days he'd leave the third floor and enter family life on the first. Sunshine thought him crude, although she wouldn't have put it that way. On the other hand, his blurred speech and odd hand gestures excited her, but she wouldn't have admitted that either. One day, standing in the kitchen door, absent-mindedly cradling her stomach, she saw him rush at her. Down the hallway that led to the kitchen one way and toward the front door the other, he came–pointing furiously, falling toward her, pulling his arms back then forward as he came, making uneven sounds. Brother, never sure of how and what to expect from Char-Lee, overturned a chair in the kitchen and rushed into the hallway to see what was happening. Lizzie, coming down the stairs on her way to choir practice, yelled at the top of her voice for him to stop. Even Miss Charlotte, who had just turned her key in the outside lock, had seen his unexpected move through the glass of the front door and had quickly thrust it open. Startled, Char-Lee pulled back–disappointed and confused. Sunshine smiled, realizing he had seen the baby jump and only wanted to touch it. And so she reached out and pulled him to her, guiding his hand toward her stomach so he could feel the next move. Everybody sighed, except Miss Charlotte, who remembered the face of her daughter-in-law as she'd seen it when she was coming in. She saw the steel flash in those gray-green eyes and the sly smile that held while Sunshine pressed Char-Lee's hands to her stomach. And Miss Charlotte wondered–not why Char-Lee had become so over-whelmed that he sank to his knees, pressing his head against the bottom of Sunshine's belly, rocking slowly, but she wondered about Sunshine's face. It glowed.

"Is Charles at home?" the sweet voice asked again. Fumbling, not sure of what to say, Sunshine managed a weak, "He's out of town."

Standing on the stoop was George. A blue-black mountain man, with a body that looked like a sledgehammer and gestures that poured tea from fragile teacups–a geisha in Wrangler jeans; the voice amber, low. It made a sound like wind chimes in the distance.

"Funny, he left something at my house last night," the sweet mountain man said. "Tell him Big Boy has something he's been waiting for," he said, pursing his lips and moving the words through his mouth seductively.

"If he comes in…you want me to…" But her remarks fell on deaf ears; the sweet mountain man was gone. She shut the door. Pressed her back up against it. Heaved a sigh, then smiled. Aunt Marian's boy "doing it with sissies"! Now that was funny. Did the ti-tongue get in the way? she wondered.

"Do ya always go to the door like that?"

"Beverly! How did you get in?"

"I always git in…where I need to."

"But…"

"But nothin'. Look at you! Nightgown ridin' up on yo' ass…"

"The doorbell kept ringing and Miss Charlotte said to make sure I let you in. Besides, I'm pregnant, Beverly. Nothing fits."

He started to tug at her gown. It tore. Her stomach loomed like some silly balloon loose at a carnival. The gown hung in jagged edges just under her belly. She was an over-stuffed kewpie doll—like the ones you win at the carnival who, too big for the dresses they wore, stood mute with frozen smiles on their painted faces. Their bellies, round and ready, stood at attention waiting to be rubbed.

"Peaches and cream, sugar and spice," the Easter-Egg-Man whispered huskily against her ear. Then running the tip of his tongue in the opening of her ear, he put one leg between her legs and moved her back against the wall. And then, through clenched teeth, breathing heavily but not very loud, "Baby…" Suddenly he pulled away. "No Black brother ready for the re-vo-lu-tion gits off on yellah pussy. This fight is for Black people! Ya dig? Not cream-color bitches in heat! I got yo' history, baby. You house niggahs spoilt every runaway. Ya'll wanted to STAY! Then STAY!" he mimicked again, pinning her shoulders against the wall. "Stay with the man. But just remember ya'll gave up this dick fo'," he said starting to unbutton his pants, "fo' a white prick."

He was pressing himself hard up against her again. Her mind, in a whirl—fear mixed with pleasure—joined his breath as it fell, hot, to her shoulders, then her breasts and finally her stomach. His hands were moving round and round her belly. And she? She was on the merry-go-round riding the red pony with the big teeth and holding the gold harness still looking for the door.

Just then one opened. Miss Charlotte came in. She stopped so short Brother, who was right behind, bumped into her. Miss Charlotte said nothing, turned and gave the situation over to Brother—with a look that said, "Where's yo' manhood now, boy?"

Easter-Egg-Man jumped up. "Ya need to keep the bitch tied, man," he said, stepping back and bending quickly, giving sudden attention to his paintbrush lost deep inside the can of yellow paint.

"Oh, Easter-Egg-Man, I need ya to have a look-see on the second floor," Miss Charlotte said, motioning him to pick up his buckets and brushes and come with her.

"Brother, it's not what you think," Sunshine said in a hurry.

"What do it mean then, 'ho?"

"He just talks to me."

It was funny how "he talks to me" slowed Brother down but didn't stop him. Just for a fraction of a second he had reacted like he did when he heard that old hymn, "He Walks with Me and He Talks with Me," feeling called upon to be reverent—but only for a second.

He shoved her into the bridal bedroom with such force she hit her back against the brass handles of the dresser drawers. The baby shifted, sending streaks of pain through her—like the end of the world.

"Send a cab to 1448 John R. Street. My car had a flat. I'm already late fo' work," Miss Charlotte said in low tones into the telephone.

The only sounds that could be heard in the old house, if one cared to listen, were the whistle of Easter-Egg-Man already busy on the second floor, Miss Charlotte hanging up the phone, and Brother attending to his wife as she lay writhing on the bed.

"*Ain't* is not a word! I'm not going to tell you again." Wop! Her mother's hand was quickly sorry, but only after—always after.

"*Ain't* is what *common* Negroes use, baby," she'd say, holding a cold towel to her little girl's face. "One day we won't have to live here, darling. You'll see."

Moving to another neighborhood was something that obsessed her mother. And because it did, her father refused to move—regaining his manhood every time he won the argument.

"No, Viola, this place is good as any."

"You spend all your waking hours trying to undermine me, don't you, Henry?"

"No, I dream dreams about stopping you, Viola."

One day, while her parents were fighting, the child split in two. And became K-a-l-i, the warrior.

Kali spoke from the mirror with a vengeance, one that smudged the child's loneliness—blurred it, sent it scrambling. Often Sunshine flipped into Kali—sometimes outrageously funny, or clever, or just plain sassy. Anything that worked and made it possible to live in an all-Negro neighborhood as a freak with gray-green eyes, a nose that didn't need pinching, a flat ass and sandy hair with a slow though evident kink to it.

When her mother stood over her, the child's voice was always one way: careful. But sometimes she would forget or Kali would lull her out of her carefulness. It was those times that her mother descended on her like the devil with a pickax.

"Only niggers use *be* for everything! I *be* this and I *be* that. You will not!" her mother screamed. And in a shrill voice, she added: "Move that thick tongue in your mouth! End your words! Cross your t's! Pronounce those d's!" Screaming again, she jerked the sandy head back and spit rage into those gray-green eyes that mirrored her own.

Viola's hatred was universal. She was a busybody without actually putting her body in other people's business. Because the neighbors were beneath her dignity, she drew her deep and abiding hatred peeping out from behind the shades at them—wishing them away. If it wasn't the shiftless Negroes next door, the loose red woman down the street, the brand-new live-in man of Pearl's, or those wayward children with slingshots breaking out the alley lights, it was, and continued to be, always *something*, and that *all* the time.

When Viola had married Henry, she had no reason to suspect that the amenities that her caste and color brought her down among the magnolia trees wouldn't continue. Though he was from the North, he was even more hi-yellah than she was.

Once up North, Viola soon realized that Henry had no intention of merging himself into her blue-blood lines. She felt trapped in the northern cycle of Negro living. "All of you live like vagabonds...from payday to payday. No Negro in this fricking town," crossing herself she went on, "owns anything but the preachers and funeral directors!"

Henry couldn't understand her need for owning. He owned his job at Ford Motor Company and that was enough. All the rest was just living.

When he had first met the very luscious and lovely Viola Maddox Brown—who batted her southern eyelashes and would have covered her face with a fluttering fan if this had been thirty years earlier—and heard that voice dripping with honey, he was hooked.

Twelve months after their first meeting, the *Michigan Chronicle* gave the following information: "After several visits to the state of

Georgia, Henry Whitfield brought back a Georgia peach from that fair state, Miss Viola Maddox Brown, and they settled in the Brewster projects in lower Detroit." The ad ran in the *Michigan Chronicle* because Henry bought space for it. He knew it would please his new bride, and she didn't have to know that he'd paid for it. At the time, the housing project on the near east side of Detroit was a place for respectable working-class Negroes.

When Viola had a daughter he thought that would quiet her—bring her back in line. But the child became the battleground they fought on. The thrust of Viola's rage filled the house with dissatisfaction and her anger became a giant face plastered in all the rooms.

Henry had little tolerance for Viola's anger—dealing as he was with his own as a factory Black. He had less understanding of southern gentility, and no understanding of the dance going on between mother and daughter that was one part fear, one part rapture, and two parts anger.

The daughter knew that her mother's anger meant *something*. But she did not yet know the legacies—long held by slave women unable to hold their worlds together. Of women afraid of not being able to keep everybody's lives and limbs together. Of being the punching bag of men who could never be men in America—and what that meant for all the black, bronze, and gold women who lived with that fact.

Kali felt all that she didn't know weigh in heavy. Of the sixty million—and more—gone. Of the children sold. Dead. Raped. Beaten. Of the strange fruit of "three-fifths" of a man hanging from a tree. But Kali knew, without being told, the need for the anger erupting from the inside of her mother, and exploding in the middle of Miss Charlotte and her sisters. And she suspected it was what kept saving them and would keep saving her too.

Kali had her own battlefield. The first round she fought with her mother, the second with the black-skinned girls on the playground whose hatred was so visceral that they saw reflected in her face the "ugly" they believed they were. One slip on her part into right speech brought the long look, the snap, the crisp collective hatred for the "albino" or the "ya thank ya cute, bitch." And as often as not, brought on the Dozens, a ritual drama the boys played on all the girls.

"Old Mary Mack, Mack, Mack
All dressed in black, black, black
With silver buttons, buttons, buttons
All down her back, back, back
She asked her mother, mother, mother
For fifteen cents, cents, cents
To put it in, in, in
I jerked it back, back, back
Cause it was black, black, black
I want some-thin' bright, bright, bright
Like some-thin' white, white, white."

Then the boys pointed to her. She realized more and more each day that she was alone. While the girls tore into her and she into them, the boys laughed and jostled each other, slapped their Detroit Tigers caps up against one another and gave each other five. "Look, man, 'em silly bitches is fightin' each other!"

So, Kali had learned to fight early and she knew that to fight on open ground she'd have to leave home.

THREE

"Mirror, mirror on the wall, who is the fairest of them all?" There stood Sweet Baby Jane at the back door.

"Yes?" the young girl asked, sticking her head out and into the face of a small, smelly, smiling, and toothless old woman.

"Mary, Mary, Quite Contrary, how does her garden grow?" Sweet Baby Jane chanted as she set an armful of tall bottles of home brew just inside the basement stairs, ignoring the young girl.

"Who are these for?" she asked. Sweet Baby Jane didn't answer, but stood laboriously counting the bottles she'd left on the basement stairs and then the ones remaining in her wagon.

Carefully rearranging the bottles in the wagon, she looked up and repeated in that odd way people without teeth sound, "Mary, Mary, Quite Contrary, that's how her garden grows." She turned and, in a heavy overcoat that weighted her down and made her step like someone landed on the moon, she engaged the wagon handle with her over-worn gloves that had the fingers cut out and went on down the alley.

"Either there's a woman in here or somebody's cleanin' fish," Miss Charlotte announced as she bumped the door frame, balancing her ever-present coffee cup. She had stood there for several long seconds watching Sunshine drying the dishes. She saw the girl from a great distance, like looking through the large end of a pair of binoculars. Still, from that distance she could see the hilltop house—abandoned, bleached boards paralyzed by the sun, ripped here and there from the main stock of the house. That day there had been a curious collection of Imperial butterflies billowing throughout the house. And she and Ricky, sweaty and drowsy from lovemaking, had watched them from the mattress they'd found on the floor.

Once Miss Charlotte came into the kitchen, the view through the binoculars vanished, but not the butterflies. By now they were odd-shaped and noisy, with iron wings that clacked as they settled on the remaining dishes in the rack.

Laphonya had the long mouth. "Folks git tired of yo' silly shit, Charlotte," she snapped, hurriedly wrapping up two halves of one fish, spilling cornmeal all over the table and floor.

Miss Charlotte hadn't known her older sister was in the kitchen. As Laphonya passed she looked Charlotte full in the face and blew the word, "Bitch!" sending a shower of spit with it. Miss Charlotte waved at her—a silly little wave—and giggled. "It takes one to know one!" she laughed—and then had to give immediate attention to juggling her coffee cup.

"Chile," Laphonya shot back, on her way through the doorway, "watch her, she's a snake!"

Miss Charlotte slid into a kitchen chair. Losing her giggle, she asked with a start, "What's that cornmeal doin' all over the floor?"

Her daughter-in-law, surprised at the suddenness of the question, answered with a raised eyebrow. "She was putting it on the fish."

"Oh," Miss Charlotte said, relieved. "She's a black magic woman, ya know."

"A what?"

Miss Charlotte ignored her. "I ain't heard ya say nothin' 'bout seein' a doctor. Have ya?" Her voice had that tone of eager concern that Sunshine could never get used to. It would emerge out of nowhere, and her eyes would soften.

"I'm fine," the young girl replied, refusing Miss Charlotte absolution today.

Charlotte shrugged it off, and in a gesture that added to the girl's continuing state of amazement, reached up and snatched off her wig. Ten thousand tiny, tiny braids tumbled out from under it. The move was funny, and weird, and tragic, all balled into one. The "thing" lay on the table like some sort of wounded animal with its undersides exposed. It lay in a mess of cornmeal still strewn all over the kitchen table, announcing "Made in Hong Kong" from the tag sewn inside.

"Yeah, I know ya stay *fine,*" she said loudly. Drawing her lips into a straight line, she demanded, "Go see the doctor anyway. 'Bout time *somebody* 'round here had a baby in a hospital."

"Why spend the money?" the young girl asked.

The question would have been too full of northern sass if Miss Charlotte had *really* heard it, but she had effectively immersed herself inside the deep and ever-deepening coffee cup. As the black and gold dragon began to roar, she stood and moved around the oblong kitchen table. Standing in front of it she fumbled inside her bosom and finally came up with a fist full of small bills. Patting herself on her bosom she exclaimed, "These here is the only two suckers I can trust!… That was meant to be funny," she explained when there was no response from Sunshine.

Still holding the money, and without warning, Charlotte gently placed an arm around what was left of the young girl's waist and thrust her other hand into Sunshine's wet one. "Do ya boogie? Naw, ya too *stiff.* Watch. Besides, this is one way to git ya to exercise," she pronounced, closing her eyes and shaking her head to some imaginary music. Then, she dropped Sunshine's hand, jumped back and clapped her hands—moving toward her doing the Camel Walk.

In fact, Sunshine did know how to dance—and very well. Without exception she learned every new dance that came out. It was her way to fit in. When Miss Charlotte grabbed her to boogie woogie, she knew just what to do.

Miss Charlotte was spinning her out now, as the butterflies nervously watched. Raising her forefinger in the air and moving it back and forth she explained, "This here is truckin'." The girl, already holding back, stopped dead still when the phone rang. Miss Charlotte reached for the receiver but it slipped from her sweaty hand and the entire phone banged hard against the floor.

The loud buzz from the throat of the dying phone joined the clacking of butterfly wings. No one picked it up. It lay in a disjointed heap on the cornmeal floor. Soon the swish of Miss Charlotte's weaving feet began to beat time in the yellow cornmeal. Sunshine edged out the door.

Ferry Street, the street the doctor's office was on, was "round the corner." Everyone on John R said that, just like they called John R.

Street "on the strip." It was, "I saw so and so up on the strip." So Sunshine decided, now that she had Miss Charlotte's money, that maybe she should go round the corner to see the doctor.

As she passed the Chinese laundry, next door to the old house, she could hear the snap of the shoeshine rag coming from Sneaky Pete's Shoeshine Stand, just on the other side of the laundry. Balladeering in front of Sneaky Pete's was Ben, the hot tamale man, keeping time with the snap of the rag.

"Git yo' hot tamale man while he hot, hot, hot!" Repeat. "Git yo' hot tamale man while he hot, hot, hot!" He looked up just in time to see her huge smile. He stopped crooning his tune to ask, "You from Jamaica born?"

She shook her head no.

"No mat-ta child, thee whites drop some here, drop some there," he sang as he dipped his hand into the heated tin container and passed a hot tamale wrapped in a steaming corn husk to her. She reached into her dress pocket to pay him.

"Child," he waved her money away and pointed to her belly, "name *he* after me!"

Brother had placed for her everybody on the strip and given everyone a name. So she knew that Mr. Ben, the hot tamale man, had been on the strip longer than anyone. That he lived in the basement of the Chinese laundry, ran the numbers and put out a small newspaper called *Ben's Broadside*.

When single action was introduced on the strip, Ben was reluctant at first, then decided that no one was going to keep colored folks from playing the numbers. He would, at least, keep it as honest as any gambling can be. He hired Tiny—all two hundred pounds of her. She worked both sides of the street and all the bars and passing cars, taking bets at fifteen minute sets, closing right before the next digit came out.

Sunshine bit into the hot tamale and almost choked with laughter when the fruit man, who had overheard Mr. Ben, shouted to her, "He cain't make a baby if Betty Crocker *gave* him the recipe! Now me? That's a different story. Here, Snow White, *this* apple's on me!"

Joseph, whose fruit stand was next to Mr. Ben's, also made homemade wine out of tomatoes. He sold the bottles along with his dreams. Everyone on the strip knew Joseph was the dreamer, and when they bought a bottle, what they were really paying for was his latest dream. They'd rush home to check the Red Devil or Three Wise Men dream books, then they could "jump" lucky.

And while he dreamed his lucky dreams, swinging softly in his hammock, Sweet Baby Jane, who lived somewhere in or near Apple Jack's stable—where the last of the ice/coal men gathered in summer and huddled in winter—swept up bruised apples, rolling grapes, smashed bananas, and any other thing living or dead dropped under Joseph's stand. After, she made and sold her home brew from her little wagon marked "Red Arrow."

Mr. Ben and Joseph worked side by side year after year. In later years they had begun to look alike. Mr. Ben was short and stocky, black and easy on the eyes. He had come from Jamaica, following, as he said, "the only man could git thee Black man movin'!" Marcus Garvey. He was on his way to New York when his hero went to jail—so he settled in the Motor City, all the while hating its hero, Henry Ford. "That white man! He vex Ben-ji-boy so!" he said. Daily he pointed his finger in the faces of the "day" people who had just been released by Ford's three o'clock whistle. "Look at ya! One day thee three o'clock she blow and none of ya here for ya all be dead! Do ya hear? All ya be dead! So ya better be playin' thee shit row, tomorrow. Okay? She lookin' good. 369. Some hits git ya out thee fac-tore-ree fo' good, gents. How much ya bet?"

Joseph was medium brown and not much taller than Mr. Ben. His manner was slow, but he smiled easily and liked more than anything else the feel and smell of money. He had been born under a lucky star. He knew he would hit one any day now.

In the meantime, along with placing their bets, the day people stopped, dipped in their pockets, and paid an array of bills for Joseph's bottled dreams. Mr. Ben, intermittently knocking a tambourine, provided the news and history lessons: Little Rock, the sit-ins, the Detroit Tigers at Briggs Stadium. Or he would stun his captive audience with "Thee Black man was the first to make thee traffic light, gents." Thrusting his paper in their faces he said, "Here, read all about it in the *Broadside*."

"Where's your manners, my man? Let the little lady in." The flimflam man waved her forward as she stood shoulder-high, in a sea of bent backs, straining to see a pea that none of them could see. The crowd parted to let her in, and remembering with a laugh Laphonya telling the one about the flimflam man stealing Jesus' cross, she was pleased.

"Pregnant ladies are always lucky," Fred "Mudbone" Smith announced to the crowd, still beckoning to her to come forward. "Come on, little lady, show 'um how the heavens smile on pregnant ladies."

And she won. By the time she realized what Three Card Molly was, she had guessed right twice and then had lost all of her winnings back, including some of Miss Charlotte's money.

Mudbone, never one to leave a lady in distress, cried out to the crowd, rubbing his hands over his chest and stomach as if he were in pain, "A saint I ain't." Then he rubbed the palms of his hands together, like a preacher after sinners. "But I never took money from mother or child. And I ain't 'bout to do both." Tipping his hat, he handed her a two dollar bill. She had, in fact, lost more.

Today the Black Muslims, energetic, clean-cut, in bow ties and white shirts, were out in force, pushing *Muhammed Speaks* in the faces of people as they passed. Sunshine, embarrassed, took one.

She walked up the sidewalk to the doctor's office with its neatly groomed trenches that separated lawn from sidewalk on both sides. She looked into the narrow trench just to the right of her. It was empty, as she supposed the other was. In summer it was filled with water from the lawn sprinkler, but now it was October and winter was coming on.

As she opened the door on Ferry Street, round the corner, she took one last look at the neat indentations at the sidewalk's edges and entered the back door of the doctor's office—he insisted that his patients enter by the back door and leave by the front.

Her feet, cocooned in furry house shoes with the backs pressed down, made sounds that swished on the linoleum. The linoleum's squares whined as they stretched themselves down the hall, climbed the stairs, and entered the second floor landing, then paused—the pattern blurring suddenly (because Aunt Lizzie had dropped some lye)—turned back to the stairs again, seeking the third floor, breathless now as they touched the third landing, keen on making it all the way to the top.

The linoleum had passed rooms on the first floor dressed in carpet, with rich red plumes tied in yellow sashes on dark blue backgrounds. The sitting room peered into another room where the carpet lay embellished in braided squares that ran the length of the room. One room had heavy velvet drapes and lace curtains that touched the tips of the shag carpet that flooded it—along with huge potted palms that were scattered about and seemed to bob inside the shag like buoys. That room was Miss Charlotte's parlor.

No one dared tell Charlotte that parlors were not the rage anymore. She might have known that if she had visited anyone. But she didn't. She expected that they would come to her. And they did. Nieces and nephews, relatives and friends (mainly Lizzie's church friends) came bringing gifts and gossip, and news of burials and weddings. Dumping out the news—as Miss Charlotte held court—glad to be the first to get a raised eyebrow along with "Girl-l-l, hush yo' mouth. Did that heifer really say that?" And the bearer of news, depending on Miss Charlotte's mood, would rear back, plant her feet under the table and place a fork in whatever food King had fixed that day. Or leave, head bowed, dismissed because Miss Charlotte had already heard the news or was just not interested. And that was happening more and more frequently.

Alone in the old house, swollen like a balloon, waiting and depressed, Kali would sometimes slip into the parlor. Once, interrupting an animated conversation, King Solomon pushed open the door to Miss Charlotte's parlor and said from the doorway, "Thought maybe Charlotte was home. Heard two of ya in here."

"No, I talk to…"

"To yo'self. I'd be worried if ya was answerin' too." He laughed.

She didn't. "Have you ever wanted something really bad? So bad it hurt sometimes?" She lifted her head and looked at him through watery eyes.

"All the time," he answered. He leaned against the doorjamb and moved the toothpick in his mouth from one corner to the other.

"Like what?"

"Come on in the kitchen, Lil Sis, that question calls for some coffee." He paused, turned around and asked, "Ya do drink coffee, don't ya?"

"Drinking coffee makes you black." She said it before she knew what she was saying.

King was startled. Then he let out a belly laugh that rippled up to the third floor and back again.

"I'm sorry, but…"

"The same bunch of lies is told everywhere."

"*She* is *so* against colored people…but I'm not," Kali hurriedly said.

"Who's that?"

"My mother."

"Whoa! Whoa, little gal. You *are* colored people. It might take a body a spell to figure out, but I'm here to tell ya, *you* is the niggah in yo' woodpile, Lil Sistah."

"I know *that!* But…but…I could never be *them*. Not at home. Not at school. At home I was *too* colored. On the playground I wasn't colored enough. First it was Catholic school," she said, reflecting. "Nothing is colored about Catholic school. Nothing! Do you know how many fights just wearing a uniform every day got me?"

No, he didn't know. What he knew was that colored people who thought they was something other than colored sent their children to Catholic school.

"Those nigger gals set my hair on fire!"

"Who?"

"A bunch of them…they set my braids on fire!" Her voice broke. "Those Black girls were walking behind me…they had a cigarette lighter and…and…they set my braids on fire."

King looked at his daughter-in-law as she sat reliving the event. He looked at her so long that when she returned his gaze, he nervously coughed and asked, "Ya want a sweet roll?"

But Sunshine had seen the tenderness in his eyes. And something else flicked there. Something she couldn't name.

It was passion born from being half empty all the time. But being empty most of the time didn't mean he didn't know the difference between passion and being in love. For he understood, and quite clearly, that the beloved is passion's motivation, the hand that finally turns you toward home. And Charlotte was home, deep with weeds to be sure, but home nonetheless. Home in a yellow cotton dress.

"I'm lonesome too," he said simply. Not because it made any sense but because he didn't know what to say.

"I expect everybody is, Daddy King."

Her calling him Daddy King pleased him but he said nothing. No, she was more than the young girl whom he had scarcely noticed. Not that he had ignored her, but she was, in his opinion, a very foolish girl who didn't know shit from shinola and he had simply offered her community when she had moved in among them.

"I don't want to be somebody's mel-low yel-low," she said, pressing down on the ends of the words. She said it much too loudly and with not enough conviction.

"Then why my boy?"

"He moved me to a place I'd never been."

He was startled by her answer. Thinking she meant John R. Street, he said, "Well, movin' up on the strip ain't..."

"I'm looking for an open door. He moved me closer than anyone...ever...didn't Miss Charlotte take you to a place you've never been?"

"Me and Charlotte don't talk 'bout doors—closed or open."

"Nobody *talks* about it, Daddy King!" she said abruptly, scooting back in the kitchen chair and giving him a stern look. "But they know it all the same. And I'll know when I find it."

"What ya, seventeen? And, without that baby, a hundred pounds soaking wet?" he questioned, more to cover his embarrassment than to get an answer. "You got all the time in the world."

"That's just it, I *don't!* I'm having a baby *now,* and that means some of my time goes to him."

"Ya don't think they gon' really get on the moon, do ya?" he asked, setting a steaming cup of coffee before her, changing the subject because he didn't know what else to say.

"Sure," she said as she swallowed the hot brew, burning her throat all the way.

"If the Lord wanted 'em up there he woulda put 'em up there."

"Oh, Daddy King, don't be so old-fashioned," she said, scolding him gently this time, touching his face.

And that's how their day talks got started. Solomon on the swing shift; she always searching for her open door.

Sometimes King stayed in his room and no amount of wishing

could bring him out. Other times he emerged looking like Bill Robinson: short, round, dimpled, and dressed in a modified zoot suit. In pegged pants (the long chain was missing) with a bowler hat made from baby beaver—a round and monstrous thing with a notorious feather—a black umbrella with a carved handle, and black-and-white spectators. When his daughter-in-law first saw him dressed like that, she didn't know if she should laugh or ask him to dance. She soon saw that he was very serious. She watched from a crack in her bedroom door as he ceremoniously removed the very bold and overflowing handkerchief from the breast pocket of his box-back suit coat with the more-for-your-money lapels. And with a soft-shoe rhythm he took off his stingy brim hat (he didn't wear the bowler hat all the time) struck the sides of it with the handkerchief and wiped one shoe, and then the other, up against his peg-leg trousers, never missing a beat. Then he crushed the bold and overflowing handkerchief back into the breast pocket of his box-back suit coat, placed the stingy brim hat back on his head, hooked the black umbrella on his arm, and all but danced his way through the open door and out into the sunlight.

Those times, when she was left alone by Daddy King, she spent hours asking herself, "What now?" She had taken to staring into corners of the rooms trying to remember something she could not.

On wintry days when the sun came streaming in through the east window of the parlor making strange shadows on the shag rug, Charlotte made as many excuses as she dared not to go to work. Especially after Christmas, when things were slow at the shop, she stayed home in the mornings. Ate sausage or bacon, soft scrambled eggs, toast with jam, absent-mindedly sipped orange juice with ice chips in it, and seriously drank strong black fragrant coffee.

Winter closed her off, made her silent, reflective, keen on yesterday. It was a time for the long leisurely baths that filled the bathroom with the scent of rose water. Yesterday passed over her like the stream that ran past the house down South. She missed that stream, and, oddly, she realized she could never recapture that feeling unless she lay in her parlor on wintry mornings masturbating in the sun.

Dropping her towel and lowering her nude body onto the rug she spread herself face down in the deep shag, gripping it from time to time when an orgasm thundered through her. With each one she remembered Alabama, New Orleans, New York, but felt cooled and unaffected when her thoughts turned to Detroit. Everything seemed to stop with Detroit.

Alone those mid-mornings, drifting through her own fantasies with whomever she wished or willed, she could, by afternoon, move into the world again, refreshed and ready.

Never were Sunshine and Charlotte in the parlor at the same time. So that day of questions must have been a dream—of Charlotte's or Sunshine's or perhaps both. Perhaps at the same time or different times. It was the day they took their questions to the somber-faced relatives—all twenty-two of them—lined up on the wall of Miss Charlotte's parlor with assorted groups of children, all at various heights and weights knuckled about them, waiting to be sentenced, it seemed, by the hanging judge.

No answers from them. The men stared out into the world. While the women just stared. Stoic faces. Grim. Not at all like the women really were. Huge women who slapped their thighs when something was funny. Or when sad, shook their heads while they strummed guitars and drank whiskey, and let out sounds that split the air.

"How can I forget that you can never be trusted?" Miss Charlotte often asked, marooned in her parlor.

Now the young girl stood alone facing the twenty-two, and speaking directly to the women, she asked, "Could you *ever* be trusted to look life straight in the eye and spit and spit and spit until you gagged and gagged and gagged? Till the hair on your necks stood out—hot-wired and alive? Like I did in my mother's house?"

"Once we stood in our mothers' houses. We believed in the hallelujahs and the amens even when our men hung from trees, as we knew our sons would later. What else was there? We beat the rage down inside ourselves. We had a debt to pay, and we, like our mothers before us and our daughters after us, are the only ones to pay it."

"But you never fought for yourselves," the young girl protested. "You never gagged, never spit until your bellies emptied. You never said, 'I been had. And in the worst way.'"

"No, you didn't," Miss Charlotte added accusingly. "You women preferred to forget that fact every day. Drinking your whiskey, playing down and dirty blues, singing loud and low (especially when the whiskey got low), and you parted your thighs and let babies drop from you till you broke!"

"Didn't you ever want to be *somebody?*" the young girl asked.

"There was *nobody* to be, *little girl!*"

"But you're choking!" the young girl countered.

"Like you?" they countered back.

"Me?"

"Babies are our birthright!"

Charlotte joined the young girl, both shaking their heads.

"Don't you want something for yourselves?"

"It isn't time," they said.

"Then when?" The two women asked in unison.

A silken cord had been enveloping the two women since Sunshine had come to the house. When they were together it felt like a noose, and they clawed at their own throats and at each other's. Sometimes when they were apart they could feel it yank, never understanding who was at the other end—they fought their worlds, but not together.

The women who hung beneath the dusty glass knew all about cords and nooses. All of them had mammoth bosoms pinned with pearl broaches that somehow reached around them and fastened their backs upright—draped in dresses that covered their bodies like shrouds.

FOUR

"Momma!" Brother yelled. "Somethin' wrong with Sunshine!"

"What the…Lizzie! Git down here!" Miss Charlotte yelled up the stairs, her voice carrying easily to the second floor.

"What happened?" was the first question Laphonya asked, looking first at Charlotte and then Brother.

They didn't answer.

"He pushed me and I fell up against the dresser," Sunshine said through broken bits of pain.

"What?" Lizzie asked in disbelief, turning the full weight of her disgust on her sister. "Mind ya, Charlotte, the boy is wicked."

"Be gentle with the girl, Lizzie. Mister Big Shit and me gotta talk," Laphonya said, shoving Brother in the chest, backing him out of the bridal bedroom and into the hallway.

"She's…she's a…"

"I don't wanna hear it, boy! Next time yo' balls gits in the way of yo' brains, I'll slice 'em off myself. Ya wanna lose that baby?"

The girl looked up into a sea of concerned faces, all three sisters floating in and out of her pain.

"Ya go on to work," Lizzie directed Charlotte. "Ain't no tellin' how long a first baby'll take."

"Git her to a hospital," Charlotte said before she left the room. "The doctah's numbah's in the phone book."

Turning to Lizzie, Laphonya said, "Watch the child fo' another minute, I gotta speak to Charlotte fo' she leaves." Stepping behind

Miss Charlotte, Laphonya guided her out of the room. "I smell a rat, Charlotte…what's he really done to her?"

"He ain't done nothin' you can't see…I gotta pee." Miss Charlotte said, her eyes very dark now.

Brother was still standing in the hall with his hands stuffed in his pockets, with what Lizzie called a "hung dog look."

"Tell me true, boy. What ain't went your way this time?" Laphonya asked.

Before Brother could answer, Miss Charlotte came out of the bathroom, passed them in the hallway, and said lightly to Laphonya, "Git the doctah."

"Charlotte, before…*Charlotte!*"

She went out, slamming the door.

Before anyone knew what had happened between the two sisters, the back screen slammed against the back doorjamb. The Easter-Egg-Man had gone out too.

Miss Charlotte hadn't reached work before Opal Henry stepped through the front door of the old house. She had never lost a baby and everybody knew it. But, so the tale goes, she almost did this time. Opal was busy doing what she does, so Lizzie said. She was pressing on the mother's stomach like she s'pose to, coaxing the baby down with soft words. Going about her business like any good midwife might, wiping the mother's face as she huffed and puffed herself into spaces between the pains. Easing her down when need be. Opal Henry was busy—too busy.

"Too careful, fo' my taste," Lizzie dutifully repeated to each cousin, even though none of them had asked. "She was not tendin' to the boy, like she ought," Lizzie announced, as the cousins agreed, more out of habit than interest.

"When she finally reached down to cut the cord, why I bet ya cain't guess?" Lizzie asked. When there was no reply, she continued, "The boy had the double skin over his face and was laborin' to breathe," she announced, very satisfied with herself *and* the drama.

Lizzie cornered Miss Charlotte on the stoop and flooded her with the events of the day. "It is my Christian duty to tell you that Opal Henry did all she could," Lizzie said so fast that Charlotte had to slow her down and ask her to repeat herself.

"Why didn't ya'll git her to a hospital?" Miss Charlotte asked, looking directly at Lizzie.

Lizzie stood still, dumbfounded. She couldn't believe the question.

"Why?"

"Because it's 'bout time *somebody* went, Lizzie."

"No need to fret 'bout that now," Laphonya said, coming in from Miss Charlotte's kitchen, meeting them as they entered the hallway.

Charlotte knew Laphonya's tone. "Why?" she asked cautiously.

"Simple, the boy got the *Sight*, Charlotte."

"Laphonya! Why ya spoil my surprise?" Lizzie asked, beginning to pout.

"Not today, you two!" Miss Charlotte spit out. "No baby born in the North got the *Sight*," she said, reaching under her dress to pull off her girdle. Next she reached on top of her head and pulled off her wig. All ten thousand braids came bouncing out.

"Charlotte, cain't you wait to do that?" Lizzie squeaked, her voice shrill now. Neither of her two sisters paid any attention to her.

"Maybe so, maybe no, but he got it. Somethin' that woulda been missed if he'd a been born in the hospital," Laphonya continued, still wiping her hands on a towel from the meal she had prepared and eaten by herself because Lizzie was too excited to eat.

"They woulda washed that second skin away like it was dirt goin' down the drain." Laphonya ended her speech with a belch and a thump against the wall. Moving past both of them, heading for the stairs to the second floor, she asked, "Ya comin' Lizzie?"

Charlotte had left her two sisters when she was sixteen, one older (Laphonya) and one younger (Lizzie). She headed to New Orleans and when she came back (by way of New York), wiser but not much older, she found them odder than she had remembered. They were secretive, sometimes seductive, and behaved like a pair of kids caught in a complex game of their own making.

They didn't look alike, and really they were not alike, and yet, between the whispers and the outrageous laughter, they settled like twins in the minds of others.

Laphonya was taller and a deep copper brown, almost black except for the red cast to her skin. She was big-boned as well as big.

With hips that moved like jelly beneath her clothes. She was small-waisted and small-busted, making her what the neighborhood called "a pretty gal."

Lizzie was, on the other hand, caramel-colored, short, and small, with eyebrows that came together and a nervous twitch that punctuated her words as she chattered like a bird. She talked so fast folks thought she was a Geechee. She was in the business of other folks' business, pecking along, ferreting out bits and pieces of their private affairs—dumping their stuff down Laphonya's throat like a mother bird. Except for what Lizzie told her, Laphonya was unmoved by news on the outside. Generally, she planted herself in her rocker and waited for Lizzie's shining face to break through the door to their room and reintroduce her to a new set of "Guess what?"

But Charlotte was the gamin' one. She came back from New York City, met Solomon, and in six months married him. She left her sisters tending the family farm. After her move to Detroit, she had all but forgotten them when she got a surprising letter from Lizzie announcing she was coming North. Laphonya would follow soon after.

Sunshine felt the weight of her—somewhere, pressing. Stirring the silence into liquid night, it started at the tip end of the third floor, covered the landing, and spilled down into the rest of the house, slipping under her bedroom door. It tugged at the sheet and felt for her face. Her eyes opened, suddenly. She waited. What is it? She turned to wake Brother but decided not to. Hadn't she just put the baby down? Fallen to sleep? Now here she was awake. Weighted by something she couldn't name. She rose, started to perch herself on the window sill, changed her mind, and thought, The bathroom is just down the hall, I'll only be gone for a minute—no real distance...

She pressed her ear to the door: the first floor was quiet. She paused, reached for the door handle, and stepped into the hall. Then looked up. No reason to look up, not as late as it was. What did she expect to see that time of night? She should hurry. Get her business done in the bathroom, and get back. She should be asleep anyway. Or, at the very least, looking out of the window as the night people hurried home, their turn over—the day people hugging their pillows for one last chance before their lives woke them up.

But she did. She did go into the hall. She did look up. She could see the entire stairwell. It rose not quite in a spiral, broken by the second and third landings. More like an exaggerated square. But as she looked up, the second floor opened like a rose, opening fully as it reached the third floor. She was transfixed by the full black figure perched on the third floor, nesting near the top of the house. Brooding. She shuddered. There was Miss Charlotte perched on the third floor railing! Rocking back and forth. Back and forth. Fiercely looking down the stairwell. Sunshine opened her mouth–ready for something to drop, something she needed, something she wanted and had to have. Her breath came in quick puffs. She could barely breathe. Miss Charlotte was pushing her, and she fell off the edge, and hung there–excited, caught, hands clinging to the single branch that protruded from the side of the mountain, that just happened to be there, as she fell off the cliff, too excited to scream and too scared not to.

"Hey Charlotte! Yo' ass gon' fall if ya ain't careful." There was Laphonya on the second floor looking from one to the other. "And ya down there...could scare a body to death. Bettah learn to turn on the light when ya walk around the house in the dark."

"I'm just going to the bathroom, Laphonya," she finally managed to say as she swung her leg back over the cliff.

"Well, turn on the hall light, will ya?"

Just then, Miss Charlotte swooped her long legs around and landed in the hall. And as she landed, her arms swung into a sudden turn and fluttered to a halt. She erupted. Her laughter, layered like feathers, floated into the hall, down the corridor of the third floor. Threatening, the laughter entered the corners of the second floor and continued to waft downward, turning into a feathered stone as it fell to the first floor. The twisting aunts stirred in their sleep and moved nearer the twitching uncles, who groaned and thought they heard one of the unsure cousins slipping in past midnight–decided no, and turned back into sleep.

Laphonya decided to mind her own business and shut her door. No need to wake Lizzie with Charlotte's foolishness. As Miss Charlotte swooped down from the top of the house and into her parlor, she heard the door to Brother's room click shut.

Sometimes, after Brother fell asleep and the baby was between pulls at her breast, she rose and looked out the window into the night. That black velvet star-studded night that ran along John R where the beautiful people lived and played. Lavish women in rhinestone face, queen lace stockings, and satin dresses that hugged wonderful asses, were all dressed up with everywhere to go! Some with smooth-talking pimps checking their early evening traps, their bodies silk-suited, hiding jewel-encrusted dicks.

There were deep dark men in Cuban heels, and white men in white-boy shoes, the kind with the double stitches, ready to ride. Men who hooked their legs into the stirrups of sanctified thighs that blessed them and kept them coming back as they moved through corridors of rotating hips and blowjobs. And pimps, forever searching for women to break and stable in order to supply the demand.

Other women with large bracelets, red lips, red nail polish, with red toes stuffed into open-toed mules, got out of slick red convertibles. But not before they flashed plump, perfumed thighs that caused the passing men to suck in their breath as the women smiled slow, revealing gold-rimmed teeth hidden behind full lips. Then, wrapping their necks in feather boas, they strolled deliciously in. The bars were already jumping!

The evening late, the night early, found the junior pimps already out, checking out Millie or Betty, and maybe Sugar to see if they were keeping their johns coming quickly and returning early. These pimps would move their hands to their mouths pretending to cough, hiding the grins they felt. "Dumb mothafuckahs," they thought. But they didn't understand yet what all this was supposed to be about. These were pimps who still needed to fuck to keep order in their stables. Daddy pimps like Monkey Dee never fucked to maintain, but fucked only to add, knowing that illusion and fear worked better than their dicks.

Sugarman, the pick-up man, hustled numbers during the day and had two hustlers working at night. The strip west of Woodward, known as the Cass Corridor, provided him with pocket money to finance his pimping and an ever-ready supply of soon-to-be-his-women to fill his corral. Not much money yet—but then, he hadn't learned the game yet.

"Look, Sugarman, I told ya from the start I been lookin' to work fo' M.D.," Millie said, the thin lines just beneath the surface of the skin around her mouth suddenly emerging, as she was making a point—a point that Sugarman missed, just as he missed her lines: it would cost him later (for he would need a replacement sooner than he expected). "I saw M.D. smile at me last night." She was a good-looking woman who knew it. A sharecropper's daughter who came North and was doing good, but expected to do better.

"Where did you see that gorilla-lookin' niggah?"

"In the Chesterfield. Say what ya will, Sugarman, but he knows how to make a lady feel…"

"Look, baby, you are *dreaming!* Get it? You are dreaming! You are so far off into a fuckin' fantasy, Disney couldn't bring you back!" Snapping his fingers, then pointing with his forefinger, he started laughing. "Yeah…look what he done to Snow White. She got the poison apple!"

"But then she got the prince."

"But ya ain't Snow White, baby, and yo' Prince ain't comin'. Not if you think Monkey Dee is he. Dee deals with nothin' but class, baby. And class ain't what ya got.

"Maybe so. Maybe no. But I got plentee ass!" she said, snapping her fingers in his face. "And that's what sells, my friend."

"Not in Dee's stable. Ya too broad, baby. Too full. Too round. Good-lookin' but that's all. And that's not enough fo' the Monkey. The kind of woman the Monkey wants… Well, they got…*something*. They brings plenty bread, baby. Lilac got a three-hundred-a-hour pussy."

"She white, Sugarman, that's why."

"Naw, baby, she ain't white, she just looks white… And some niggahs will pay anything fo' what they *think* they gittin'."

"Look, Sugarman, *I been around.* I know white when I see it… All them crackers down home. Don't tell me I don't know white!"

"Baby, you just named the problem. You know white from down home. This ain't down home, country gal. This is the big ci-ty! And you trying to read Big D from a down home book!"

"What niggah got that kind of money to pay fo' a three-hundred-dollar piece of ass?"

"Ya would be surprised, *my friend,* what some big-time preachers and small-time politicians will pay fo' admission to Disneyland. Next time, country gal, git up close and take a good look at Lilac. Maybe she'll give you some tips."

"You one simple-minded fool, *my friend*. And why I worked fo' you remains a mystery to me. What workin' gal gon' let another gal git close to her working space?"

"Don't worry 'bout it, baby, ain't no contest."

"I'm gon' work fo' the Monkey one day, ya watch."

"Dream on, baby. Suit yo'self. But in the meantime, listen up."

"You listen up, Sugarman. And come here."

"Look, baby, I ain't got no time…"

When Sunshine rose in the night and stared out, the window came alive and so did she—moving down John R. Street, a satin doll with a wonderful ass. Held high in high-heel shoes, seams straight, with perfume splashed between her thighs and rubbed between her breasts, she went into the Chesterfield Bar, ordered whiskey and water, laughed and nodded to the female impersonators already on stage, who, even while entertaining on stage, would envy her wonderful ass pressed onto the barstool. The whole time they were stripping down to their G-strings they envied her. That wonderful ass, edging the barstool, ready for the night to begin. For no matter how clever they were or how they wore their makeup, tied their G-strings, removed their body hair, or gestured, they knew, as she did, they could never be the real thing. Yet each wondered about the other. She, with the wonderful ass, tried to guess how they hid their disturbing dicks; and they, with inquisitive dicks, eyed her wonderful ass looking for elusive clues that might explain the mystery of it.

Or maybe she would go to the Frolic or Flame Showbars, where tiny bits of mirror were fitted together behind the bar, forming one giant reflection for all the customers—some to check a moustache, others to wipe away the lipstick smear from a top lip. But none passed their reflection without looking, for that mirror was the only lie they could count on. All the other lies up and down John R. Street were subject to change, depending on who told them, what time of day it was—or night—which way you were standing when it happened, and who you owed a favor to. But the broken bits of mirror remained a steady voyeur, looking into the lives and the faces of the converts along John R. Street.

All the moustaches would smile as they felt the hot breath flow from beneath them, their eyes watching the razzle dazzle of the female impersonators. The moustaches announced that they were *real* men, some who worked in the foundry by day, fucked and re-fucked women before coming out for the evening, and then fucked women in between sets.

But still they enjoyed the real life in the bars watching unreal men do their "real thing." As the sculptured male asses paraded in front of them, laced with one gold G-string, they sat on the edge of barstools, pulling at one pant leg and then the other, kicking one foot out and then the other, revealing one silk sock and then the other, and felt a feeling like none other—rise as their silk stockings rose, stopping suddenly at the knee. But the feeling continued on up—rising, caressing their muscled thighs, moving into the main chamber, where their disturbed dicks, still inquisitive, got caught in the swish and sway of the sculptured asses with the golden G-string.

And all the wonderful asses would, in seeing themselves inside the broken bits of mirror behind the bar, pause, and check their over-penciled eyebrows and under-penciled beauty moles, suddenly not sure if they wanted to remember what life was like outside of the bars that struck the night in flares.

Morning signaled and the syncopated rhythm began. From each door emerged the arthritic aunts and palsied uncles moving from third to second to first floor. The uncles filed past with their black cannons topped with the silver handles—inside, cold potato salad and yesterday's chicken. Chicken was a welcome addition to the lunch pails. No longer did northern coloreds wait for Sundays, and the preacher, to fix and eat chicken. No, this was the North and yesterday's chicken, be it Tuesday's or Wednesday's, in the black lunch pails with the silver handles, was a sign of Negroes on the move.

At 5:45 the yellow streetcar clamored up, leaving a trail of steel gray ribbons in the deep dark asphalt. Overhead, the umbilical cord was taut, tied into the main line. Sometimes sparks flew—crack! A lash, as a steeped memory deep inside the psyche slid out and other images of other lashes and other chains tangled in the umbilical cord. All were dazed by the rash of stars, by the comet's tail—the amen, the alpha and omega. The aunts with the jigsaw joints and the jittery uncles and the some just-glad-to-be-here cousins waited on it to go somewhere.

But they couldn't go somewhere, nor could they go over there, as if they could amble over there with no particular time for getting there and back. No, they had to go up there, not down there, for that was where they had just come from and smart meant knowing where you came from. And no, they couldn't go from here to there, and no they couldn't go back there either. And even going right there wasn't possible, because if they were all going right there, they could have walked, cause there ain't no need for colored folks to take a streetcar right there. No, everybody was going up there. All except Kali who didn't know where she was going...yet.

The up there forked at ten miles. The dislocated aunts went to the right with their black-strapped leather shopping bags stuffed with a second uniform, just in case, and store-bought shoes with the sides slit to release corns, already weary from the streetcar ride.

The men went to the left, toward the plant. This time it was metal they picked, not cotton. The metal would roll out as they "picked" their way through the field of Henry Ford's new invention–the assembly line. So new, in fact, few saw the metal grow up around their feet and demand the life from them even as King Cotton had done.

"Where's my grandbaby?" asked Miss Charlotte, not bothering to knock on the bedroom door but once. Never giving her time to say, *Who's there?* like people say who own the space they live in.

"There. He scoots in the corner of his crib, Miss Charlotte."

"Those yo's?" Miss Charlotte asked, pointing to a series of quick hand drawings that were taped to the walls. "You got a good hand," she acknowledged, moving about the room, tipping over one of Brother's shoes with the end of her stockinged toe, which was neatly polished, flipping open a magazine, closing it, and finally she turned toward the girl who had been watching her all the while from the mirror she was sitting in front of.

"Ya just wash yo' hair?"

The house blinked. Felt cold then hot. It needed something cool. A fan blowing on a bowl of ice cubes. An open window perhaps?

"I was tryin' to let it dry before I pinned it up."

"Leave it that way."

"What way?"

"Down."

Miss Charlotte slipped the hairpin from Sunshine's hand while in midair. Then she slid it between her teeth and picked up the hairbrush, humming softly.

The hum entered the back door of Sheppard's Place, where women big and small, black and tan, sang the Blues. One gold tooth with a diamond star blazing from it flashed through the smoke. It filled the bar where Big Maybelle sang—getting the women ready on Friday night for what they were gonna feel Saturday night when their men failed to come home, *I Got a Feeling Somebody's Trying to Steal My Man.*

But she hadn't come to New Orleans in search of a man or the Blues. No, she was in search of something better. And if not better, certainly different. She found it leaning up against the piano every Thursday in a tight, tight dress singing in a small voice.

"Is that a halo 'round yo' head?" Charlotte asked, sure she was seeing one, and reached to touch it as the two women sat at the bar.

The small woman with the small voice smiled, leaned forward stroking her slender fingers along Charlotte's thigh, and answered, "No. Is that a line meant to get my attention?"

"Uh huh."

"Not a chance." They both laughed.

"I swear I see a halo ever' time ya sing!"

"What do you see now?" the small woman with the small voice purred. She straddled a naked Charlotte, who was breathing heavily. Rivulets of water cascaded down their bodies—both still wet from the bath they took together. Charlotte lay watching two water droplets— backgrounded by lamplight—ready themselves. They teetered on the tip—enlarged and enlarging—ready to burst from pink nipples. Hungrily the small woman mouthed Charlotte's dark nipples, crushing the hanging water droplets on her own, filling her mouth, rising, thrusting her body forward. Placing one pink nipple in Charlotte's warm, dark, and wet mouth, she rocked back, still on all fours. She moved the tip of her tongue along Charlotte's body, trying to dry it.

"At this rate we'll never be dry," the small voice whispered, the loudest sound it had made to date. Charlotte groaned, lifting her dark body to meet the wettest tongue from the wettest mouth in the world. Tumbling on the bed, they were night then day as each tumbled over the other, like winking stars creating first light in the darkened bedroom.

Charlotte had found Sheppard's Place on her day off and heard this woman with the small voice sing. Not a great voice, not deep and rich like her own, but a voice.

Now, in the dark, drowsy room, she asked the small-voiced woman her momma's name and all her sisters' names, all in one breath.

Laughing, the small voice asked, "Why do you want to know my mother's and sisters' names for?"

"Cause if I wake from this dream and find ya gon', I'm gonna git on the first thang smokin'. Coming for yo' momma and if she says no, I'll start on yo' sisters."

"*Girl*, you outta be shame!"

"No, Ricky, Ricky, Ricky, Ricky!" she huskily repeated. Each time the name moved from her lips and out into the darkened room it layered itself, building as it went. "I want ya. And I'm here to stay." And they stayed together, even when their new act got discovered by a big-time agent and they went to New York to do a show.

The young daughter-in-law tried reaching for the brush but was stopped by Miss Charlotte, who moved the young girl's hand away and placed it back in her lap. Then touching her own index finger to her mouth, shook her head no.

Sunshine watched, fascinated by the ritual reflected in the mirror. Finally, the older woman pulled the hairpin from her teeth, collected the sandy hair that was beginning to curl, and pinned it on top. Dropping her face near the rose tips of her ear, she asked in a low whisper, "Ya got pink titties too?"

"Too?"

"Like Ricky."

"Who?"

"No, never mind."

She left the room closing the door softly.

Sunshine sat for a long moment after Miss Charlotte left, placing her arm across her breast, wondering, who was Ricky?

FIVE

"You pussy-whipped mothafucker! Get your redneck leeching suburban self home to your prune-pussied wife!"

There stood a white man who had appeared from nowhere, suddenly cussing and chasing a speeding white car.

"You sure you're all right?" he asked, holding his throat with one hand, trying to catch his breath.

"Me?"

"Who else am I looking at, honey?"

The white man moved toward her as she stood struggling with two pillowcases—one full of dirty clothes, the other full of baby diapers. With her mind on last night's hard conversation with Brother, she hadn't seen him come up the first time. She had been on her way to the laundromat when a sports car, some two-seater with wire wheels, had slowed down driving alongside of her. A redheaded man leaned over, rolling down the passenger window, and asked, "How much?" Suddenly, the car jumped into gear and took off as this white man took off running, chasing the car. Now here he was, back again.

"Don't be so chicken shit. I asked how *are* you? Those *bastards!*" he screeched, turning from her and shaking a fist toward moving traffic.

"Why do you have your head covered up, honey?" he asked as he lifted his hand to remove the cloth wound carefully around her head.

She drew her head back.

"This is a wrap." She had seen them in *Sepia* magazine, where she had flipped over the dark and lovely African women who wound these colorful swirls about their heads.

"You gotta be a student."

"I wish."

The white man was surprised by her quick step back. He was, after all, the only white man who was permanent on the strip. He lived among these dark people, never thinking that they might not believe in his commitment to them. He dropped his head just a little and ran his long, slender, manicured hand through his hair—just like her father did. She realized with a stab how much she missed him. Especially his: *Hey, Dumplin'. How's trix?* And her reply, *Solid!,* as they gave each other five.

She had grown used to Brother's hair, which was stiff as a board and did not move.

"I like my hair covered," the young girl said and started to struggle with the two pillowcases again, losing one of the dirty diapers in the process. He reached for it, pinching it with his forefinger and thumb, stretching his arm full length, and turning his head to one side.

"How do you *stand* doing these things?"

"I suppose just like your mother did," she remarked.

Huh! A sassy little bitch, he thought. "*Girl,* don't you just *hate* those bastards?" he asked, flipping into an impersonation of himself, limp wrist and all.

"Why should I? I don't even know them."

The white man paused for a moment, decided that this was one woman best left alone. Still, he said, "You look just like my mother, Mary."

She smiled, not because she believed him for one minute, but because he was so ridiculous and, ultimately, harmless. She found herself enjoying him. And he, catching the feeling between them, asked for no particular reason, "Where did you get that nail polish, honey?" He refrained from touching her this time.

"Nail polish?" she asked, impersonating him. Making a wide grin and batting her eyelashes.

"Come on, honey. The one ya'll wearing. Try and think *real* hard where you got it."

"From Laphonya."

"What's a *Laphonya?*" he screamed, smacking his thigh.

"Laphonya is not a 'what,' she's my *aunt*. Well, not mine, but my husband's aunt. And she got it at Maxine's."

"On Woodward?"

"Uh huh."

"That heifer!"

"I beg your pardon, not *my* aunt!" she yelled, her face starting to break up.

"No! No! I meant Maxine." He was rolling now. "She promised to call me when it came in," he finally managed to say.

"Oh," she said, grabbing his hands and examining them carefully. "That color ya'll wearing matches your eyes perfectly. Bloodshot!"

"I do nails," he said, regaining some composure. "The girls come to me before showtime."

"Showtime?"

"At the Chesterfield. I do hair, too." This time overstepping his boundaries and successfully removing her head wrap.

"It needs a conditioner," he announced, managing to pull apart a few strands of her hair.

"Do you mind?" she asked, furiously trying to rewrap the material, even though she knew it was impossible without a mirror.

"What did you say your name was, sugar?"

"I didn't."

"No matter, Mary."

She had seen him before from her nightly perch on the window sill. He belonged to the six-block stretch of John R. Street where everybody who was anybody came to play. He worked, she knew, in the Gotham Hotel, which was just across the street from the old house. The house that stood alone among the beer gardens, fancy clubs, and barbershops.

The six-block strip of high rollers, some just up from the South, some never having been there, was like the white-man-who-belonged-on-John-R.-Street: out of place, made to fit in on a street of misfits; out of step but not out of the minds of the dutiful people downtown who, in order to turn attention away from money received under the table, needed to start a campaign to clean up crime and corruption in Detroit City. And John R. Street would be next. In the meantime... Now white folks, who came to buy, mixed in with the caramel-colored high rollers, the Black-get-back dapper daddies, and all the in-betweens.

The whites made their business short and sweet on the strip, but inside the clubs it was a different matter. They ordered drinks like they ordered women—or men. Saying, "Scotch and soda, that one with the black skin and gold teeth. Jack Daniels and water, that one with the high ass."

Some preferred men, like the slender reed of a man, the lone one sitting at the far end of the bar—waiting, sipping slowly. The one who drank only Black Bull straight up—when there was money enough. And had the red scarf tied at his neck. There would be a wink. A recognition. Another drink. Another. Then an absent barstool left spinning.

And their money bought it all. Reefers and booze. Deeper drugs that did deeper things, leaving them smelling the sweet roots of places they had never been. Ordering life and lives to suit their wallets.

There were young women, some on drugs, others just to buy bread—all wanted to stop turning tricks in doorways; older women on the way down, terrified at the thought of returning to the doorways and street corners; young boys who wanted the latest pair of Stacy Adamses; or seasoned fags—in drag or not. But the white-man-who-belonged-on-John-R.-Street took his time—and he moved that way. He knew about time, like colored people know about time. They know life takes time and they slow down for it. Time's not something you aim for, but something you live. This white boy was either a fool, she supposed, or southern. Not too many white men let time move them, Laphonya said, most think they move it, except some few southern whites who know about colored folks and time. Most hurried into the bars quickly, and when they came out, they came out suddenly. Led by women who laughed, or colored men who didn't. But this man lingered and stood timeless under the streetlight just to the left of the door of the Gotham Hotel. Very still.

Then, one night as Sunshine sat watching from the sill, into this stilled time a movement dropped from a long sleek white car that pulled in front of the Gotham. A white expensive coat—cashmere maybe?—draped about shoulders that rocked on unsteady legs. It passed under the dim yellow streetlight, avoiding the red rhythm of the neon signs. The long white arms of the white coat—cashmere maybe?—were flailing in the white fog, empty arms dangling, star dust raining out of his pocket.

The moon, already on its back, offered itself—illuminating the winter frost collected around the rounded circles of the sewer grates. Shimmers. The grates shone like new money. The night hushed as the car moved away, slowly at first, then faster, white smoke pouring from its tail and joining the low ground fog just beginning to swirl, both circling the sleeves of the very expensive, perhaps cashmere, coat. As the white smoke from the car joined the low ground fog and merged with the after-trail of the red tail lights from the car, the poem began. The night heard the recitation begin, softly at first, then more labored, as it breathed in quick puffs at the sight of itself mirrored in the glints of tiny snowflakes that were slowly falling—everything else was in deep freeze.

The speeding car was gone, but the flashing red lights remained hanging in the cold night air, and merged with the neon signs from the clubs. The red warmed in her mouth as John R stood motionless for a moment, caught in the on-beat from the neon signs and released in the off-beat.

There was a waver but no break in the movement, even though it rocked on unsteady legs. Before it climbed the stairs of the Gotham, it bowed on bent and bowed legs as the flashing red lights that weren't supposed to be there merged with the neon signs that were and created a strange marriage, illuminating the face of the white-man-who-belonged-on-John-R.-Street. Who stood aside to let the movement pass.

Everything about that face was severe. It was severely white. The nose was severely narrow. And the mouth was severely thin. But when he smiled, his hawklike features descended into a broad, white smile that disarmed the dark inhabitants on the strip.

As the thin white smoke and the white ground fog descended into the sewer grates, the movement pitched forward and the white-man-who-belonged-on-John-R.-Street reached to break its fall.

"Do she wash?"

Brother didn't answer his mother. He decided that it was better to finish his cereal and get her on to work.

"I asked ya, boy, do she wash?"

But before he could figure out just what she meant, she answered her own question.

"Bet not. I don't hear no tub water runnin' no time. How ya stand a woman don't wash?"

"Shh! Momma, she can hear you."

"Don't shush me in my own house, boy. Besides, she's a lady of leisure; she ain't up till noon."

"Momma! She's got the baby to see 'bout."

"Shiitt! She'll stick a tit in his mouth and he'll be out fo' the count."

"Momma!"

"Let's go. I'm gonna be late. There's a new shipment comin' in." Miss Charlotte grabbed her purse and her coffee cup and went out before Brother, talking as she went. "She was fryin' chicken the other day and she didn't wash that chicken off fo' she floured it. She just threw it in the grease! I thought she was gonna set fire to the kitchen!"

"What are you *gettin'* at, Momma?"

She turned slowly and looked at him as if he had asked the dumbest question ever.

"Woman don't wash no chicken fo' she fry it don't do much washin' no other place either."

Just then the front door opened and King came in.

"Where ya comin' from, Solomon?"

"Charlotte," he said her name with some disgust, "I been workin' swing shift fo' years—six months on and six off. I'm on second shift." In fact, he had been on second shift for a few weeks now but Charlotte hadn't taken any notice.

"Then why you comin' in the door this time of mornin'?"

"I cain't sleep. Did you?"

Brother could feel the question his father was really asking, and hoped, just this once, his mother would hear it too. He started to push past them, annoyed with the extra weight his father carried.

The door to the bridal bedroom opened and Sunshine floated

out with her hair in long braids falling past her shoulders. She wiped her eyes with both fists like a child. She looked so young. The child ignored Charlotte and Brother and spoke to King.

"Are we going to do it today, Daddy King?"

"Sunshine!" Brother moved toward his wife. "Did we wake you up?"

"Do what?" Charlotte turned to face the young girl, who recognized that she had on a new wig.

"Is that new?" she asked, pointing to the wig. She knew that was a question women reserved for each other, in their own space, and only if they liked each other.

"Do *what*, Solomon?" Charlotte asked, turning toward her husband.

"Corn fritters, Charlotte. Little Sis wants to learn to make corn fritters."

Brother looked directly at his mother, who was looking at him, waiting for him to say something. He shrugged his shoulders.

"And where will *you* be when all this is goin' on, boy?"

"Out," he said, gaining courage as he looked over at his father, then smiled at his wife.

"Well, maybe it's *best* that *all* of ya'll kiss my black ass!" she shouted, snatching the car keys out of Brother's hand. She dumped the burning contents of her coffee cup down her throat and stormed out of the house.

The day had been cold. The house creaked all day. The wind played music in the rafters inside the attic. Music, the house remembered, like Char-Lee had first played that day when his mind came back to him. He had been grieving all these years! And nobody knew it. Or even suspected it except the house. It watched him sit for hours playing with his whistle and waited till the boy came back to himself.

After the third floor miracle, as King liked to speak of it, he began to take the boy, now in his middle teens, everywhere he went. And it was one of those times that Charles Lee, leaving King in an animated conversation with Black Muslims over an article printed in the *Amsterdam News*, wandered over to a lone musician standing in back of the Frolic Showbar blowing his horn. Char-Lee fell in love. He stood electrified by the sound. No one—at least then—paid the boy, or the horn player for that matter, any attention; no one, least of all the day people, realized they were hearing the birth of Be-Bop.

But Sunshine couldn't have known all that. Now she heard music coming from the rafters and wondered why no one else heard it. The rafters played music inside the attic, just through the paneled door, off the stairwell of the third floor. She had waited all day for John R to toss off its day clothes with the slow throbbing beat of a stripper. Finally, 'round midnight, she moved from her bed and onto the secret sill and peered out. Wafts of broken fog clung to the neck of streetlights, creating a haze of luminous cobwebs spun about the lamps. She felt privately like the old woman who chained herself to the prophet while he slept and wouldn't let him go until he gave her a blessing. The strip held something for everyone who entered the boulevard of beautiful people and dared to stay. What about her?

She saw Vanderbilt at his usual station across the street at the entrance to the Gotham. No one would have guessed that Vanderbilt Rockerfellow Ford, the cool white boy, had come from a small town in North Carolina that was full of marching bands and Saturday football games. At age eighteen, he had joined the army and then moved North after his discharge. This move had given him an inexhaustible supply of Black men.

His first look and taste of northern Black men in boot camp brought this southern sissy, he wrote, *to Boy's Town. And life ain't never been the same!* *They have,* he wrote in his fifth 100-page diary, *bodies that wink, like cool serpents; others move with a kind of "jitty."*

Jitty, he explained in his notes, *is a kind of walk that only northern Blacks do. They carve it out of the cement prison they live in! Why don't they kill every whitey they see?* he asked his notebook. Then he put an aside, in large print, *Shit, that would be me. I love the walk and talk of them. And all them southern peckerwoods would too if they only knew. Arm stiff at the side with the hand pulled back, fingers failing. Then step. Other arm stiff, hand and fingers failing. Step. Repeat. It's a song.* (He tried it once but Dee told him his swish got in the way.) *It is "hip" and they are cool, these fast-talking fast-moving Dee-troit Blacks.* And he finished the page with *I love it!*

He had followed his first real love back to Detroit. The love had fizzled but not his taste for these beautiful black butterflies, cocooned on John R. Street, trapped in the six-block square.

Monkey Dee descended the stairs of the Gotham, his white cashmere coat still draped on his shoulders—the sleeves moving in hypnotizing rhythm—his shoulders pressed back as an electric current snaked through the movement in his body. Taller now somehow, he grew with each step he descended. Even the night fell back as the flashing tail lights rounded the corner toward him. He passed Vanderbilt, smiled, and tipped the brim of his white fedora he had pulled down over one eye. Lilac was with him and so was Ruby Red. He got in the long sleek white car that had appeared. The women getting in behind him seemed bunched, braided together—Lilac, white with full purple lips, and Ruby Red, black with no lips. Lilac turned and pressed her face against the back window of the long sleek white car, distorting her features like a child making faces. Ruby Red looked straight ahead. The driver pulled away quickly, but Monkey Dee, looking backwards over the heads of the two women as the street fled before him, tipped his kid gloves against the brim of his white fedora, smiled, and sank back into the cushioned seat.

Struggling again with her laundry bags on her way to the laundromat, her attention was drawn to the street, and so were all the day people along the strip who stopped and gawked. Willie "Chi-Town" Wilson was passing in his black on black in black Cadillac—followed by lesser makes of long white cars. Even without being on the strip proper, everybody knew when Chi-Town and company were in town. Suddenly all the boosters everywhere would have all kinds of "hot" clothes to sell. Chi-Town provided the locals with the latest leathers, suedes, silks, and satins. His car stopped briefly, and from the back seat a copper brown woman with a blonde wig stared at the girl on the sidewalk trying to lift both bags of dirty diapers. The woman sucked in her breath and placed a gloved hand up against the closed car window. She mouthed some sort of coded message that was lost on the struggling young woman. The procession passed one way and the laundry bags another.

Outside the laundromat, she rested for a moment, setting down the sack of diapers. Through the window she could see Easter-Egg-Man going toe to toe with Jesus, who was in the middle of a sermon about white blue-eyed devils.

Mabel's Washtub was a gathering place—warm in the winter, warmer in the summer. It was a womb that carried everybody, no matter who and what you were. The sweat from dryers and people steamed the windows. If she had known Easter-Egg-Man was going to be there she would have waited…

"Yo' daddie's rich and yo' momma's good-lookin'," a wino sang and played his harmonica just outside the door. Sunshine picked up her bags again and walked in.

It was hot inside. But she grew cold when she saw Beverly look at her. Jesus made the quick connection, for he saw everything.

"I died for your sins."

"Ya'll ever seen a black Jesus before?" Beverly turned to the laundromat audience.

She blinked and thought about reaching again. The crowd laughed and Jesus groaned, covered his heart with long slender fingers, and looked about him—his eyes luminous, his beard snarled, his knotty braids hanging almost to his waist. Now, silently, he began to move around the laundromat—his robe swinging, stopping short at his ankles, his feet hard and crusty from walking barefoot. He moved among the people, glaring at them through glassy eyes. Finally he returned to his spot opposite the Easter-Egg-Man. The crowd paused—waiting.

Beverly had not been to the house since the baby was born. Well, yes he had, he had come only yesterday while she was upstairs with Lizzie and Laphonya. If anyone had asked he'd say he'd been away.

She hadn't known he was in the house. But he had left his telltale can of paint in the hallway. This time Charlotte had him painting something in King's bedroom. The paint was black.

The banter with Jesus continued but had slowed down, the Easter-Egg-Man was growing weary in his head. Only Jesus noticed; the crowd didn't. They loved Jesus, but were afraid of him. Goodness they questioned. They could never trust it. Evil they understood and made room for. They also loved the Tempter, Easter-Egg-Man, but had no fear of him.

What colored people expected goodness? Or could trust it even if it came? Better to have what you knew, and the Tempter they knew. He tempted them with women and strong drink. Somebody's husband. He got them to play numbers and gamble the rent money away. Laughed at them when they went down to witness the popular, talented, and expensively-tailored Reverend Lawrence and his "Ship of Joy," the good Reverend's Sunday night radio broadcast.

"I'm waiting on the *Quiet* money to talk, chil'ren... Hear me now. Uhmm...Uhmm... Can you hear me, JEE-sus? Praise God!" He shouted, skipping about—pausing and catching himself on the hem of his gown. Pulling it up, he shouted again, rubbing it between his hands like he was using a washboard. Then, dropping it, he began to strut. The loose gown waved back and forth as he went from one side of the pulpit to the other, like a rooster in a barnyard.

"PRAISE GOD! Hallelujah! PRAISE GOD! Gimme, Gimme, Gimme that *Quiet* money." He whooped. "Gimme, Gimme, Gimme, Moneymoneymoney! Mon-NEY should *never* make a loud noise unto the Lord. Hallelujah! Praise Him!"

The little old sisters would drop their coins back into their pinched purses and reach one more time, in the name of the Lord, for the paper money that "don't do no loud talkin'." They placed it on the floor, where the ushers swept it up into bushel baskets.

Easter-Egg-Man made all the noise they would not. But he profaned the scriptures, something they dared not.

"Let him without sin throw the first stone," Jesus, arms outstretched, was speaking to the crowd.

"*Man!* You gotta quit." There was real pleading in Easter-Egg-Man's voice. "We gotta git offa our *knees!*"

"Repent! He who looks at a woman to commit sin with her has already committed adultery in his heart."

"WE GOTTA BE READY WHEN THE MAN COMES, YOU GOT THAT, MAN?" he yelled, grabbing Jesus by the neck of his robe. The crowd groaned. Beverly closed his eyes for only a minute to get his bearings and stomp himself out of a frenzy. Dressed in that African stuff with a tiki dangling from his neck, he looked just like the wild man they were afraid of becoming. He was Cheeta. Or the darkies they saw in Tarzan movies who always ask the white man in *their* jungle, "Which way, Bwana?"

When he opened his eyes, Jesus had gone out from among them. Beverly couldn't remember releasing him. The crowd dispersed. This round they awarded to Jesus. Tomorrow was another day.

SIX

⟅⟨⟫⟆

Shitshitshitshitshitshitshit, Solomon! Shitshitshitshitshit. SOL-omon! Shit, shit, shit, shit, shit! Shit! Shit! Shit! Shit! Shit! Shit! Shit! Shit! Shit! Shit! SOLOMON!

Miss Charlotte was at it again. Her *shits* rose in perfect pitch from first floor to second then on to the third. Soon the drum beat of her *goddamns* would join the first, second, and third floor *shits*.

God damn you, Solomon! God damn yo' rusty hide! God damn! God damn! God damn, ya son of a bitch! As the octave change of the perfect pitched *shits* gave way to the lower boom of *goddamns*, they broke the naps of the arthritic aunts and confused the not-so-sure cousins.

The sounds of *shits* and *goddamns* sometimes rustled the pages of the jangled uncles, blurring the tiny print of the *Detroit Times*. And entered the wash basins of the snarled aunts crinkling the water of today's soaking uniform. They went on to confuse the confused cousins who had no idea why Miss Charlotte's perfect-pitched *shits*, and the low boom of her *goddamns*, started in the first place. She'd reached for the phone on the first ring. "Hello?" she said. Click. The caller hung up when they heard her voice. "One of Solomon's BITCHES again!" she screamed.

Every month or so the drama was the same. King retreated to the bedroom and everyone else to their own small rooms, while Charlotte broke every dish in the kitchen. Cups. Then glasses. She even tossed the silver. Then a final crescendo like cymbals being wildly struck as the pots and pans hit the wall.

She had a special vendetta against the kitchen. Colored women lived and died tied to a kitchen. Theirs or some white woman's. She tore the kitchen up every chance she got.

Anybody wading into Miss Charlotte's kitchen after one of her battles would back away, wondering why King let her get away with it. Maybe her time in New Orleans made her act this way—ornery. Tale was she had done some singin' down there. But she didn't sing in the church choir. Miss Charlotte, for that matter, didn't even go to church! So what kind of woman was this? And rumor was she had been with a white man.

It was late, as usual, and Sil Silverstein's office was clogged with fabric samples, as usual. He had been at his desk—mostly on the phone—for twelve hours, hadn't eaten all day. And now he was about to fire someone.

"You want to know why I hire colored people?" Sil asked the not-so-young and obviously defiant Negro woman standing before him. "You think anybody cares why I hire colored people? Even colored people?"

"Yes *sah*, Mistah Silverstein."

"You think that the whole world is caring that Sil Silverstein lives? Or colored people? Why do you give everybody always such shit? Why, if you can tell me? You been here...for what, two months?"

The rather tall, dark woman was ill at ease, but said nothing.

"I'm the friend of the colored people. Ask anybody about Sil Silverstein, they can tell you!" Looking up and into her hostile face, he said, "God forbid you should smile, lady. Are you listening?"

"Yes *sah*, Mistah Silverstein." The Negro woman looked down at him and gave him the famous darky smile—one that he knew and she knew he knew.

"It's enough, already. You're fired."

"Kiss my ass!" the Negro woman said, suddenly erupting, "Mistah Silverstein!" She turned to go, her hips as defiant as her face had been.

Sil stood up and shook a fist at her back. "That I should live to hear such anger wasted on me. If *we* had had such anger!" He stooped over, beginning to cough and choke.

"I hope it ain't catchin'," she said and turned back to help him move to the small sofa in his office.

He waved her away, finally clearing his throat. "Go ahead, leave. I should die in peace."

"I ain't ready to leave now that I'm fired."

"I have a question," he said, easing down onto the sofa.

"I ain't got to answer." She still held him under one elbow, steadying him.

"When are you people gonna get off of your knees? And put that anger to work?"

"When fuckahs like ya git yo' foot offa our necks." And that began the love affair with Sil Silverstein.

He said once, "I wanna see with these eyes here," pointing at his eyes then pulling at his jowls, extending them like balloons stuffed with water, "you people taking to the streets—demanding... You think I can live so long, Charlotte?"

"Not unless you gonna dump some money out there, Sil."

"You always make the joke."

The affair had been discreet. Done when Solomon was on the second shift. Few calls were made to her on John R. Street. Seldom did Miriam, Sil's wife, come down to the business. Silverstein was dying—a little every day. And when he did, three years after the affair had begun, Charlotte stayed on to run Sil's upholstery company. Charlotte, as it turned out, had an eye for color and fabric and a sense of what would sell to Sil's mainly Black and poor white customers.

"He never got over surviving," Miriam had explained the first day she and Charlotte ever talked.

Each knew Sil's guilt. They slept with it as they woke him from his tortured dreams, afraid of his screams and afraid for him when the anguish ripped through his body.

When Sil left Charlotte a piece of the business, Miriam didn't like it but she was wise enough to know who really kept the business going as Sil's health declined.

"Sil left things good for me." The truth was that Miriam loved her husband. "Like the first day I met him, I still love him." And she had respected him and his decisions. Even this one.

"My Sil wanted that she should have a piece of the business. So what's so terrible?"

"Brother, 'for ya go out, tell Sunshine to bring the tea." Brother turned and left the doorway of the parlor as his mother settled back in her wing-backed chair and entertained the ladies from the Pastor's Aide. As a rule, men didn't come into Miss Charlotte's parlor. Not that they could not. They did not. King and Brother kept their distance and so did all the rest.

All seven of the women from the Pastor's Aide were there, more for Lizzie's sake than Charlotte's. Laphonya knew that. Why, she thought, did Charlotte play this game? These women bored her. Charlotte was forever with the lifted coffee cup in her hand. Why the women came, Laphonya could never figure out. But they did. Lizzie's face was shining. Glowing. Everyone was talking about the electrifying Reverend Midas, everyone but Miss Charlotte. She just smiled and looked over the edge of her coffee cup—never able, no matter how often they came, to remember the names of the women there. She sipped the brew and proceeded to wipe the corner of her mouth with one of the linen napkins she used for such occasions. Soon now, Laphonya knew Charlotte would find a way to get them out. Just as soon as she got whatever Charlotte wanted from them. Laphonya suspected Charlotte of some special dislike for these women and the way they stuffed themselves full of church. "Men or church," Miss Charlotte would say. "One or the other. Never both."

"Charlotte, that's a precious grandbaby." The lady with the brown hat went on, "He's got his father's way. I know you're glad 'bout the first being a boy. We womens know how our misters feel 'bout boys." She gave a little cough and went on. "Why, Mr. Woodrow complains—bein' in a house with women. Jesus knows how hard I tried, but he wouldn't come. Many a night I fell down on my knees..." The woman with the brown hat's voice was rising. "Cried out to Him! Jesus lift this affliction. Did I do some thin' to offend ya, Lord? Have mercy, Je-sus! But the girls kept on. Four girls is all I could stand," she lamented, shaking her head. "But Mr. Woodrow won't sign for my tubes to be tied. Even though the doctor says..."

"Don't let it git you down, girl," the woman in the green dress said.

"You can talk! You got a house of boys! Yo' mister ain't blaming ya for jinxin' him," she said, turning her focus back to Miss Charlotte. "I know ya is blessed."

"Momma's *baby*, Daddy's *maybe*," Miss Charlotte said, very slow and very deliberate. The women all froze.

"Charlotte! Ya don't mean ya thank...?" the woman with the brown hat started to ask.

No one but Miss Charlotte had heard Sunshine come in. Brother had left the door open.

"What!" she shrieked. She seized the opportunity to fling down the silver tray she held. The milk went flying one way, the cookies another. Hot tea spilled on the nyloned legs of the women from the Pastor's Aide. They all screamed, and hurriedly wiped their legs.

Miss Charlotte looked up slowly, drained her cup, wiped her mouth with the linen table cloth, and said, "Maybe all of you better leave now. Little Miss Sunshine seems upset."

The house heard thunder. The rain started up again. It had been feeling bad—and the rain didn't help. But it had received a new coat of paint earlier today—something in King's room. Charlotte had ordered black paint. But even with that it couldn't shake the Blues. The door to Brother's room had been closed all morning and most of the afternoon. Was she in there?

Then the door had opened; feet, moving weighted and slow on the cool linoleum floor, had gone into Miss Charlotte's parlor. Wielding a large brush, with bold strokes, Miss Charlotte's daughter-in-law had written in tall black letters on the yellow walls of the parlor: *My name is KALI! My name is KALI! My name is KALI!* And then she had left the house.

No one knew what to say about Miss Charlotte's parlor. Charlotte just sat, sipping coffee, and stared at the black-stained walls. Finally, Lizzie asked, "Charlotte, want I should ask the Easter-Egg-Man?"

"Not yet," Miss Charlotte said, and kept on sipping.

"That chile cain't even spell her own name," Lizzie said. "C-A-L-L-I-E spells Kali, don't it?"

"Not just yet," Miss Charlotte said again, sitting back in her wing-backed chair, feeling a tug at her throat—her eyes watering.

SEVEN

She walked into the Gotham streaked and spotted in black paint. She almost bumped Dee on his way out. "What the fuck! Don't get that shit on my *coat!*"

"Where's that white man that's always looking after you?"

"What *do* you mean?"

"Just a minute, young lady," a woman said from behind the hotel desk.

"Hold on, Mildred, I know this painter who gets more paint on herself than on the canvas," Vanderbilt said, emerging from the back of the hotel. "Mary, what are you doing here?"

Still caught in the drama just ended in the old house, she screamed, "My name is KALI! Do you get that? KALI!"

When she woke, she was lying on something that moved every time she did. It sounded like newspaper. Perplexed, she raised herself on her elbows and felt beneath her.

"You didn't think I was gonna put you and all that paint on my good couch without a cover, did you?" She just blinked and lay back down.

"If this doesn't feel like a bad movie to you, it does to me. So I'll supply the dialogue because you are in no shape to do so. First the action: you act out on me, looking like a crazed woman costumed in black paint, I pick you up, black paint and all, mess up my good shirt, I might add, and bring you in here. Your line, 'Where is here?'" Vanderbilt mimicked in a high nasal voice. "Here is in my room," he said in a deep voice. "The place where good girls don't come. The place where people do the nasty… 'My dear man,'" mimicking a high nasal voice again, "'I don't go to men's rooms unchaperoned. And I *never* do the nasty. Wait till my father hears of this. He will have you drawn and quartered. You cad. Take this!'" He picked up her limp wrist and slapped his face with it; she couldn't help but laugh. "Don't worry, honey, women aren't my thing."

"I know."

"*How* do you know?" Vanderbilt asked, pointing a deliberate finger at her.

"Because Monkey Dee is."

"Now, just wait a minute…"

"Don't try and get out of it. I know more than you think I do."

"Just what do you *think* you know?" Vanderbilt reached over to the cigarette box on his coffee table and pulled out a thin brown cigarette.

"Lots."

He picked up a lighter in his hand and leaned towards her. "What *are* you talking about? Color me white and dress me in purple, I am the flaming faggot on John R. Street…everybody knows that!"

"I know. But he likes you." She shifted a little on the couch and the newspaper crackled.

"Dee likes everybody. Besides, what's he got to do with it?"

"Everything…and nothing…"

"What kind of double talk is that?" Vanderbilt drew deeply on his cigarette.

"I'm tired. I really am."

"Look, before you pass out on me again…your aunt…what's her name…Laphonya?…said don't worry, she'll give the baby a sugar tit. Come back when you're ready. What happened over there?"

"How did you know?" she asked, too tired to think straight.

"I know everything and everybody on this street. Including you. I know something went down over there. And I even know what a sugar tit is."

"Kali, my name is Kali," she whispered, just before she went back to sleep. Vanderbilt brought a damp cloth over from the sink and attempted to softly wipe the paint away from her face and neck.

"You have to rub harder than that, my man."

"Dee! How long have you been there?"

"Long enough to witness this tender scene. Callie, huh? I hope you've got her under control so she won't freak out again."

"She's scared, Dee. Real scared."

"So is half the world, my friend. So is half the world. But don't be so sure about that one. Mark my word. She's jailbait, remember that."

She woke with a start, then drifted back again. Hooked into some invisible pain, she finally came fully awake. It must have been hurting for a long time. Yes, she was sure it had. But she had been too tired. Now her breasts were throbbing. She moved her hands across them; tiny drops of milk wet the black designs of the paint streaked across her front. The pain was bad. She had dreamed of kittens—no, lion cubs—nursing. She needed the breast pump. And fast. Where was it? She started to raise herself, thinking it must be on the dresser, when she felt the gentle force of a hand pressing her back down.

"What's the matter?" a male voice said next to her ear.

"What?" She lifted one hand from one of the seeping breasts, shaded her eyes to block out the light so she could focus on the voice which she did not at first recognize, and said, "I hurt."

"From what?" the voice continued, and finally merged into Vanderbilt and the memories that got her here.

"The milk."

"Milk?"

"My milk, stupid. My titties hurt like hell! How long have I been here? And how long have you been sitting there? And what time is it?" She could smell his cigarette smoke now, mixed with paint and her own sweet-sour smell.

"Whoa! One question at a time. You've been here since five this afternoon. It is now ten. And I've been sitting here, off and on, all evening." He blew a smoke ring at her.

"Why?"

"Because I was afraid if you woke and found yourself in this fabulous apartment you might steal all my clothes. And how could I continue to be the flaming fag on John R with no clothes? Besides, you know how darkies steal."

"What kind of shit is that?"

"Joke, honey. Joke." He waved a hand at her.

"No joke, *white* boy."

"Look, little *girl*, I live on the strip, just like you do."

"What little girl are you talking about? My name is Kali… Look, I'm tired. My titties ache. I'm carrying a lot of things I don't understand yet. Understand?" She looked around Vanderbilt's room, an odd combination of old Victorian and quirky things. There was an old barber's chair in the corner.

"Didn't I hear someone else in this room?" Kali asked.

"Like who?"

"I don't know," she said, moving her knees up toward her chest and back again. She was beginning to stiffen.

"You heard Dee."

"Uh hum."

"Look, he works out of here and…"

"I need to go." She shoved herself slowly up from the couch.

"Your aunt said for you to come back when you can." Vanderbilt got up too.

"I'm not married to my aunt. And I hurt too bad."

"Where's your husband?" He reached out to steady her as she weaved a little.

"Gone into work; he just started a new job."

"Whee! I'm glad he is. I don't need him punching me out because of his wife. You know how crazy niggahs can be."

"There you go again."

She tried the handle and the door came open. The big oak door of the old house just opened. Why wasn't it locked? True, she had left the house suddenly, running away from the parlor, excited by all the drama. Now what? Funny, she could remember the sound of her footsteps like rapid drumbeats against the linoleum as she ran out of the old house. But nothing about her could remember why she didn't think to bring the key—since it had taken forever for Brother to make her one. And she would not have gotten it then if Miss Charlotte hadn't spoken up, telling him in the way she said most things, "Git the girl a key, boy, ain't nobody got time to knock the door down!" There it was again, a tiny opening. Miss Charlotte concerned—letting her in. A key was placed in the palm of her hand the next day without so much as a word from Brother. But here she was without it.

Who had left the front door open? It must have been Laphonya, she thought, as she let herself in. Miss Charlotte passed by the front door and went into the kitchen. She had to have seen her standing there, framed in the doorway. The stoop light was on, the door not closed yet. But she just passed her like she didn't see her and went on into the kitchen. Oh well, tomorrow would be soon enough to take on Miss Charlotte. I wonder if the baby is asleep? Did he give Laphonya a fit with the sugar tit?

"He only sleeps for an hour at a time," Laphonya said as she entered the room, closing the door softly behind her. "He misses the tit all right. If ya wanna git any sleep tonight better wake that boy up and feed him, cause soon as ya settle down, he gon' wake up."

"Laphonya, I…"

"I had thirteen of 'em. I should know. Too many, I s'pose."

"Laphonya…" She stopped, not knowing really what she wanted to say.

"Tell me when ya a mind to. Wake that boy up. And sit with me a spell."

"Won't we wake Lizzie?"

"Lizzie and me been sharin' a bed since we was girls. And when she sleep, it's like somebody done put a hammer to her head. 'Sides, I gits lonesome sometimes."

"What about your children, Laphonya? Don't they help?"

"I never see 'em. They bein' taken care of better then I coulda ever done. Or wanted to do. It wadn't no skin offa my nose. Didn't cause me no worryin'. I was young and Lizzie and me had a place that needed tendin' to. And I knowed I was gonna have a Jones baby. And that baby was gonna have a daddy—and twelve uncles—all them hands and arms would take care of it. And we didn't have no real worryin' to do."

Just like us place being takin' care of. Lizzie and me couldn't do all that needed doin'. Listen. Sarah Jones had thirteen sons and two daughters. The gals took off as soon as they got their monthly and felt good about gettin' it—married theyselves off to two brothers in the next county. Me and Lizzie wadn't 'bout no marryin'. We was a-bout our farm. Now how was Lizzie and me gonna work a farm by our selfs? We was on neighborin' farms from the Jones? Our folks was dead and me and Lizzie was left. (Charlotte by then had done run off to New Orleans.) 'Em sistahs left all they brothers farmin? Cain't blame 'em though. Farmin' ain't no life fo' no womens. Plowin' fields like a damn mule. I ain't no mule. And Lizzie ain't never had no appetite fo' much hard work either. What was a body to do? We was all neighbors. And mens do anythang fo' womens when they ain't enough of us to go around. And it was thirteen of 'em. Mens needed women. Lizzie agreed at first till her baby died. I had done took off and had so many already. We was just like Leah and Rachel in the Good Book, and Lizzie was patient. The Lord was gonna bless her, she knew. So she waited. And waited. Smilin' every time she was auntie to a new youngun. But wantin' real bad to make some kind of contribution. So she waited. And I was on fire, and Lizzie never had none. Until... Laphonya stopped, rose in her chair to look over at the sleeping Lizzie, and went on. *And she was real happy, her and New Hampshire. Then the baby died. Her and New Hampshire was real sad. Well, when it came time fo' New York, Lizzie up and said no. I asked Lizzie straight out then. "Lizzie," I says, "ain't ya gon' try no mo'?"*

"Naw, Laphonya, I ain't," she up and says. "I ain't. I ain't never been too particular 'bout no mens. Maybe I kinda likes New Hampshire, but no, I ain't."

"But Lizzie," I says, "if it be New Hampshire ya wants to be real special to, we can work out a way. And a-nother baby will come. If ya don't wanna bother with New York or Delaware. I ain't never cared fo' Delaware myself. Come to think of it, Pennsylvania either."

"Naw," she says, "it ain't 'em. They is all right. All thirteen of 'em. I likes Pennsylvania. He snores, but he gentle. But I want babies. Not mens. And the Lord don' took the onlyest one I had. I ain't gon' bother no mo'."

So that left me with the thirteen brothas. Each named after the thirteen states. Sarah Jones' husband only went to school fo' eight months of his life. The lesson fo' that time was the first thirteen states. He learned 'em. All of 'em. Then he had to get back to the farm cause it was harvest time. So he took what schoolin' he got and named his boys after 'em states he had learned. Never went to school no mo'.

Laphonya sat for a moment musing, rocking back and forth in the old rocker with the flat arms and the red cushion, looking every bit the older sister of Miss Charlotte. But that was a role and Kali knew it. She had seen the other role Laphonya played–the one she watched from her bedroom window. The first time she saw the back of the full figure in the blue suede coat and matching hat emerge from the old house, she thought it was one of the rambling cousins from the third floor easing out after dark. But no, there was something smooth and steady about the strut in tall boots, the polite pause of the figure that waited for the yellow taxicab to empty out the laughing white couple. How the figure moved across the street, the way it flicked the heavy ash from the red-tipped cigarette—that was too familiar. As the ash scurried in the wind and landed on the slush covering the asphalt, the figure reached the other curb, and, about to enter the neon doorway with the arrow pointing downward, stopped and lifted a hand, gloved in kid leather, to wave at someone. The red light from the blinking arrow outlined the face and Kali had seen that it was Laphonya.

This woman who sat before her now, whose face and body were framed by age, was not the one glowing under the red neon sign that read "eat here."

She watched the rocking figure before her for any tell-tale signs of the shifting motion of the rolling hips just under the smooth suede coat—saw none, then her breast began to hurt again. She moved uncomfortably, reached to pull the boy from the warm arms of Laphonya to give him the full tit. Laphonya stirred and handed over the baby and continued the tale.

Well, where was I? Oh, yeah. After Lizzie done quit, that left me havin' a baby every year. Well, I be damn! There I was repeatin' Sarah Jones. I had nothin' but boys, though. No girls to ease me and Lizzie's lonesomeness. The baby boys had all daddies and all uncles too. Each brotha would go and try to convince Lizzie to change her mind. She say no. And I'd say, "That's my sistah. I'll blow the first fucker's balls off who tries to take it." And I would have. But more important, they was scared I'd shut down too. And where would they all be? With no woman, and no chil'rens to carry on they names.

No other womens would come out to where we was stayin' fo' no length of time. They would come but none would stay. New York, as I recall, went and took a wife once. She was a no talkin' woman, and like I said, Lizzie and me wanted some company. When she did talk she didn't have much opinion 'bout nothin'. Too quiet fo' my taste. 'Specially round men folks. Servin' food. Cookin' and cleanin'. But quiet. Me and Lizzie ask her if the cat got her tongue. She smile. And still say nothin'. Then one day she was gon'. And New York kinda suck his breath in and say, good riddance to bad rubbish. And none of us question what he mean. At least not to his face. But Lizzie and me knowed she didn't do no measurin' up to what a woman needed to be 'round here. New York didn't leave the farm to run after her, fact none of 'em boys leave the farm much. And Lizzie and me ain't too keen on leavin' our farm, at least not then. Who is a people if they ain't got no land? Besides, we was held in 'spicion by both the colored and white folks. Well, not so much Lizzie and me but 'em Jones boys was. So, no folks came out much to bother with us and our farms. And we all liked that real fine, exceptin', some time Lizzie and me git lonesome.

The white folks treed the Jones' daddy after he don' put fifteen of 'em on the earth and woe out their motha in the begittin'. That made the Jones boys very wary of white folks. Like most niggahs, I 'spect—wary of white folks. Real wary. But could I say if 'em boys cared 'bout white folks one way or the other? They just stayed out they way. After that little mealy-mouthed woman of New York's run off, Virginia told all 'em, "If ya cain't wait yo' turn with Laphonya and live with the hope that Lizzie gon' change her mind, then ya bettah leave the farms."

He knowed what he was doin', all right. How could Negroes leave they farm? The onlyest thang to own in the world? White folks own everythang else. Don't they? They sit on top of the whole world and shit on the rest of us. And we gotta take it, but we don't got to take it on us farm. And we got the onlyest farm the white folks leave 'lone. "So many of 'em big niggahs lives out there, 'sides they 'bout crazy just like they Pa. Ya know don't no acorn fall far from the tree," they say. "Leave 'em alone."

Laphonya paused, reached for her spit cup, spit, coughed a little, wiped her mouth with the back of her hand, then continued. What they was really meanin' was leave 'em crazy niggahs alone. What bothered 'em local town's folks was the body. Ol' man Jones' body. The Ol' man's talkin' body. That had hung from the tree till it was dead. They had already lit the fire and decided the funnin' was over. Took 'nother random look at ol' man Jones fo' they was to return home. The ol' man was hangin' and burnin' just fine. And they was all pleased and gatherin' they picnic stuff. Then he righted up. The body went to talkin'! Seen it myself. I was feelin' real sorry fo' the family. And wonderin' what now? Turns out I didn't have nothin' to worry 'bout. The dead body was talkin' and what's mo', it was cussin' and cursin'. It commenced to pronouncin' every curse ol' man Jones ever knowed, and some I 'spect he made up as he laid 'em white folks low. Hallelujah. Bless God!

"No-doin' no-'count white folks tryin' to take my land," the body kept talkin'. "The Bible say the bottom rail gon' rise to the top! Just like the Hebrew chil'ren gonna, Negroes gonna rise too. And I been summoned by the Lord hisself to take the lead." And he went on to make a crook road straight. 'Em white folks was plenty scared. He said they could kill the Lord but he didn't stay dead. And neither was he. Then he went to quotin' his favorite text, "The Lord is my shepherd and I shall not want. He gon' have a second comin'. And I gon' have a second one too! Can I have a amen? In the meantime I is prepared to haunt ya'll. Watch out, ya real sons of Canaan, the curse gon' fall on ya! Ya'll been put on notice by Ulysses Eloisus Jones!"

And they all was so overcome some of 'em white folks ran off. And coloreds too. Quakin' in they shoes. But I ain't nevah don' nothin' to ol' man Jones so I knowed I was safe. Others stood mute. After he finished his cursin' and cussin', he gave one long sigh and died a second time.

Well, the white folks started to have all kinds of trouble. First it was the crops. Then some of they wives took to drinkin' afternoon "tea." Got quarrelsome and took to shamin' they husbands in public. Especially when they husbands shut the still down. And then the white womens quit makin' like wives. I ain't sho' what that mean. Cause white womans mo' like spoilt chil'ren to me. Or crazy like C.C. who run up and down the strip with a hatchet under her coat.

"Who?"

"Ain't ya heard 'bout crazy Carrie Cobo runnin' up and down hollerin' 'bout demon rum?" Kali gave her a blank look and Laphonya went on. Some say the mayor's daughter Susie Brown had a baby that looked 'spicious. All the negroes knowed she was after every buck on the place. Many had trouble with they chil'rens learnin' in the new school house. Some say the new school marm threw up her hands and left town, sayin' to Mattie, who came once a week to help out, "these is the dumbest bunch of chil'ren I ever done had the displeasure to teach." But nothin' really happen till they pocketbooks got infected, when the bo' weevil come through and wiped many of 'em out—then they remembered us farm. So a gang of 'em came stormin' out to the farm demandin' that we take the curse off, or they was gonna take the farms. Can ya believe that? The ones with the curse gon' demand the one who done it (well not the real one, fo' he was dead) take off the curse or else!

Well, when 'em Jones boys emerges—some out of the house, some out from the back, some over by the well and some back 'cross the road—all lookin' just

alike, all the same height, all the same colorin', all wearin' the same kind of
Farmer Jack overalls, the white folks thought they was seein' doubles. And mo'
doubles of ol' man Jones. Ha! Scared 'em crackers to death! They ain't had no
be-cause to come down in the hollow and mess with nobody out us way, any-
way. We guess it was the combination of all 'em look-alikes comin' round all
at once and all 'em lookin' just like they fathah and they remembrance of the
curse on 'em that caused 'em to hightail it out of there. They was movin' fas-
tah than the bo' weevil done done. We had a hoe-down! Lizzie got on the fid-
dle and I got on the jug. And everybody dance. We broke out the coon dick
and everybody got drunk. All 'ceptin' Lizzie, of course! She don't do no
drinkin'. That girl ain't nevah knowed how to have a good time!

So the two farms growed together and so did all the babies. Till every
brotha had one he could claim. And me and Lizzie had all us plantin' and
plowin' done on us place. And the chil'ren helped. The farms took care of all
of us. And the white folks left us rub-belly niggahs alone. "Gettin' 'em babies
like mongrel dogs," the visitin' preacher man would shout in the pulpit on
Sunday. Lizzie would always go and hear 'em preacher mens. She had some
fondness fo' preachers, and still do. Seem like she got some special need fo' fire
and brimstone.

Then all us started to worry her some. Me and all 'em babies. And the
thirteen states. She loved the babies. And she loved the thirteen, but she say the
Lord don't a-gree. Still, our farm was goin' good. Our stomachs was full. Our
chil'rens was well. And the white folks left us alone.

"Ain't that sign enough fo' ya, Lizzie, what else do ya wont?" I asked one
day.

"I wanna go North and be with my sistah Charlotte now that she got the
house."

So when I finish weaning Wee-Little, I caught the fastest train North to
be with Lizzie. How I s'pose to live without my sistah?

"How ya just run off leavin' yo' baby?" Lizzie asked, lifting her
body up and swinging her legs around and sitting next to Kali on the
bed. Laphonya stopped, spit tobacco again into the can next to her
chair, and waited.

"How ya 'spect this baby gon' eat?" Lizzie asked, turning now,
directing the question to Kali.

"We done done all right, Lizzie, the baby ain't come to no
harm," Laphonya said. "Besides, she cain't go too far cause her titties
woulda drew her back. Ya remember 'bout how they hurt, don't ya,
Lizzie?"

"I ain't had but one. And the Lord took him."

"How old was he, Lizzie?" Kali asked, suddenly sorry for Lizzie.

"Don't seem fair, somehow." Lizzie began to shake.

"Lizzie, don't cry, we got all the rest…"

"*You* got all the rest. I ain't got nothin'… He was such a little thang," she said, explaining it to Kali, her face wet and shining. "Just stopped breathin'. And I had all that milk left." Then with sudden anger she said, "And this boy here suckin' for the milk that ain't here. While ya run off and leave yo' baby hungry."

"Lizzie, ya bein' kinda hard on the child."

"I wanted my baby. I had milk and no baby to suck. It was a frightful time."

"Well, Lizzie, that ain't quite the truth. We was in the birthin' house…"

"Birthin' house?" Kali asked. She wasn't sure she was hearing right. Such a night, so many stories, and she was so tired now.

"When the baby drop we make the house a birthin' house. The rooms got to be washed down. Special candles an' prayers. A place where only womens be. No men. Not till the quarter moon."

"You serious? I've never heard of such a thing."

"My milk had no place to go." Lizzie was staring straight ahead.

"Lizzie, honey," Laphonya was straining to say, "if ya gon' tell it, tell it right. We found some place fo' it to go. And we took care of yo' pain. Till the herbs could work. Didn't we?"

Kali watched both women, amazed, and pressed her baby tightly.

"Laphonya, you ain't never cared what the Lord say," Lizzie said, looking directly into Laphonya's face.

"I don't give two shits 'bout the Lord, but I care 'bout ya. And ya was in pain. And I wadn't gon' leave ya like that. So I did what I knowed to do."

"But it wadn't the way the Lord say, Laphonya… Ya coulda went and got New Hampshire. He woulda come."

"What happen, Lizzie, when a baby calf die? Huh? Tell me if ya know?"

"I ain't talkin' 'bout it no mo'."

"Oh, yeah, we gon' talk about it. We gon' talk a-bout it this night! When a calf die, what happen, Lizzie?" Lizzie didn't say anything.

"What happen, goddamn it!"

"Ya git some other calf to suck," Lizzie said under her breath.

Kali leaned forward, hoping to hear this time.

"Say it loud, Lizzie."

"Ya hope ya got 'nother calf to suck."

"Was there 'nother calf to suck, Lizzie?"

"There was New Hampshire! He woulda done it."

"You said git another calf to suck, not a bull! You cain't in-vite a bull to no china shop! I told ya I don't care two shits 'bout what the Lord say. But I *do* care 'bout ya, and the birthin' house. And it ain't no place for mens, not till the quarter moon. Ya know bettah than that, Lizzie! Did I ever in-vite mens into the birthin' house 'fore the quarter moon? Did I, Lizzie? Did I?" Laphonya was up out of her seat with her finger pointing into Lizzie's face. "How we gon' act a fool and disregard what we know to do?…Lizzie!"

"I read once that women used a nursing cat or puppy… Didn't you have plenty of them on your place?" Kali asked this question in earnest and Laphonya looked over at her in disgust. She never thought of that, but now wasn't the time. It was clear that Lizzie had removed herself. Laphonya dropped back to rock in her rocker; its rhythm joined the two women together, their minds pulling away from this unfamiliar place. Their two shadows rose, passing from the room, each moving from beneath the eaves where icicles hung like knives. Their memories linked—going South. And they spoke to each other in the chatter of little girls playing house.

"Pass the tea, Lizzie… Everything *up* there was too sharp, like steel, wasn't it? Sugar? I'm glad to be home again. Yes, I know you missed home too. Cream?"

Their voices floated on. "No underbelly. Just edges, wasn't it, girl?"

They were back where there was marrow in the bone. Lazy summer days where the sun means heat. Where everybody knew to stay out of it. Where women, if they had a mind to, opened colorful parasols because it was hot. And treated the heat with respect. Or found trees that hung with shade. Where were the trees up there? Only in the park, for Lord's sake! Who was gonna take a streetcar and go to Belle Isle just to sit under a tree in the shade that you didn't need cause the sun don't get hot enough in the first place? "No, chile, my sistah and me didn't like it up there one little bit!"

The baby stirred, losing the nipple. Lizzie reached absent-mindedly toward the spot where he had been asleep. Lizzie, turning to face Laphonya, spoke to her with a voice not like her own. "I ain't asked ya to come North, Laphonya. Ya coulda stayed. Havin' all 'em babies just like a mongrel dog–just like 'em womens we see out there on the strip…"

"That puts ya high up on a hog, don't it, Lizzie? But if I hadn't sucked yo' milk out, you woulda died. It had run inside, under yo' arm. Don't ya remember the knots? Ya was talkin' out yo' head. Seein' folks that weren't there. Talkin' to Momma, even though ya knowed bettah. Did ya wanna be dead just like her? Being *good* coulda cost ya yo' life."

"You shoulda let me die!" Lizzie said. The bed began to creak and the twitch began to rupture her face. Her toes brushed the tip of the floor as she rocked back and forth on the bed. "It woulda been bettah than rememberin' what didn't need to be."

"Lizzie! Ya woulda died! And if there wadn't no babies, how we gon' git our farmin' done?"

"I shoulda died. What go 'round come 'round. Now ya done brought that curse back on our heads with this baby here suckin' on a sugar tit cause his momma wanna be like them womens on the strip."

"That's cold, Lizzie. Real cold." Kali spoke low in her throat.

"What? What ya say, girl? If ya gon' speak, speak up like a woman!" Lizzie demanded, waiting for Kali's answer.

"I'm not like those women on the strip," she said. "And even if I was, they enjoy life better than you do stuck up here in this house or up in the preacher's face," Kali said, surprising herself.

"Chile, ain't no cause to talk to Lizzie like that. She's my sistah…"

Kali began to wrap the baby hurriedly, and, turning to both of them, said, "I don't know what the answers are, but it's for damn sure…"

"Watch yo' mouth, gal."

"…you two don't have them," Kali managed to say on her way out the door.

"Don't let the door hit ya in the ass when ya leave."

She turned back. "I won't, Laphonya, and thanks for nothing. Next time you slip across the street, wake Lizzie up, she might want to go with you."

"Git outta here, ya yellah heifer, and take that devil's chile with ya...fo' I break..."

"Laphonya!" Lizzie yelled, jumping from the bed, pressing her sister back into the rocker which had almost tipped over.

"Cocksucker!" Kali said.

"What!" Laphonya was up and out of her rocker.

"Laphonya! She got the baby!"

"Git that baby bitch outta here fo' I..."

"Chile, git," Lizzie said, shooing Kali from the room, all the while trying to hold her sister back.

Miss Charlotte heard the door slam on the second floor and heard the baby crying. By the time she reached the hallway to see what the ruckus was about, the big oak front door had slammed shut.

EIGHT

Mrs. Wintergreen sat at the window across from the old house, the reflection of her small, thin frame staring back at her as she watched the streetlights along John R go out, not all at once but one at a time—like someone was moving between them, pulling at one chain and then the other. All the streetlights, that is, except the one just below her window. It only dimmed. She had visions, and sometimes nightmares about all those kilowatts the city was wasting leaving that light burning. Who went to sleep and forgot to turn it off? Why didn't the day man snuff it out? Or warn the night man that something was wrong with his kilowatts? All of those watts left burning—like the lone flame under a single cooking pot—bothered her, left her strangely annoyed as the sun rose and entered her back window, waking her plants and disturbing the insomnia she suffered.

It would be hours till she slept, if then. Her neighbors filed out into the sunlight, their small rooms left unattended, as they emptied into the alley from the backs of buildings whose sides, like an enormous stomach cramp, pushed them forward. They moved slowly, edged into a stream that trickled, then flowed toward the trolley stop.

In the distance they could hear it. Almost smell it. The reel ⌐ sway of the streetcar. A yellow lady all dressed up to beat tʰ No matter what the season, she came, all smiles. They ⸱ as she opened wide, probing, pushing till they reᵣ When she whispered to them, "This is the greaᵥ they got excited, shoved themselves toward the baᵥ small rooms and airtight lives. They listened only to the soft whispers of the seductive lady, who blew in their nostrils the smell of money, covering the smell of crank shafts that swung high and low as they worked Henry Ford's assembly line. Confusing them. Life was better, she said. But was it better or just different? And as they loosened their faces and thought about money, the yellow streetcar roared off, sparks dancing overhead, leaving them to grab for the leather straps and hang on.

The clubs along the way tipped their hats to the daredevil streetcar and the neon signs winked shut. Too bad the city didn't come down and watch how the clubs killed their kilowatts, Wintergreen thought. The swish and sway from the yellow streetcar was enough, and blink—the neons went dead.

The only light still alive on John R, as Mrs. Wintergreen looked out, was the one just below her window and the lone light left burning in the parlor window of the old house across the street.

Just about the time the lunch whistle blew—and the men unlatched their lunch pails and the women stole their first break, the one they took because the mistress of the house went shopping, leaving a list of things that Jesus himself couldn't do, the break where they propped their feet up and removed their shoes, cut just right to make room for their corns—Mrs. Wintergreen would finally sleep. A crazed sleep full of broken bits of things. Small things. Rows of burned candles with the centers gouged out. Shapes shifting in one direction and then back. Needles and pins searching for patches to patch. Blue patches, banging up against green ones, while yellow patches, suddenly freed, turned and sped away.

Then near six o'clock, she woke to watch from behind the full glass window as the last streetcar rocked its way down John R. Street. It dumped people out with a loud belch. They would stand there for a moment—dazed, trying to adjust to what they had come home to.

The women walked together towards their rooms, in a slow-moving group. They were women who stopped and asked, "How's Buddy today?" And waited for an answer. Not some quick Yankee reply, but an answer that answered the question. "How is Buddy?" meant how is he *really* and what can I do to help, even though one more minute on my feet will be my last. But I need to know about Buddy and what can I do? Cause next week it will be my Joe. And I will need for you to ask how Joe is and help me help Joe.

Each entered the alley slowly–mindful of how tired they were. The alley, all tongue and gossip by late evening, had a lot to say, but seeing the women's fatigue, said little. Things like: the children played all day; Robby pulled Brenda's braid and he took her ribbon; she broke Miss Miller's window when she threw his ball through it.

Meanwhile, old Willie put Georgia Skin on notice that he was one greedy son-of-a-bitch, who didn't re-spect nothin' and nobody. "One swig, man, not the whole mothafuckin' thang. I-I-I-I said *one*." Willie said, putting one finger up. "Can you count?" He grabbed the bottle back with the other hand.

Georgia Skin, turned actor, carefully wrapped the faded lapels of his coat together and left the alley, stage left. But not before he streaked himself from knee to shoe top with his warm pee, strong enough to sting the nose and bring water to the eyes.

The children playing in the alley knew when it was time for momma or grandmomma or Big Sis or Aunt Josie. They would stand on tiptoe and reach in the tall black leather shopping bags for some clue that showed them it was all right to work for white folks. And they knew it was all right cause the shopping bags would be stuffed with some shoes that just needed to go to Johnnie's Shoe Repair, or maybe a blue-eyed doll with only one toe gone or an arm. Maybe an erector set with all the pieces almost there.

No need to hurry, the alley reminded the women, your rooms are still here, shut up tight–waiting. No need to hurry and nobody did, except Mrs. Wintergreen, who hurried, as best she could, on tiny feet, as she went from her apartment into her club downstairs.

She wound around the back stairs, hobbling down, and told herself that John R. Street was all she needed. And she was almost right.

Wintergreen gave her club class. Many of the patrons had seen dated pictures of the lovely Wintergreen in the pages of *Ebony* magazine. They forgot, as they watched the ageless small woman, that those pictures were from a different time when a very young woman, smooth, almost white, danced in places they had never heard of. Then a breezy Wintergreen was off to the races or posed on top of a piano, eating cake, drinking champagne out of a slipper–a short, smiling woman with penciled-in eyebrows and low-fitting flapper hats, on the arm of men who looked like men in the movies. She had class, all right, and class was what kept the blue lights on and cigarette smoke rising from the tables. An arm would lean out of the blue smoke with a cigarette between the first and second fingers, and a voice would drift through, "Hey, Wintergreen, sing 'Foggy Day in London Town,'" and she would smile under the stage light and nod. Another voice from the curling smoke would say, "One more time," and she would tinkle the keys like Count Basie and go into a medley of all the songs that were like "Foggy Day." The crowd would take a tour of London, Paris, and Rome, shake their heads, drum their fingers, and rock their thighs—Wintergreen would be on! Afterwards, someone would order themselves a drink and send her one. When the stage light went out, she groped toward the end of the stage. The stage door johnny, distracted by the stage light suddenly on again, would lose eye contact with the shadowy figure. Then he'd find her at the end of the bar, lift his glass in a toast, and she would make the quick decision whether he would be the one tonight. Later, long after Mrs. Wintergreen had gone up, he would wind himself up the back stairs that Jake, the bartender, had pointed to.

In bed already, she hurried the lovemaking. Excited by her nakedness, the intense tongue or the startled foot of her lover would pull back as it touched the socks she wore to bed. Some paid no mind and thought it was a new kink, others slowed, still others would try to unravel the mystery under the guise of passion. With the latter, she would tense, scissor her legs closed, and say, "No more tonight, sugar." Some left bewildered. For the ones who got angry, annoyed by her sudden disinterest, she would push the buzzer by her bed. Jake would be up the stairs and through the door in seconds, and the man who had just been called a sweet sweet daddy, or had just heard daddy daddy daddy, it ain't never been like this, would find himself dismissed in a hurry.

Some nights she sat at the end of the bar joined by the man in the red scarf. She'd order him shots of Black Bull if he was low, and realize, as she counted the house, that she was having a good time.

Her face was white gauze some days, like organdy stretched too tight—a tightness that lifted her cheekbones and narrowed her eyes, made her hair fall in short bangs across her forehead. Other days her face was like cream velvet, and as it lengthened, it drew her shoulders into a neat square that lent weight to small breasts, like round puffs

stuffed inside a low-cut dress. On stage she layered her face with silver, gold, crimson—sometimes blue glitter that reflected in the stage
lights—covering the beginning of bags beneath her eyes and the
unmistakable hint of jowls slowly drooping with age.

Some nights she wore a shirt and tie—hair slicked back, cigar lit.
Pulling the sleeves of her jacket up, she'd play a Fats Waller piano like
nobody's business. Or she'd sing the Blues, and the diamond cuff
links, odd-shaped buttons emphasizing long, slender fingers, dazzled
the eyes and picked up the glint from bridgework behind the blue
smoke.

When the joint got to jumpin', she would douse the cigar and
remove her jacket (to the delight of the crowd), revealing the pinstriped suspenders with diamond-studded garter belts on each sleeve.
She would toss the garters one at a time to the crowd. They went
wild.

Her torso was contained in the circle of the stage light—the rest
of her never entered. The upper half did not obey age and moved on
cue—as long as she sat. Her voice would lift out of that small chest
and boom! A gravelly voice, low and liquid some nights, a tainted
soprano others. No one knew if they were hearing a slight southern
drawl beneath the lyrics or the nasal twang of a New York accent
playing with the melody.

After a few moments with Wintergreen between sets, men with
overripe smiles who had heard and seen everything and laughed at
everything everywhere would come away with the curve of their
smile suddenly straight. Fractured by her stage presence and entering
her space for a brief moment, they needed to prove to themselves
and the crowd that they could stand before this fabulous woman and
come away still intact. Instead they came away with their smiles lined
out like the beep of a heart machine that registers the patient dead.
They weren't angry, not even annoyed; they had been caught by the
best smile in town, and they knew it. A smile that had inched its way
into their personal lives, and all they could remember was the slow
move of a tongue which asked, in a touch of French, "How are you
this evening? Are you having a good time?"

Women would, after leaving, remark about her perfume. Make
a note to change their hairstyles—not to imitate hers, that never
occurred to them—but suddenly they felt naked or exposed,

wondering if they had put on too much eye shadow or not enough rouge and if they dared try wearing glitter.

From a distance, black-skinned Black women would whisper among themselves, turn their collective bitchery outward, saying things like *She thinks she cute* or *Half-white heifer!* while the hi-yellahs, light and medium browns who heard felt divided—devastated by the wasted venom.

Wintergreen knew how hurt they felt, even though they could never speak of it, not even among themselves. She had decided years ago that this was not her battle and she would have no part of it. She did, however, feel sorry for all the hi-yellahs and the light browns who roasted under the attack directed at her but spoken only within their hearing, the remarks slapping them across the face, echoing once again the division between Negro women.

Finished with her set, Wintergreen sometimes stood briefly, but then her upper body would bend while her feet took over. The body now tuned to pain would begin to curl. Her feet moved against her in an attempt to gain control. She would shift her weight to her heels. Pain would flee her body, exiting through the eyes, narrowing them to shining slits that shone like silver. And she would brace herself against the piano. After one bow the stage light would go off immediately. The stage, dark at her end, would light at the other end for the visiting singer or musician or comedian, who always came on last, no matter what.

They knew they needed to play Wintergreen's, and going on last meant they had arrived. To play Wintergreen's meant the *Chronicle* would review their act in Jodie's column, and people along the strip would ask, "How's trix? You catch so and so at Wintergreen's last night?"

The darkness of the stage on her end would blot her out as she hobbled to the side of the platform, where Jake or the man in the red scarf, who usually sat at the end of the bar, reached for her when she stepped down.

After the club was closed, the money counted, and the place cleaned to her liking, Mrs. Wintergreen would watch John R. Street from her window in the morning.

Dawn would find her still wired but not alone. Now there was the pretty brown boy—she, of course, never allowed men to stay in her apartment overnight. The boy had come with his young mother to stay with her for awhile. Wintergreen knew a lot about the people in the old house across the street and why someone like Kali would leave. But it was the baby boy that had sealed her on cleaning out and fixing up her second bedroom. He had come just in time.

She couldn't remember the exact day she felt the ping—the seeping hole beneath her left breast—but it was there, filling her lungs with water while little bits of air escaped into the room. Little puffs that floated toward the ceiling, leaving her feeling limp. She felt the leak start and grow, but when she looked down she saw nothing. Then there was the day it felt like a dam had burst, the day she had allowed herself to remember: how she had always surrounded herself with children wherever she lived. In Paris, Vienna, Italy, it was the same. She would spend her mornings visiting the children's hospital, or the orphanage. Or a family with nothing but children. What she had allowed herself to remember, after breaking into long and deep sobs, was that she was lonely. It was a strange feeling after living her life so long alone. An entertainer *is* alone. That she understood and accepted—almost gratefully—and didn't mind. There were too many people everywhere and she enjoyed the "star" separation from them. But this new feeling had emerged one day unannounced, and she had cried a long ribbon of tears. It was only after she had slept long and hard, floating out on the raft in the middle of a hazy river, that she woke feeling what she never felt: loneliness.

When Mildred called from over at the hotel and explained about Kali, Wintergreen jumped at the chance to take on the pretty brown boy whose mother would be falling in here any minute, bone-tired.

"I can't go?" Kali was standing behind the Gotham front desk and had caught Van on his way to his room.

"To the Chesterfield? You got to be kidding, sweetie."

"Why, Van?"

"Sugar, come on." Vanderbilt leaned up against the desk, his eyes bleary from lack of sleep.

"Come on. Come on. You're not my daddy, Van."

"Thank gawd," he drawled, rubbing his eyes.

"Aw, come on, don't be so hard. I wanna go."

"Kali, you're tacky," Vanderbilt managed. "Look at your hair." He reached across the desk, picking up one of her braids. He shook his head. "Chile, you oughta be shame," he said in his best southern dialect.

"Hair...? You do hair." Her eyes lit up.

"Don't do me no favors. You got a cigarette by any chance?"

"Van, that's cold. What'll you charge?"

"To you? Nothing. With your looks and my talent, the result, my dear Scarlett, would mobilize the South a-gain!" he said, bending at the waist and removing an imaginary hat.

Kali, laughing, leaned over the desk to give him a kiss. Embarrassed, he pulled away.

"When?" she asked.

"Now." He waved her in the direction of his room as he started to move away from the desk.

She held out her arm to stop him. "Mildred, remember? She'd have one fit after the other if I leave early."

"God, don't let that woman start."

"Oh, she's not so bad."

"Hush my mouth and call me gummy. God don't take to liars," he said, striking her arm with a limp wrist and putting his other hand on his waist.

"This evening?" Kali asked in a little girl voice, placing her forefinger in the corner of her mouth.

"Miss Scarlett, Miss Scarlett, what shall we wear?" He put both hands to his cheeks and rolled his eyes.

"Why, Brett, honey..."

"Rhett." Vanderbilt raised an eyebrow.

"Rhett? Oh. Why, Rhett, honey. The South shall rise a-gain!"

"I do Ginger at four; come at five," Van said as he reached for his key and yawned. "How do you work this graveyard shift?"

"It's called 'Baby needs a new pair of shoes.'"

Kali's braids lay on the floor. At first she refused to look at them. Just as she got up enough nerve to look in the hand mirror, Dee walked in. He spoke briefly to Vanderbilt and, turning toward her with a broad smile, asked, "Have we met before?"

Kali looked up and then at Vanderbilt. "Scarlett," he smiled at her, "they can never keep a good woman down."

"Oh, Brett…"

"Rhett…I knew the South would rise a-gain!"

"Is this a private party or can anybody play?" Dee asked.

"Not this time," Vanderbilt said, suddenly very serious.

"M.D., it's me, Kali."

"Well, well, well, what have the scissors wrought? Callie-girl, no one would have suspected. Remember," he turned to Vanderbilt, "when she *dropped* into the lobby of the Gotham for the first time?"

"I remember. Right to the floor." Vanderbilt smiled, touching Kali's hair softly.

"Why," Dee said, taking a long look at Kali and then turning to Vanderbilt, rubbing his hands together. "This must be my lucky day."

"Over my dead body," Vanderbilt said. Each man glared at the other. Kali, feeling the tension, sat quietly.

"We'll attend the funeral. Won't we, Callie-girl?" Monkey Dee quipped, breaking his gaze from the glaring Vanderbilt.

"Kali, Wintergreen's at ten," Vanderbilt said as he bent low and spoke directly in her ear.

"Out front?" she asked, raising her voice on purpose.

"What? A rendezvous?" Dee asked.

Kali, deciding that the war between them was best left that way, got slowly out of the chair, picked up her things, and went to the door.

"Red would devastate them, baby! Don't believe what they say…Cinderella wore red and she got the prince," Dee said, delighted with his version of the fairy tale. He pulled a gold case from his breast pocket, opened it, and carefully picked out one ivory toothpick from among many. He took his time putting it in his mouth. Kali smiled as she hurried through the door, deciding that she liked the fairy tale the old way. She left the door open.

Vanderbilt, grimacing, ran his hand through his hair and started over to close it. Just then Ginger came rushing in, his hair all over his head, his face bruised, his nails broken. "Van, you gotta do it again. That son-of-a-bitch! No more johns before showtime. Who would have thought that little lowlife son-of-a-bitch got his kicks…"

"Man, I haven't got time to do you again!"

"Here," Ginger said, handing Vanderbilt a fifty dollar bill.

"Obviously the fucker paid."

"Obviously. But I wouldn't charge you a thing," Ginger said, placing a hand with broken nails on Vanderbilt's crotch.

"You never quit, do you, man?" Dee said, irritated.

"What's it to you? Six one way, half a dozen another. You make yours one way, me another."

"He makes his money any way he can. Next it'll be old women and children," Vanderbilt said, annoyed, hurting himself to say it.

"Now that sounds like an exit line to me. See you around," Dee said, and slammed the door on his way out.

"What will it be, Ginger?" Not waiting for an answer, Vanderbilt picked up the brush and raked it across Ginger's head with a vengeance.

"Hey, man, be cool! One rough mothafuckah in a day is enough."

"Mrs. Wintergreen, do you have anything red?" Kali asked, rushing into the room on full volume, unaware that Wintergreen and the baby were asleep in the big chair before the window. The baby jumped and so did Mrs. Wintergreen.

"Shhh, sugar, go back to sleep," she whispered as she stroked the baby's head. He stirred again and then settled back against her shoulder. "He just went to sleep. Why are you yelling?" she admonished Kali.

"I'm going to the Chesterfield tonight with Van!" Kali said all in one breath.

But Wintergreen wasn't listening. "Go look in your room, I've got a surprise for you."

"Did you buy me that new bedspread you promised?" Kali asked as she raced to her room. Wintergreen could hear her tearing boxes open and the rustle of paper. Slowly Kali walked back down the hall and entered the living room clutching an oversize teddy bear. "Thanks so much for all the baby clothes. He sure could use them. Who picked them out?"

"I called J.L. Hudson's and told them what I wanted," Wintergreen said, surprised by the question. "They delivered it."

"I didn't think they delivered down here, to an all-Negro neighborhood."

"They don't. But I know J.L. He comes into the club from time to time. What do you think?"

"I thought you said you had something for me?"

"Next time, Kali. Besides, isn't *for* the baby for you?"

"Not exactly," Kali said, folding her arms around the teddy bear. "I'll make this mine."

"Don't you think you're a little old for a teddy bear?" Wintergreen asked, half-kidding.

"No."

"Oh…" Wintergreen wished she could say something or invent something to say. They fell silent. "Where did you say you're going?"

"To the Chesterfield. With Van."

"The white fag? Are you old enough?" Mrs. Wintergreen took a good look at Kali—started to say something but changed her mind. Wintergreen offered the baby to Kali so she could take him into her bedroom and put him down. Kali gathered him up in her arms right along with the teddy bear.

Later, when she returned from the bedroom, Mrs. Wintergreen asked, "Who's going to take care of the baby while you go out with a white fag into a bar full of black ones?"

"You don't work Thursdays, Mrs. Wintergreen."

"Don't you know how to ask?… Who cut your braids?"

"You like it?" Kali asked, happy that she had noticed. "Van. I haven't seen it myself." As she rushed toward the bathroom, she stepped on the baby's bottle. It broke.

Mrs. Wintergreen looked at the bottle, then at Kali, but said nothing.

Kali raced to the kitchen for the broom and began to sweep the glass up with the milk.

"Try picking up the glass first, Kali. Then get a damp cloth."

"Oh, yeah. Okay." Wintergreen always made her feel like such a fool. She hurried back from the kitchen with a dustpan.

"No question the white boy's got a jones for Black folks," Mrs. Wintergreen said, almost to herself. "I don't like it. He's working from what he *thinks* he sees."

"What?"

"Men do it all the time," Mrs. Wintergreen said, again to herself, because Kali was already in the bathroom.

"What's wrong with it?" Kali asked, looking in the mirror.

"When I was a little girl, my father took me to one of the neighbors to get my hair done. He had a mental picture of what *he* wanted. I came away looking like a fool."

"Thanks. Is it that bad?" asked Kali, who had pulled herself away from the bathroom and was now standing next to Wintergreen, looking at her reflection in the window.

"No, it's just not good."

"Well, *I* like it. You ever let Van do you?" Kali asked, looking down at the very fine, light brown strands of Wintergreen's hair and deciding that she was glad she went to Van.

"Once. Oscar comes in."

"Is he any good?" Wintergreen understood from that question what Kali really thought about her hair.

She reached up to touch it. "*I* decide what I like."

"For what? You never go out," Kali said in that off-handed way she said things. "Do you?"

"What do you mean? I work," Wintergreen bristled.

"I mean *go* out," Kali said, forcing the *go* between her lips.

"Work is out."

"I mean *out* out."

"For what?" Wintergreen asked, as if she was genuinely surprised at the question.

"But there is a whole world out there!"

"Like the Chesterfield?" Wintergreen asked, laughing, crossing her shapely legs and placing a slim cigar between her teeth, then stopping—as though waiting for a light. Kali picked up the silver cigarette lighter from the coffee table and handed it to Wintergreen. She took it but made an awkward business of lighting the cigar. After a few deep puffs, she blew the smoke into the air and said, "I've been in a thousand Chesterfields."

"Where?" Kali asked, almost as if she didn't believe her.

"Everywhere."

"New Orleans?"

"Why?"

"Miss Charlotte has."

Mrs. Wintergreen cleared her throat. "Speaking of your mother-in-law, have you seen your husband since you moved here?"

"Once."

"Can't you talk to him?" she asked.

Kali looked down and said nothing.

"Answer the question."

"Is it important?" she asked, lifting her face and looking directly at Wintergreen with that odd bit of sass she was capable of.

Wintergreen chose to ignore it and said softly, "Kali, take some time to talk. Brother feels something for his son, doesn't he?"

"I suppose."

Mrs. Wintergreen sat musing to herself, puffing on the cigar and rubbing her palms together. "Red. Why red? It's all wrong for you."

"Oh, somebody said to wear red."

"Who?"

"Somebody."

"Soft colors, sugar. Never advertise."

"Yes, ma'am."

Wintergreen heard the sass behind Kali's *yes, ma'am*. She straightened in her chair and said, almost coyly, "Let me dress you."

Kali, surprised—not knowing if it was intended as a question or a final statement and not knowing what to say—asked, "Would you?"

"Only if there are *no* changes," Wintergreen announced, glad on the one hand that she could give something to Kali, and on the other that she had some control back.

"It sounds like I could be sorry."

"Bring the brush and the baby powder."

The news was bad. Whenever Mildred stepped from behind the front desk, the news was bad. Monkey Dee wanted to say and would have, "Don't bring me no bad news," but Mildred was right there, eager. And so he said, instead, "Can't it wait, Mildred?"

"Not unless you don't care that Lilac's got a problem."

"Not again."

"She refuses…"

"She refuses? She refuses! Nobody who works for me refuses!" he said, lifting the glass paperweight from off the desk and thumping it down very hard.

"Well, you better tell her that."

"Did you introduce Callie-girl to Mrs. Wintergreen?" he asked, throwing Mildred off, giving himself time to regroup and reassess the situation.

"Yes."

"Why?"

"Well, her people across the street in the old house…"

"Her people live across the street?" he asked, growing more and more interested. Mildred noticed and was glad she knew something he didn't.

"Well, not her people—her in-laws."

"She's married? Where is her husband?"

"He's there."

"Well, what is he doing about his wife living with Wintergreen?" M.D. started playing with the paperweight, rifling through the papers under it.

"And his baby."

"She has a child?" He stopped and looked up.

"Six months or more," Mildred said with obvious satisfaction.

"Makes sense…" He looked back down.

"What makes sense?"

"Wintergreen. Women, no matter what, from eight to eighty, stop dead for a baby." He had picked up a bill and was reading the due date.

"Not this Callie. The baby, according to Vanderbilt, only gets in the way." Mildred made a wry face.

"Eventually they all stop… What does he know about babies?"

"He knows. What about you?"

"Anybody who hates dogs and children can't be all bad," he said, throwing back his head and laughing loudly.

Mildred frowned and rushed back to the news that would upset him again.

"Maybe you wouldn't be laughing so hard if you knew that your big moneymaker is not making you any money. And by the time you persuade her to, by whatever means you do that, the Congressman—the one who owns the funeral home, and we both know who I mean—will miss his supper this Sunday. Lilac, I'm willing to bet, will *not* be ready."

"You love putting nails in my coffin, don't you?"

"Personally, I wouldn't bother putting you in a coffin. I'd bury you alive."

Dee slowly smiled, removed the toothpick from his mouth, and said, "Mildred, now I seem to remember…"

"I wanna go home, Dee."

"Where is home, Lilac?"

"Upstate New York."

"No, baby, home is *not* there. It is here. You live here. And where is here?"

"Detroit."

"Wrong again. You live in the Cadillac Towers. At fifteen hundred a month."

"I'm not impressed with fifteen hundred a month. Money is not my thing. Besides, we were not poor, Dee."

"But we were, little girl."

Before Lilac could respond, he climbed onto the table and began to scratch himself beneath his armpits just like a monkey. She didn't know what to do, now that Dee was making chimp sounds and demanding that she laugh. So she did.

"You turn tricks because you hate daddy, little girl… I turn you because I love you," he said, stepping down from the table and placing himself at her knee.

"Dee, come on, I didn't mean…I just…Well, we're not close like we used to be…"

"What are you getting at, my little cupcake?" he asked, cupping her face in his hands.

"I want that again."

"What?"

"Us."

"I do not, and never have, fucked whores," he said, as if he was surprised that she didn't know. "Love and sex never mix."

"Dee!" He was now squeezing her face as he drew it toward him. Looking directly into his eyes, she finally whispered, "Dee, you're hurting me."

"Baby, I'm so sorry." He dropped his hands and reached for her hand, brought it to his mouth and kissed it. Slowly he removed his lips, and still looking into her eyes, he pressed the small finger of her

left hand all the way back, snapping it like a twig. Lilac froze. The
pain was trying desperately to catch up with her surprise. Just as it
broke through her lips, he slapped her unconscious. She lay on the
floor in a heap. The finger hung limp, apart from the hand; blood
oozed from her mouth. He picked up the phone, dialed, and heard
a female voice answer.

"Doctor Fields' office, may I help you?"

"This is Melvin Davis. Is the doctor in?"

"Sorry, Mr. Davis, the doctor is with a patient. May I help you?"

In a commanding voice he said, "This is an emergency. I want
the doctor *now*. Understand?"

In less than fifteen seconds a deep, resonant voice spoke from
the other end. "Doctor Fields speaking. Mr. Davis, what can I do for
you?"

"One of the girls has had an accident. I'll pay your usual fee."

"I'll be there in an hour."

"No, now! She will be hysterical in an hour. Your fee is doubled
if you come now. Come immediately to the penthouse."

Monkey Dee slammed the phone receiver back in its cradle, causing the phone to slip from the table top and drop onto the floor. He
grabbed up both receiver and phone and with one giant swing threw
them into the wall.

Mrs. Wintergreen lay against the back of the blue velvet fainting
couch as Kali gazed into the oval mirror above the honey-
colored dressing table. The table had inset drawers but no handles.
They opened from the sides where cleverly hidden crevices, once
pulled, swung the drawers outward.

Kali turned slowly and said, "I look like a boy."

"No, you look like me in Paris in '24."

Kali turned back to look at herself in the oval mirror, tugging at
the white satin legs of the trousers. Turning to the side she looked at
her profile, following it from neck to shoulder to arm. Then she
pinched the satin trousers trying to form a crease.

"They were meant to flow freely," Wintergreen remarked.
Looking past Kali into the mirror, she remembered when no one
expected trousers to have a crease. When everyone understood that
wearing Norma Shearer satin trousers was the in thing.

She boarded the train for Berlin wearing a mean hat tilted forward, gabardine riding breeches, and long leather boots touching at the knee. She smiled and there were the usual explosions of reporters' flashbulbs.

"Are you off to the races, Wintergreen?" a reporter asked.

"No, I've been, and I won. Can't you tell?" she questioned, raising her voice to a boo-boopie-do pitch. Her words booping through the perfectly painted bow of her lips.

"What are these pants made of?" Kali, now seated on the lushly padded dressing chair, asked as she rubbed her hands down the front of the trousers.

"Satin," Mrs. Wintergreen answered in a soft whisper, "white satin."

"How do you keep from getting dirty?"

"No one who wears satin trousers gets dirty."

"Oh," Kali said, not sure of what that meant but liking the sound of it.

Wintergreen, her attention returned to the warm compartment of the moving train, sat quietly.

Underneath the gabardine riding breeches and the silk underwear, and even beneath the perfume at thirty dollars an ounce, she felt in her heart of hearts and said out loud, "Berlin is too far." Jake mumbled something and went back to sleep. Far from what? the Wintergreen in the train window who was looking back at her wanted to know. From two people terribly young exploring…everything…

"We're taking the show to Paris, France. Do you want to come?"

"Are you kidding?" she had asked. "Sure I do. Is everybody going?"

"No, just you."

"How come? We're all part of the show." Everybody knew she was not the best dancer, or the best singer for that matter. She had her own way but the real singer was…not her.

"But," they had explained, "we want you. You have the 'look.' New York's been good but Paris is better!"

Sure, she was good but everybody was. Frick and Frac were funny as hell! Tiger Lily could make them all cry when she let out a song. The Coon Boys

made tapping a step toward heaven. And there was Charlotte. With deep
dark arms and full round breasts and hips that flowed like a river. Who, once
she got going, could sing better than anybody. Anybody.

"Just wait," she had said to Charlotte, "they'll change their minds and
realize this ain't a show without you."

"Is this what you really wore in Paris?" Kali asked, pulling the
matching shirt out of the trousers and stuffing it back in again, drawing Mrs. Wintergreen back into the room.

"When I wore anything."

"What?"

"Sometimes I went nude."

"Naked?" Kali asked, turning around to ask the question, suddenly aware of the blue-trimmed eyelet ruffles along the hem of the
bedspread.

"Yes, silly. What else does nude mean?"

"But why?"

"I was a dancer. Who sometimes danced nude."

"Paris," Kali said softly, picking up the mother-of-pearl hairbrush
trimmed in gold. She brushed her hair absent-mindedly.

"Careful, you'll kill the waves, sugar."

The face with the rakish hat shimmered in the train window again. The
image–hat still tilted over one eye, a cigarette glowing off and on in the long
ivory holder–asked, Is this what you want, Wintergreen? Going
between Berlin and Paris? Performing like a trained seal? For people
who, at best, think that's all you are? Some white cracker said as
much...while I was at...was it Bricky's?

"We keep all our niggahs in the kitchen," he had said. The other
Americans thought it was funny. The French didn't. Brick Top, on hearing the
commotion, came rushing in from the kitchen with a silver ladle still in her
hand, soup dripping down her brand-new dress. She had the redneck from
Manhattan thrown out. But Paris was beginning to squirm with his type. So
much money.

"When did you start singing?" Kali asked, still looking at herself
in the oval mirror, starting to like the look of this reflection, starting
to bend her body...

"When I stopped dancing."

Kali's face began to melt in the oval looking glass, just like hundreds of faces in all those clubs had begun to melt—like wax from candles.

So she had said to Jake, "It's time."

"Time for what?"

"Time to go home."

Jake's Mediterranean looks had made him more and more vulnerable each time they went to Germany. There was always someone "interested" in his heritage. Paris wasn't much better. But she had wanted to stay on a little longer to do a show, a new club in Berlin that just had to have the "golden one." So she made Jake promise to go back to Paris and to ship out immediately on the next boat to the United States.

Though he had never intended to, he finally did leave for the U.S. without her.

For her, a little longer had turned out to be too long. One beautiful spring morning, uniformed men entered the house of the family where she was staying. When they left, they took her with them.

NINE

"There's a white woman out here to see you," Jake said, between puffs on an ever-present cigarette he kept between his lips.

Mrs. Wintergreen looked up from her desk, and, after checking her calendar and flipping through several dates, said, "Ask her what she wants."

"I did. She wants *you*." Jake smiled, pointing at her like Uncle Sam had in the army recruiting poster.

"Tell her to come in."

She was already standing behind Jake. "I'm in... How do you do?" The white woman walked towards her, offering her hand–which Wintergreen didn't accept. The woman sat down without being asked. "I didn't expect to find...I run an escort service."

"Find what?"

"I didn't realize you were quite so..."

"White? I'm not. Creole. I'm sure you understand. A lady pimp has got to understand..."

"Illusion?"

"Exactly. Jake!"

His cigarette smoke entered the office before he did. Jake was short and muscular–dark for a white man; it was impossible to tell what he was. His face appeared with a two-day-old beard, rubbing against the mahogany door.

"Yeah?"

"Vodka stinger for me, Jake. What will you have?"

"Southern Comfort."

"Ah, the difference between us," Wintergreen said.

"Meaning?" the white lady asked.

"I jab."

"While I block," the white woman tossed out. They laughed: a stiff kind of laugh both knew well. The battle lines had been drawn. Wintergreen with her sting; the white woman hiding in her comfort.

The office walls framed the two women as the light from small windows revealed evening coming on. The alabaster walls rose slowly in that light, rounded in the corners, and flowed out into the high ceiling. There it inched along, interrupted by an elongated design filled with fat angelic figures that romped and played, carved in heavy plaster. In the center of play there hung a small but elegant crystal chandelier that looked as though it had been an original fixture in the seventy-year-old building. In fact, Wintergreen had asked Jake to take it to the United States when he had left Paris for good. It had hung in her dressing room at the Folies and was only noticed by everyone else who worked there once it was gone.

A few months after she had returned to the United States, Wintergreen sat in her soon-to-be office, in one of the deep depressions that often hit her since she'd come back. She sat on a lone chair among the fabric designs and carpet samples, thinking out loud that the room needed something special, some focal point. Suddenly, Jake remembered the chandelier, gathering dust in the basement.

Jake had bought this club on John R. Street during the war. However, much of his time the last three years of the war had been spent going to every official he could think of, trying to find out what had happened to Wintergreen. He was reminded that she had chosen to stay, and they had more to do than concern themselves with what could only be a Nazi sympathizer. He had complained–and vigorously–but they knew about Wintergreen and her notorious life in Paris and had more important things to do, they said. "Don't you know there's a war on?"

One wall was covered by a French tapestry, gaudy by everyone's standards but Jake's. He found it, he said, in a little shop along the Rue de Rogier. He liked it. She didn't, preferring instead the Ibo masks that hung upstairs in her living room. The opposite wall was vacant, giving the room a seesaw look–the one side weighted by the tapestry and the other upended, it seemed, by the weight of nothing. The few visitors who entered her office sometimes commented on the imbalance. Wintergreen would simply say, "I left everything in Paris." Which, of course, explained nothing.

There was one small photograph in the wall's center. It was a picture of Jake, standing alongside a ship. The caption at the bottom read, *S.S. America, October 15th, 1939.* There was Jake waving and smiling, a bottle of champagne tucked under his arm, a cigar in his mouth. As it turned out, the ship he sailed home on was the last one, before the Nazis entered Paris, that would carry U.S. citizens home.

The white lady, who'd been fishing for her pack of cigarettes, shook her hand "no" when Wintergreen offered her a reefer from a silver case she kept on her desk. Shrugging her shoulders, Wintergreen rolled her thumb across the flint tip of a cigarette lighter. The white woman leaned forward and lit her cigarette, drawing the smoke in deeply and exhaling a shimmering blue screen into the evening light, her eyes fixed on Wintergreen as she settled back again in her chair. Wintergreen smoked nothing when doing business with strangers, even in her own club.

"Who's that?" the woman asked, pointing with the lit end of the cigarette to the playpen where a pretty baby boy slept.

Jake brought him down, playpen and all, every Thursday afternoon while Mrs. Wintergreen went over the books. He and Cook had him out at the bar until he got fussy.

"He's mine."

"Oh, *really?*" The white woman smiled, lifted an eyebrow slowly, and said, "I've come to do business."

"Oh? Do I know you?" Wintergreen sat quietly still, self-contained, watchful.

"No. But I know *you.*"

"Oh?"

"Never formally. I've been in the club a few times. But everybody knows the lady never mixes out."

"But she does do business."

"I want your club."

"Oh?" This time her mouth made a perfect circle but no sound.

"Is that Edie Piaf I hear?" the white woman asked, surprised by the sudden sound of the very sad French voice.

Wintergreen explained, "We were friends once." She pointed to the small speaker, one of four wedged in the corners, fronts covered with heavily brocaded cloth. "Then we fought... I was young, you understand. Young boys were her weakness," Wintergreen volunteered and then shook her head. "She kept an interesting nursery. Not unlike yourself, I bet." Wintergreen looked directly into the white woman's eyes but failed to get a reaction. "Jake puts her on from out front."

"Some of my clients want a private party while their husbands are out of town."

"Their husbands are generally here," Wintergreen said.

"Oh," the white woman said, in spite of herself. "They know. But if they don't name it, it doesn't exist. Illusion again..."

"No, it's *de*lusion this time," Wintergreen offered matter-of-factly. The white woman shrugged her shoulders. Wintergreen shifted forward and asked, almost in a whisper, "Who's in your nursery?"

"A Negro boy, a white, and an Oriental... By the way, what's your name?"

"Mrs. Wintergreen."

"Of course. But I mean your first name?"

"Mrs."

"I see," she said. "I forgot you drink vodka stingers."

"But I never forget that in Dixie you drink Southern Comfort."

"I'm not from the South, Wintergreen."

"All American whites are from the South. Twenty-five hundred and I'll supply the booze."

"*Dar*-ling, you were in Paris too long," the white woman mimicked Tallulah Bankhead's voice and gestures.

"Maybe we should forget the private party and book you for impersonations."

Without giving ground, the white woman countered, "Twenty-three hundred and we'll supply our own booze."

"Done. Tell me, who makes the most money for you?"

"Why, Wintergreen, don't you know?"

"Mrs."

"Why would white women exchange one white boy for another?" It wasn't really a question.

"Then why the white boy?"

"For bored Negro women… You'd be surprised."

And Wintergreen was, but didn't show it. She asked, "Why me? And why here?"

"For southern comfort. White and black."

"And the Oriental?"

"For diversion. Big and black is what most want. You know the reputation," the white woman said. They both laughed, more relaxed now.

"I'll call you when I work the date out," the white woman said.

"You can't have just any night. I run a business here."

"They'll pay the difference, Wintergreen. Besides, it's not my money. I'll call you," she said, getting up from her chair.

"And *you're* not concerned about money?"

The white woman stopped at the door and turned. "Money is an illusion. If you understood that, you wouldn't waste time hating me. It burns energy."

"The worst sin in America is not having money. And *you* got it."

"No, Wintergreen, the worst sin in America is having no love. And you *got* that. Maybe you should *listen* to the songs you sing, sugar."

This time Wintergreen flinched.

"You need some comfort, honey."

"What's your name?" Wintergreen asked, not intending to. She would have preferred leaving this white woman as a face attached to a business card, unimportant until needed.

"Samantha. Sam for short. My father wanted a boy."

"He got more than he bargained for," murmured Wintergreen to the retreating back.

Kali waited until eleven o'clock outside of Wintergreen's. She didn't have a watch to know how late Van was, but she had been waiting so long the doorman, who at first thought she was Mrs. Wintergreen, asked if he could hail her a cab or reserve a table for her inside.

"No," she said. He must be new, she thought. She explained that she was not going into Wintergreen's, she was going to the Chesterfield, and later perhaps to the Frolic or Flame Showbars. But not Wintergreen's.

"Too bad," he said, "this is the best place to be on a Saturday night in Dee-troit city."

Having explained that she already knew where the best place to be on Saturday night in Detroit city was, she said, "Anyway, this is Thursday, not Saturday." She heard herself explain further that she was not from out of town, as he probably thought she was. She was from here and she knew the best place to be on Saturday night in Detroit was *not* in Wintergreen's. Besides what did he know, he was from Memphis.

"No," the doorman had said, he was not from Memphis but his best friend was. It was a place he had always wanted to visit. How did she know that, he wanted to know. So, she had found herself saying at last, what did she care about him, or Memphis, or his friend either? He then revealed he was really from Alabama and found the stories untrue about how cold Yankees were. For example, how nice he thought she was, even though she tried to appear mean but was really a nice person even though she wanted to look like a boy. She stopped the conversation then, realizing that she was standing out in front of Wintergreen's arguing with the doorman about Memphis, his best friend and Saturday night in Detroit, when it was really Thursday. She shook her head and walked quickly away, leaving him shouting at her back about how nice she really was and the next time she was in town she should visit Wintergreen's.

Kali hurried into the Gotham, right past Mildred at the desk, and knocked on the door of Vanderbilt's apartment. She knocked long and hard. Finally the door cracked and a sleepy Vanderbilt peeked out. She moved right past him into the dimly lit living room.

"Van, you *promised.*" That's all she could think to say as he stood in the middle of the floor unable to speak, chest bare, a sheet wrapped around his waist. She thought she heard a noise in the bedroom, but Van, though sleepy, moved quickly past her and shut the door. Not, however, before she saw, in the rose-colored light of the bedroom, what she thought was a white coat, definitely cashmere, carefully laid across a chair. She focused on the loose button on its sleeve, amazed that it hung there at all–limp and near to being lost forever in the rose-colored light of a sleepy friend who had promised her her very first night out. And had broken that promise.

"Was that Callie-girl making all that noise out there?" a voice asked as Vanderbilt returned to the bed and moved into the arms of the voice that hushed his reply with a warm tongue snaking across his narrow lips.

A deep groan entered the rose-colored bedroom and held.

Kali hurried down the hall of the Gotham past Mildred again, who looked up long enough to say, "Our policy here is to stop at the desk and make inquiry about our guests, not go rushing past."

"I know what the policy is, Mildred."

"Callie, is that you?" Mildred cried.

"Mildred! Come on."

"You come on, Callie. I can't believe it!"

"Well, she said she could do it," Kali mumbled to herself.

Mildred, never one to miss anything, said, "I don't know who *she* is, but...where are you going?"

"To the Chesterfield."

"Don't tell me you perform there too?"

"Mildred!"

The moon hung low—a yellow ball. The trees, entombed in cement, created strange shadows against the upper windows of the Palmetto Hotel north of the strip. Kali shivered and slowed down to examine the night. The moon had drawn everybody out.

Carrie Cobo, in a red-hooded cape, starch-white makeup, red painted circles on her apple cheeks, and purple fingernails, rushed past on her way up the strip.

"Hey, Little Red Riding Hood, can I go with you?" somebody asked from a passing car. The night rider had missed the shiny object she carried under her cape. It was that kind of night.

When Carrie Cobo had first shown up some years ago along the strip, no one had paid any attention—until one night she entered the Frolic Showbar with a raised ax, shouting, "Down with demon rum!" The customers scattered. And Carrie axed the counter of the bar—spilling drinks and breaking glasses. All anyone knew about her was that the next day a generous cashier's check, more than covering the damage, appeared in the mail and Carrie Cobo had vanished. Some said that in the confusion she had simply disappeared down the alley. Others swore she got into a long black limousine that appeared just at the right time. Still others claimed she escaped through the same front door she had come in. No matter. The story ebbed and flowed every few years. Like a river running into the shops, stagnating on the street corners. In between thumb and forefinger, along cue sticks tipped blue, the tale continued.

One other night, after Emmett Till had been lynched and mutilated in the South, she chained herself to the door of Wintergreen's, her sweat mixing with the makeup rolling down her face, spoiling the overripe circle of her apple cheeks, her purple fingernails broken. The club didn't open that night because the people who had been milling around outside "somehow just didn't feel like goin' in," even after Carrie was sawed loose. The next day, Mrs. Wintergreen received a large cashier's check that was at least twice what she would have made if she had opened. Carrie Cobo was released from jail within an hour of her incarceration. No one would say—downtown or otherwise—who had paid the bail, or where she had gone. That's when all the clubs added doormen to their list of employees. Only then did they realize it was a nice touch.

Carrie Cobo was soon lost in legend on the strip because Negroes were beginning to listen with one ear to that southern boy Ma'tin Luthe' King. But they were *really* listening to the message from a homeboy, who had been Detroit Red before he went into prison and Malcolm X after he'd come out. He had white folks by the balls and people on John R liked that better

Carrie Cobo passed by Wintergreen's, did a double take, and set the head of her ax down on the sidewalk, the handle still covered by her long cloak.

"Red, where's yo' picnic basket?" the doorman asked. When he looked into the sober face of the hooded woman he changed his tone. "Uh, Ma'am, can I give ya a hand?... No, I'm not from Memphis... Yes, Ma'am, Alabama... Nice night. Yes, Ma'am... Full moon. And warm, too... Can I get ya a table inside? I hate to see a nice lady like you sitting at the bar... Yes, Ma'am, this *is* the best place to be on Saturday night in Dee-troit City... "

Kali slowed her pace even slower, and finally she stopped in front of Luigi's, which was on the other side of Fawnsworth Avenue about a block from the old house. She stopped to hear Melvina, the street poet, talking and sermonizing the blues about men and bad times.

Jesus was coming out of Mabel's Washtub, this time at the side of Easter-Egg-Man. They walked along John R, their arms folded: one, the Black Christ, in a long robe that brushed the top of his bare feet as he walked; the other, the infidel at his side, eager to communicate.

Kali heard Beverly, loud and animated as they passed, unmindful of her, make a point. Jesus was surreal and occasionally offered an "amen" while Beverly explained scripture with large doses of blue-eyed devils mixed in.

As Kali reached the door of the Chesterfield, the doorman said, "Entertainers enter through the back entrance." She stood there uncertain.

"She's with us," a woman behind her said. Kali turned to her. The woman had on a string dress, one-inch platform shoes and queen lace stockings, with her name, "Dixie," spelled out on a wire broach pinned over her right bosom.

The man at the door smiled at Dixie in the one-inch platform shoes, ran his eyes along the queen lace stockings and up into the strings of the dress as they tossed in the night, and said, "Uh uh uh, all the Dixies I know are made outta jelly, cause jam don't shake like that!"

She laughed and grabbed Kali's arm, while the white man in horn-rimmed glasses at her side remained bored and unaffected.

"What's the matter with him?" Kali whispered, nodding her head toward Dixie's friend.

"Private school—always messes them up."

Dee entered the Chesterfield, went up to the bar for a drink, and stood surveying the crowd. Suddenly his attention was attracted by the tip of a silver wing-toed shoe and white silk stockings emptying out from under white satin trousers. But the crowd moved like a wave, obscuring his vision. He craned his neck, lifting it like a pink flamingo, dressed as he was in a white coat with a dark pink handkerchief billowing from the breast pocket, a daring silk scarf, with bits of that same pink, draped from his neck, and white-and-black spectators protruding from under sharkskin-gray trousers. As he longed for the silver wing-toed shoe, Ruby Red, sensing her cue, floated to the bar like a big-boned dancer, reached for the phone, and in 2/4 rhythm, with the tip of her long red fingernail, dialed a number. The response was immediate. With one hand Ruby placed the receiver back into its cradle, while her other swung open the door. She melted through it.

The wave moved again, and the profile with the silver wing-toed shoe came into focus, as everything else, for Dee, went out of focus. The shoulder curled and edged toward the table as the palm struck the table in gentle pats, seized with something funny. Laughter erupted. The wave crashed, obscured, cleared again. Dee squeezed his eyes tight before he could once more dare to look. The sight, and not the sound, of what may have caused the boy to move forward then back filled Dee with something so sharply sweet he dared not keep looking, for fear the scene would vanish. The tables, chairs, drinks, smoke, conversations—everything else disappeared. He felt himself fading.

The profile registered all things for Dee. And he was becoming nothing, and that gladly, as he always became when first he fell in love. And he always fell. At first. In love. And, as he said to himself over and over again, he did everything for love.

And once he was in love, any scene could make a lasting imprint. Bittersweet emotion would fill his chest, and he would declare the scene to be the best ever. It didn't matter what it was. The feeling could be just as strong if, rolling down his car window to buy a newspaper from Blind Tom, he heard the singsong of the tamale man against the screech of brakes and the jabber of, "Mothafuckah, cain't you see where ya goin'?" Over everything he could still pick out the tamale man's voice, "This yo' hot ta-ma-lee-man; git me while me hot." The song, the smell, and the clang of change heard along the strip could find a slot on his lists of to-be-remembered best outdoor scenes and, depending on how recently he had fallen in love, could move him to tears.

It never occurred to him to question why he kept lists and ranked things in his head that could send him to his knees, crying out, "Hallelujah, Father!" He would cry, and often did, in full view of everyone, like a preacher touching the heads of sinners at the moaning bench—big bursting tears that ran down his cheeks unchecked.

Because he was Black in a violent country where only white men are men and allowed violence, he grieved. His sorrow permitted him the space to be a voyeur to the tiny explosions of the unique in things, which he daily recorded. In order to tame, arrest, control, and otherwise own the dramas and scenarios of life, he would file these scenes away and reimpose himself in them at a later time in his fantasies, where he could be a man's man—tears and all—erasing the grief he felt in his heart for his denied manhood.

And the drama featuring the boy was unfolding, starting to draw itself in his mind part by part, though quickly. Like the hurried strokes of a caricature artist. First the eyes. They must be luminous. Then the nose, always aware of where Dee stood and forever ready to turn instinctively to him. And only him. And, of course, there was the mouth, ever ready to respond to the sounds he made with his own, as he fed it the best things to eat and taught it the right things to say. And the chin must not be weak. A strong chin was a must! How could he love a weak chin?

He felt the crackle in the air. Kali felt it too and turned. Dee smiled, winked, and settled again on the curve of the silver wing-toed shoe, and the animated caricature.

He was interrupted by a hand on his shoulder. Someone who wanted to talk. He turned reluctantly, but came alive when he saw the young man standing in front of him. "Willie Chi-Town Wilson, my man!" Monkey Dee said, giving him five. "What blows you in from the Windy City?"

"Money, nothing but the smell of money," the young man said. He looked like a young W.E.B. DuBois. If he had arrived on the strip some years earlier, he would have sprouted a Vandyke, worn spats, and strolled the strip tapping his walking cane as he went. Now, because it was a different time and styles change, he wore a tailor-made virgin wool overcoat with a hand-woven white scarf neatly tucked inside the coat's lapels. Dark blue pinstriped trousers showed beneath the coat. He hated the bawdiness of the role he played as a big-time spender blown in from Chicago. But he knew that Black folks spend money on shiny things and hand it over to people who look like they have money or know where to get it. He learned that when he sold life insurance on Chicago's south side. He worked his debit driving a Cadillac, new every couple of years, collecting the nickels and dimes of his policyholders. He learned then that they would never buy or keep up their insurance from someone as poor as themselves. It was true he had to sometimes be preacher, counselor, lawyer, and adviser to them—but he sold more insurance than anybody. And he *was* a shiny thing. Very handsome and well-mannered when he needed to be.

Wilson preferred the look and manner of a conservative business man. Negro people lived their lives either influenced by W.E.B. DuBois or Booker T. He dressed like W.E.B., but as an Alabama boy he knew that property—not the vote—made the man. In his heart he sided with Minister Malcolm (as Wilson liked to call him), and, like Malcolm said, we gotta have our own. Chi-Town owned half a block in Chicago.

"You still dealing with them farmers turned factory workers?" Dee asked, laughing as he said it.

"They like clothes and women. You keep on taking care of the women, and I'll keep on taking care of the clothes. Deal?"

"Deal," Dee said, giving him five again.

"What's goin' on in Big D?"

"Nothing but the rent, my man. Nothing but the rent."

"Well, I'm a man on a mission. Catch you later, 'gator."

"Where's the fire, my man?"

"I'm crossing the street to Wintergreen's to break her heart for real this time." The young man flashed a pretty smile, removing him from the serious demeanor of business, turning him into a young man who knew how to have a good time.

"That old broad?" Dee said, just to get a rise out of Chi-Town.

"One man's meat is another's poison, my friend. You be cool now, you hear?"

After Chi-Town left, Dee felt like he was drowning again. Soon, though, everything came back into focus—the white stockings snug against the slender ankles, the sandy hair brushed back from the face, the intense conversation with the people at his table—poof! everything went out of focus again.

The crowd in the bar moved as a single unit hushed by the boy with the white satin shoulders that curled when something was funny, and patted the table with soft gestures that Dee filed under

The Best Ever. When the silver from the shoe merged with the glitter of the diamond cuff links and the silver stripe from the suspenders, he gasped. A diamond jubilee scene worth forty carats, he thought, as he sucked in his breath and bit his lip.

The house darkened before he could list more. The last set was starting. As he moved the images through his mind, it suddenly struck him what was unique about the boy. He was not a boy at all! The sharp realization of that filled his mouth with prayers that made no sound, like a saint mouthing the five mysteries. My God, he repeated a dozen times, who is she?

As the passion for this woman filled his mind and flowed into his heart, it skipped a beat. For only his heart knew what Dee didn't: that the exquisite feeling it held was not love but, in fact, hatred. A rare form of hatred so intense it held itself back for just such a time and then sliced him in half like a cleaver separating fat from the bone.

Dee held up a twenty dollar bill to get the bartender's attention. "Send a bottle of champagne over to..." Dee pointed to the table where Kali was, but before he could finish, the bartender said, "Any more champagne sent over there and that table'll drown."

When Kali looked up, a single rose was held out to her by the waiter. She raised her eyebrows in a question, the waiter pointed toward the bar. There was the face of Monkey Dee looking back at her. She smiled, placed the rose to her nose, and turned to sip the champagne that was in her glass. His heart pounded. Then the bar erupted. People scattered everywhere as an ax slammed down, splintering the counter. Monkey Dee moved quickly, but the second blow nicked him on the shoulder and tore a hole in his coat. His selves split. Wham! A third blow to the counter. Then another. In seconds the bar was ruined—and so was Dee's coat, because, in all the bedlam, he had ripped it off and torn it to shreds. As if a cadre of moths was loosed in a cartoon, nothing was left but powder. Carrie Cobo slipped through the crowd, and Kali, hearing the confusion, stood up, knocking over her chair and the bottles of champagne. Still carrying the rose, she headed for the bar.

"M.D.!"

The crowd, seeing that "the Monkey," as they said, "is loose!" was moving out of the way. "Shiiit, that niggah's crazy. You see him waste that coat, man?" And somebody, remembering how it all started, shouted, "Catch that woman!"

"M.D.!" Kali said again, not understanding what was happening. Dee heard her voice this time, and the rage left as suddenly as it had come. He dusted himself off as casually as one removes lint from the shoulders of a favorite jacket. Looking at the astonished faces of the remaining crowd, he straightened his shirt sleeves. "Set them up, bartender, the drinks are on me."

"Set 'em up? You gotta be the craziest niggah in town. This bar is ruined."

"No need to use language like that, my man. Carrie Cobo always pays for the damage."

By now the band had started up again. Dee strolled over to Kali, smiled, and asked, "Callie-girl, is that really you?"

TEN

Recently there had been an epidemic of Cheshire cats in the old house. No, perhaps it was only one cat. Brother couldn't tell. They appeared and disappeared at will. They stayed on and then went off, like a changing traffic light. He couldn't remember if he'd ever seen two on at a time. Soon he stopped wondering, less concerned with their number than why they were flooding the old house. A cat would appear, shit-eating grin intact, its striped fur turning from dusty pink to fuchsia—then poof!—it disappeared. Its body was always surrounded by an olive green light, which gave it an eerie look. But somehow Brother knew that it was there not to scare him but rather to tell him something.

Sometimes it sat on the mantel and other times on the chiffonier in his bedroom. Many times, emerging from his bedroom, he found it on top of the first floor banister, glowing—its dusty pink stripes shimmering in waves.

The very night Sunshine left (no one thought she could or would), it had appeared. With that grin that said, "I know something you don't."

Lately, the Cheshire cat brought things lodged in its mouth, the shit-eating grin submerged, dumped them out into Brother's out-stretched hand, and disappeared. Hairpins and ribbons, crayons and candy.

Brother, accustomed to his mother roaming the house at night, was surprised that she made no mention of seeing the pink and green

Cheshire cats as she floated through the house tugging at her throat.

"I be goddamn, all ya'll is pussy-whipped!" There was Uncle Bubba, King Solomon's brother, rared back in King's chair in King's room—legs crossed, slapping his thigh. He had taken off his beret and his coat in the hallway, hung them carefully on the hooks of the coat stand, and placed his umbrella in a stand already filled with umbrellas of every size and description.

His beret never ceased to get folks talking. It was Bubba's style and Bubba's war memento—a reminder that he had been in the fighting 369th, one of two Negro units that fought with the French because they couldn't fight with American white soldiers in World War I.

Bubba had entered King's room in a recently pressed suit, his shoes shined and his legs carefully greased with Blue Seal vaseline. But his ankles were as bare as a baby's butt. Hot or cold, rain or shine, he never wore socks.

"Beat 'em. That's what they need. Beat 'em."

The war, everybody said, had made Bubba a hero but also left him down a few screws. King knew that Bubba was "touched," but that wadn't enough for crazy. It made him jes loose.

"Charlotte ain't been right since you married her," he whispered to King, his left leg crossed over his right, swinging back and forth, his bare ankles exposed, his Florsheims shining like new money. "Not to mention them sisters of her'n. Now Brother's wife done done whaaat?!"

Brother and King tried to explain about Kali and the black paint in the parlor and the move to Wintergreen's, but Bubba kept interrupting, exclaiming in disbelief, "Saay whaaat?!" When a break came in the conversation, Bubba shot upright in King's chair, his dark face glowing, his feet pressed to the floor. And looking directly into Brother's face, he chanted,

"Peter, Peter, pumpkin eater,
had a wife and couldn't keep her.
Put her in a pumpkin shell
and there he kept her very well."

When he finished, King looked at Brother, who had covered his mouth with his hand to keep from laughing. Bubba recrossed his legs and, unintentionally, his foot struck Africa and scraped across Japan, two of the many stickers King had plastered on the side of the steamer trunk he kept in his room, on end and ajar. He stuck some sweaters in the old trunk but mostly he used it as a way to keep track of Char-Lee's travels. Bubba's swinging foot sent the trunk over with a crash. Still talking, he jumped and tried to pull the trunk upright. "Find her and beat her, son... Saay what?... She 'cross the street? Man!... She beggin' fo' a beatin'."

"Bubba, what shit you pullin' in there now?" Charlotte yelled from the kitchen, in response to the crashing trunk.

"Bubba!" Charlotte yelled in again. Brother looked at the kitchen door and shook his head.

Charlotte, with Laphonya as her partner, and two of the other aunts were playing a mean game of Bid Whist. They had started out playing Tonk, but Lizzie had come down unexpectedly because she heard Bubba's voice in the hallway.

Lizzie wasn't a gambling woman, and because she wasn't, people in the house tended to respect that. Hearing her on the stairs, they had quickly dumped their chips in their apron pockets, hoping Lizzie would go to bed early.

"Bubba," Miss Charlotte yelled, "git yo'self in here and git some of yo' brother's bread puddin' fore it's gone. Lizzie, Laphonya, and the rest of us is waitin' to hear all yo' new lies ya gonna tell."

His father's tone was well-meaning, or so he first thought. And they had had this conversation many times. But this time there was in it an applied pressure, a fixed place, that left a lump in his throat. Listening was hard for Brother. And talking to his son was hard for King.

"You cain't have her livin' 'cross the street right in yo' face. What ya gon' do 'bout it?" King never waited for answers from him, he only asked questions.

"What about it, boy? It don't look right. Smacks against a man bein' a man, don't it?"

By now, the younger man wanted to say, if he had known what to say, "The world is bigger and badder than you ever dreamed, old man. And I got a chunk of it caught right here in my throat." But he had no way of knowing what he meant. He only knew that he was trying to forget what he supposed didn't matter. "And you," he might have said, "even you left that Alabama dirt farm, old man, knowin' it wadn't real. Gittin' family to work it. And ya left cause bein' *in* place wadn't the place *to* be. And you musta been lookin' for somethin'. But I need to know, old man, compared to what?"

"Daddy, Daddy," he would have cried if he could, "do you know how I slept last night? Do you care that I don't sleep most of the time? Sunshine is gone, and I can't be a man when it hurts so much. And it wadn't supposed to matter, was it, Daddy? And if I dared to tell you that, you would say, there is more where she came from, boy."

"I'm not asleep, Brother."
"I heard ya snorin'."
"That's the only way to keep you from joogin' all the time."
"Joogin'? Don't talk like that."
"That's what Laphonya calls it."
"Did she tell you to pretend too?"
"Things are different things to different people."
"A lie is a lie."
"Not when I need to protect myself."
"From me?"
"I feel violated sometimes…"
"What d'ya mean, violated?"
"I want some say about sex."
"What else is there to want sides gettin' some?"
"Some? What about the rest of me?"
"I never had no complainin'."
"Maybe you've never listened. Besides, how many beds have you been in before me, Brother?"
"Plenty… Tell me it ain't good."
"It is and it ain't."
"What kind of girl are you?"
"I need to be warm with you, Brother. Not just hot."
"Warm?
"Like me and Glo."

"Like *who?*"

"Like friends… We're not friends. We're something else."

"Oh, like old folks," he said, starting to tickle her. "Where he too old to get it up. And she too forgetful to remember the last time he did… What's that got to do with us, Sunshine?"

She moved uneasily. Then out of reach.

He lay back, his arms behind his head. "The first time I saw you in study hall, all I saw was sunshine. The sun was well…like a kiss."

"A kiss?"

"Yeah, a kiss. Nothin' like the sun. Nothin'. Ya know what I mean?"

"No," she said, turning on the pillow to look at him.

But Brother didn't seem to hear her. And said almost to himself, "Sometimes, I make believe."

"You mean you pretend too?"

"Well, not in the same way you do."

"Pretend is pretend."

"No, it ain't. You involved another person. I only pretend to myself," he said, beginning to understand what she meant. But not wanting to give in.

"But you said pretend is a lie. And a lie is a lie, isn't it?" she asked, rising up on one elbow to accuse him.

Brother laughed just then, reaching for her as he kissed the top of her head. "Do you wanna hear the rest of this or no?"

She smiled and cuddled close. "Yes. Now this is warm."

"Give me a break, will ya?" he said with a grin. "Well, I pretend to myself *alone* that I land on a island. Damn! Ya know what?" he said so suddenly that Kali jumped.

"No, I don't know what you do when you go to a desert island, *alone.*"

"Make love."

"You and who?"

"Me and the sun."

"Oh, I see."

"No, you don't. Understand, Sunshine, we make love to each other."

"How?"

"Never mind, we just do."

"Aw, come on. Don't stop at the juicy part."

"I guess I've been lookin'...but not really knowin' that I was really lookin' for you...and there you were. In that off-the-wall, paint-peeling, rink-a-dink study hall. Angel house. Just the place to find you. The mellow yellow."

"Brother..."

"Shh, baby, I know how good we are together."

"Suppose I wasn't sunshine but more like black thunder clouds?"

"Who do ya know wants black thunder clouds?"

"You need thunder clouds, too, Brother."

"Not me, baby. Not me. Shiiit! I gotta have some change fo' my dollar. The first time I got some of that yellah stuff I couldn't breathe. God, I couldn't breathe! I knew I had died and gone to heaven. I got stuck inside 'em cream-colored thighs on my way to the promised land. When I finally got in, I had already burst. Remember? Just like I did when I waited fo' the sun to come up while I was on that island."

"Brother..."

"Shh, baby. Come here. Ya know how good we are together."

Brother knew that his father was never far from the pain of his mother, which was lodged between what a man was supposed to be and what his real feelings were. So they played this game of "let's pretend." Let's pretend we don't know what Sunshine's leaving feels like, and we don't care how Charlotte's indifference leaves a bitter taste in everyone's mouth.

The older man droned on and Brother didn't know what he could say, even if he had known how to say it. He settled into what didn't matter, trying hard to remember to answer King on cue, while scenes of what used to be filled his mind.

Most always there'd been an eight-foot note of harmony in the shape of a bass fiddle in the center of King's bedroom whenever he and Brother took the baby boy in there. Before Sunshine had left, taking the child, father and grandfather had kept him in there for hours. Diapers were changed and bottles given with no thought of bothering his mother. After a time, mother would appear, a soft light from the alcove framing her in the doorway, asking in without making a sound. Just as suddenly, grandmother would appear at King's other door—the one that led to her parlor—the potted plants and sea-green shag carpet forming a backdrop to her entrance. At such times, Lizzie and Laphonya might bring in a mess of greens and a side of cornbread. Maybe a stray cousin or two or some of the aunts would bring in potato pie. Evening would gather the family together, in a note of harmony.

Unmasked, their faces yawned and stretched—like actors with their makeup off, dramatic lines forgotten—revealing a tenderness between them that deepened as night fell. Nighttime was the right time for King, and, as night settled, it added to his dark face a soft-ness that influenced everyone, pronouncing them happy. Family meant a lot to them, no matter what. But to King it was special because it was in those moments his wife would come and sit where he patted the bed beside him. She came with all the embarrassment of a school girl, and with that loose ripple in her hips that never ceased to tense his organ as she sat beside him on the bed. At first Sunshine had been unsure where she fit, but watching Miss Charlotte she had moved onto Brother's lap and he had gathered her in his arms, contented like his father.

The pretty brown boy had as many laps and arms as Brother could want for him. Brother had inherited that specialness for fami-ly from his father. All their faces shone in that darkened bedroom—their key light on, radiating warmth among themselves.

The bass fiddle played long into the night, low notes by an unseen tuxedoed man who accompanied the chatter of the family nestled in the old house on John R. Street.

Nothing was making any sense to Brother: not work, not life, not the flood of Cheshire cats. Nor King, who was in the middle of explaining how one monkey don't stop no show. "Do it, boy?"

"Daddy, don't."

"Don't? Don't what, boy?"

"I want my wife to *want* me... Not like Momma does you..." Brother raised his head and looked King straight in the eye.

King stared at a naked reflection of his own pain from this son he had never allowed room for. He could remember when he was born that he wished for Char-Lee. He knew in those early days that he kept imposing Char-Lee's face on the boy, and he realized with a start that he had never stopped doing that.

Now, this intertwining of the two pains, one numbed, the other raw, had awakened in him a sadness that was bottomless and left no room for talk. Slowly, shaking his head, King turned and left the room.

ELEVEN

The old house had one foot firmly planted in the alley while the other settled neatly up against the Chinese laundry next door. The muffled sounds of a giant flatiron (sometimes two) could be heard late into the night, thumping up and down against heavily padded ironing boards.

The weather had been unusually cool that summer, but people were out anyway. The strip hummed, but the beat was different—more subtle, like a low-grade fever that remained steady but couldn't be controlled. Even the greeting Miss Charlotte ritually exchanged with Mei Ling next door, when both chanced to be in the back of their buildings at the same time, was different. Their eyes held longer. A dozen years had passed before each could speak to each other in any discernible way. Miss Charlotte and Mei Ling took turns feeding Tom, the yellow-striped alley cat. He ate in both places and each woman knew this. Unable to communicate in words, they did so through the care and feeding of Tom. Mei Ling would bow while Miss Charlotte would throw up her hand in a wave.

Today, the ritual was aborted by the loud sounds of a man's voice in full rage, using words like slicing razors as he swished them at the woman who stood opposite him. The two stood on the edge of the parking lot in back of the Garvey Hotel, close to the sidewalk that formed a boundary between the lot and the back of the old house. The tirade was about money, the money the junior pimp supposedly was not getting from the woman whose face registered terror. Both women saw the terror, and the woman saw them see it. Mei Ling turned her attention to the string of white shirts hanging on the line, while Miss Charlotte stooped down to give Tom his second full meal of the day.

As the man's words continued to cut at the woman in big swoops, he shoved her. Both Miss Charlotte and Mei Ling stopped what they were doing. One arm of a dazzling white shirt fell on the ground, picking up a ring of dirt about the cuff; the other stayed pinned to the clothesline. Miss Charlotte, emptying leftovers from the chicken dinner King had cooked last night, missed Tom's dish. The food landed on the narrow sidewalk, mixing in with the loose gravel.

By then, the man had snatched the woman's purse and angrily dumped the contents into the alley. She was near hysteria, moving backwards. Miss Charlotte engaged the woman with a look that registered total disgust. Where's yo' guts? her eyes demanded. Mei Ling, in black satin trousers and tiny black slippers, though frozen at the clothesline, seemed detached. Each waited. The woman stopped moving backward and the raging man kept on. One more step and he would be on top of her. But before that could happen, the woman moved her body forward, raising her knee so suddenly that the man's disbelief registered at the same moment the knee landed in his groin. His face flushed. His eyes bulged. His mouth opened as the veins in his neck expanded—he went down clutching his groin.

The terror fled the woman's face. Surprised, she looked down at the pimp doubled over in the gravel. Slowly she picked up her things from the ground and moved toward the strip. After a few steps she turned around and retraced her steps. He was still trying to get up off the ground. With great force she kicked him back into the loose gravel and hurried away.

Miss Charlotte and Mei Ling smiled to each other. While her neighbor continued to hang the shirts, Miss Charlotte went into the old house humming a tune.

If it had made some sense, Charlotte wouldn't have minded. But it didn't. And she was tired. And fast gettin' out of the mood. The walk from her back door through the graveled parking lot and up the alley and across Woodward Avenue had put her out of breath. She was sure nobody else on the strip or back of it had to put up with this shit. Living in the old house put her in the business zone, which meant that in order to vote she needed to go up on Wayne campus and register in one of their old houses. The campus had swallowed up, one by one, the houses on Fawnsworth Avenue for classrooms. Whenever somebody up and died or somebody's chil'ren decided they old folks would do better if they sold out so they'd have some money, the campus snatched up the house.

Votin' was not much to her likin'—not since Roos'velt had died and Truman—but here she was thinkin' 'bout it again. Kennedy was brand spankin' new and she was, as most folks said, tired of tired politics—Mamie Eisenhower's bangs and Ike's penchant, as all Republicans since Hoover, for reducing the number of jobs for colored people. It was time for a change.

Her steps were hard on the pavement and she was aware that her lively breasts kept the center button of her dress popping open. With one hand she rebuttoned the dress, and she straightened her dark auburn wig with the other, thinking that her next one would be black.

Woodward and Fawnsworth were crowded with yesterday's winos hangin' in front of Barthwell's Drugs today, exchanging rounds of who owed who what from the last time when...

She didn't exactly see what happened. What she saw was a yellow parking ticket fly into the air, the winos freeze in their deals with each other, a crowd gather, and she heard the hard edge of a southern voice say, "Pick it up, nigger!" Oh no! He didn't say that! She knew better. The crowd knew better. And he knew better. So why did he repeat it? And pull his nightstick? She saw him raise the nightstick. It came down again and again, then a hand or hands stopped it, and it popped into the air over the heads of the crowd where the piece of yellow cardboard had just been seen. The policeman lunged for it, but it rolled and stopped at the tip of her feet. Miss Charlotte stepped on the black stick as the policeman bent to retrieve it. She looked first at him and then at the blood that was oozing from the young woman's head. The angry crowd pulled back as the student held her head and went into a series of motherfuckers, and mother, motherfuckers. The leathered arm of the policeman tried to lift the stick. When it could not, he slowly lifted his gaze from the foot holding the stick to the hem of a long black dress, up past full but shapely hips, a small waist and rounded breasts, and into a black, black face with very white teeth and a pink tongue. "Why you..."

Miss Charlotte jerked back her shoulders, annoyed at being grabbed by another policeman who'd pushed his way through the crowd. "Uhm uhm, white boy, not today!" she told him. The crowd moved in and the policeman dropped his arms. She addressed the policeman at her feet. "What I wanna know is why ya beatin' up on this chile?" Next a wino, not at all concerned about what was happening with the police, grabbed at a bottle of wine held loosely by one of his buddies. In the struggle for possession, the bottle fell and broke on the pavement, and a policeman who had just arrived hit him with a nightstick.

The crowd went wild. Voices high and low blended with the large shattering sound of glass, as Barthwell's came tumbling down. The plate glass window was in daggers, and the cheap crepe paper in the window display—which a moment before had surrounded smiling cardboard people, all in white face, suggesting important remedies like "take Bromo Seltzer"—was left in tatters.

The Easter-Egg-Man was in the crowd, as he always was when something went down in the city. Watching the reactions of the winos and other "concerned citizens," Beverly began to see and to understand how things could go down apart from student protests. Before that, he had been like most people he knew—thinking that only students, like those in Greensboro, North Carolina, had what it took to get things moving.

When a bank blew up on the east side of Detroit in Grosse Pointe, an all-white suburb, he didn't think much about it, but he did think the media overreacted. *Communists Infiltrating Negro Communities Responsible for the Attack on American Institutions.* Or *Colored Bolshevik Female Seen Fleeing the Scene.* Or the column read, "A Negro woman was seen leaving the scene, the same woman, it is suspected, who was responsible for tossing a Molotov cocktail from a speeding car that fell just short of the front door of the Dearborn Police Department." But nobody on the strip or the residents of Black Bottom, which was further downtown, believed the columnist, because Black people were not allowed in Grosse Pointe or Dearborn after dark.

"This ci-*tee* is some monstrous thing! Like an iron lung!" Mr. Ben had started saying, while he flapped his arms and filled his cheeks with lots of air that he blew out in rhythmic intervals. "Not even Sister Kenny, may she rest in peace," he hurriedly made the sign of the cross, "could heal such a vexation!"

Waking people up was a problem. The saying was "If you cain't make it in Detroit, you cain't make it nowhere." And "Detroit is good to its Negroes." But a few people like Mr. Ben remembered the days of Marcus Garvey and pulled the Easter-Egg-Man over to one side. "Hey Brother, say we talk some." This was the day that Beverly began to see the movement.

Lorraine Hansberry's play *Raisin in the Sun* had been turned into a movie and it caused some stir in the community, but Miss Charlotte found it boring. She had her own opinion, not only about mingling with whites but, in particular, about the Supreme Court decision in 1954 that put Black children in schools with white ones. When Little Rock and the fearsome nine had been all the news a few years back, she had followed it like everybody did—called Governor Faubus everything but a child of God, like everybody did. Stayed glued to the television, like everybody did. But still she wondered, like few did, what was going to school with white folks sayin' about bein' Black and I'm proud?

Detroit was getting ready but it would be a few years before it was put on the map for more than motorcars.

TWELVE

Laphonya was moving down the stairs as quietly as she could, but the stairs, used to the commotion of the cousins on their way out long after they should be in and quiet for the night, creaked, signaling Miss Charlotte from her parlor. The light came on so suddenly that Laphonya jumped.

"Ya on yo' way out?"

"Uh hum."

"Where to?"

Laphonya's short hair was brushed back and the overhead light in the hallway caught its hint of red color. Annoyed, she asked, "Come again?" She wore a shirt and necktie, a jacket with a vest underneath, and a chain going in and out of the vest pockets on either side, and a long skirt and high boots.

"Do Lizzie know ya be sneakin' 'cross the street to Ricky's every time she got 'Girl's Night In'?"

"Who?"

"Rick…Wintergreen's…If Lizzie knew…"

"Raisin' grown folks twice don't suit ya much, Charlotte."

"Lizzie'd raise hell if she knew 'bout…"

"It ain't Lizzie none of us gotta watch."

Charlotte ignored the accusation and reached to pick a thread from Laphonya's jacket. Laphonya, never sure of Charlotte's intentions and feeling like she'd been caught, jerked her shoulder back and said, "Ya been playin' Miss Rich and Propah Bitch fo' a long time now. The question is, what *you* gon' do tonight?"

"Me and Solomon…"

"Cut it, Charlotte, ya and King ain't never had nothin' goin'…"

Autumn was early this year and filled the air with an immediate chill, causing a riot of color in the few trees that lined John R. Street. Normally, summer delayed its exit in the Motor City, and with that delay came the gratitude of its southern immigrants who wished it would stay just a little while longer. This year, however, deep purple shadows signaling an early winter had appeared unexpectedly behind the buildings along the strip.

Northern Blacks, unused to fields and forests, rejoiced in the winter air that cut them like a knife. In those moments when the sharp intake of breath made them dizzy, they reached for the unremembered feel of baby rabbits buried deep inside the blue haze of winter. Only, for them, the rabbits of their imagination turned out to be romping tin cans, outdated newspapers, discarded paper bags, damaged paper cups, crumpled potato chip bags, and wax paper on the rampage that guarded, if only for a few seconds till they blew on, the entranceways, doorways, and stairwells of the inner city.

"*What*, Wintergreen, do you want?" Samantha demanded when Wintergreen returned her call.

The white woman had called because she wanted the club the same night as "Girl's Night In."

"Another night," Wintergreen said, into a stubborn phone that didn't seem to be conveying her message very well.

"What do you expect your receipts to be?" Samantha asked.

Wintergreen named some astronomical figure, and, to her surprise, Samantha raised it by five hundred dollars. The white woman started to set up schedules and was making arrangements for when she would be over with the liquor and the money when Wintergreen surprised herself by interrupting. "Just one minute, white girl, this is my club, and I decide." She slammed the phone down and let out a slew of French, English, and Arabic she had learned one long night in Morocco sipping sweet Turkish coffee.

Wintergreen was not in the mood. The crowd was smaller than last year, and her mind was on the money she was not making, when Laphonya stepped through the door, not in a good mood either.

Each looked at the other, Wintergreen from her piano bench and Laphonya from the end of the bar.

"Richelle." The name slipped into Laphonya's mind and softly through her mouth. Not because she willed it to, or even because she was thinking about it. It just came. The stack of letters with the funny stamps, Charlotte glaring at the letters each time one came. Silent on the subject of New Orleans and New York even when she talked non-stop about everything else. So this was Ricky.

To cover her mood, Wintergreen had put on the pink cut-away tuxedo and white top hat, and carried a pearl-handled cane. Tonight she wouldn't play piano. The surprised crowd watched as she tipped her top hat to them, then carefully setting it down on one side of the piano bench, she slid to the other and picked a saxophone out of its stand. This was going to be a hot night!

Women came in from everywhere to attend this affair. "Bitches Bite" was how the contest was billed in the neighborhood. Each year, signs were posted up and down John R. Street. Every telephone, lamp, utility pole, and shop window had "Bitches Bite" glaring out from it.

Former winners arrived early, each wearing "the look" that had won her fame. There was as much excitement from the crowd over them as there was for the hopefuls. Women would line up outside to watch as Julius Caesar, Bo Jangles, Billy Eckstine, Houdini, or Satchmo emerged from sleek cars. The Kodaks went wild.

As the contest began, former winners, some of them judges by now, others part of the crowd, began to whisper about the newcomers, who didn't at all, as far as they were concerned, know a butch look from a soft dick–wearing things that they, even in this time in their lives, wouldn't be caught dead in.

True, styles change, but the hopefuls were crass, and taste *will* always be taste, they whispered. "These bitches, or, excuse me, honey, Lay-dees, couldn't find a look if it walked up and smacked 'em in the face." There was no excuse for cheap imitations of Satchmo's horn or Houdini's cape or Caesar's toga.

Each fall, Wintergreen's was the place to be. A place for women who were unable to tell the lyin' mothafuckahs they lived with–or the women they didn't–that being who they couldn't be most of the time felt good. But other women, like Alvira the telephone operator, came in every night and sipped a short brandy, waiting patiently for Frankie, the practical nurse, still in uniform, to arrive—hurriedly, and always out of breath. They would linger as long as they dared, talking quietly, occasionally laughing—Alvira tossing her head back while Frankie lifted Alvira's open palm to her mouth and tenderly kissed the inside of it.

Alvira never came to "Girl's Night In" but Frankie did. By the time Frankie was on drink number three, she was unbuttoning the fifth button of her nurse's uniform. By drink number four and five, her nurse's whites were draped over a chair, a bar stool or a tabletop, and Frankie, on top of the bar by now, would be doing the splits. By drink number six, seven, and eight, Frankie, keeping time with the music, would be "laughin' like a big dog" and lassoing women at the end of the bar with her garter belt.

Then, too, there was the nightly collection of "blues" women, like Lucille, who didn't *have* nobody, didn't *want* nobody, and came in even when the bitches didn't bite. There was Joey, her bluesy self dressed in three-piece wool-worsted suits, who placed her pinstriped trousered leg and short leather boots between the unsteady legs and high heels of young girls, turning them on and out. And Big Baaad Delores was there to split up couples every chance she got. Not to mention Jonnie Mae Brown, who owned and operated Brown's Barbershop where "real men," it read on the door of her shop, "meet and greet the baadest lady barbers in Dee-troit city." The blues women were there nightly and when the "girls" flooded the bar during "Girl's Night In," they tugged at their trousers and straightened their ties and shook themselves all over getting ready to Booty Green and Walk the Dog.

Jake stayed for the night to work in Wintergreen's office. And Cook had his wife come, in his place, to prepare the food. Aromas coming from the kitchen were strange. Many of these women were cooks and fed fickle children, demanding men, and whimsical Miss Annes, but none dared to question Cook's wife and what she served. To complain would be betrayal. Besides, they were glad to be served for a change.

After Wintergreen surprised them with her saxophone, Laphonya joined the small band of women who hovered over

Wintergreen on the piano bench. Laphonya said, "Ricky, let's dance."

It had been that way with Charlotte too, Wintergreen remembered. During rehearsals, no matter what somebody was doing or about to do, she would blurt out the impossible—and just that casually: "Let's dance" or "Let's fuck." She'd let out a yowl, and, because Charlotte was Charlotte, she got away with it. Even if the scene had to be repeated, or the song resung, or the dance routine danced again.

Now here was Charlotte's voice, wink, and impulse, after all these years. Wintergreen slowly took in the face that was filled with Charlotte and just as slowly drew the face to her with her hands and her eyes, and said, "I don't dance, sugar. But I do smoke, so why don't you light my cigarette, and tell me how you know my name is Ricky."

The club was filling up. It was almost time for the sisters-in-law, billed as the Berry twins, to go on, but they were held up at the door by Sappho, the bouncer, with the hysterical pregnancy. Twenty-seven months.

Sappho didn't seem to mind that she was the butt-end of some cruel jokes. The baby, she said, was due any day now; and if they would sing "Stormy Weather" tonight, she was sure her water would break.

"Not while *we're* on," the sisters said in unison, as they rushed through the door to their dressing room.

"I don't dance," Ricky was repeating. But Laphonya had decided to ignore her.

"You mean you won't dance with me."

None of the women encircling Wintergreen knew if Laphonya had jerked her off the piano bench, or if during the exchange, she had gotten too close to the edge of the bench and fallen off. Laphonya had managed to down a few straight whiskeys before insisting that Wintergreen dance, and she was just a little out of hand. However it happened, Wintergreen tumbled.

Loose fragments of the past entangled her. She crawled toward a dark corner of a small cell. The cold cement floor seemed, in the odd uncertainty of the moment, to be the place for her to give birth. But she was not only giving birth, she was dying—both at the same time. In the cold night air, she trembled, and she wondered why her mother, sitting in the opposite corner of the cell, spoke but made no sound and watched her squirming in her own shit.

The past was real. She was in a cell and crawling in shit. She had been left in it for days. As she rolled to put her weight on her knees and finally her feet, the damp cell fell in around her.

Whatever it was—a jerk or grab or slap—that brought Wintergreen off the piano bench and onto the floor, the sight was funny at first. Until Laphonya and the crowd realized that she couldn't get up. She was trying to raise herself up on one knee, smelling herself again, as if the pink tuxedo with the purple cummerbund had become one big scent. In the process, the cummerbund unsnapped, snapping Wintergreen, who crawled back away from it, eyeing it like a frightened dog. Then she suspiciously crawled toward it, sniffing. It lay loose, like an afterbirth still pulsating from its bloody run. They were all amused at first, until tears began to streak the perfect face and fall onto the bowed mouth painted like angelic wings, a perfect pair of lips now parted and whimpering.

Jake, never noticing noise, exploded out of Wintergreen's office at the loud silence thumping in his head. He saw her, half crawling, half falling. He charged into the crowd of surprised women while they stood attracted and repulsed by Wintergreen, powerless as a beetle on its back.

Jake scooped up the small, trembling Wintergreen. Her eyes were closed, her pain descending into his large arms as he carried her off-stage and up the winding stairs. He shouted back to the Berry sisters-in-law to get on with their act. "Goddamn it! And now!"

Upstairs, Jake set the inert Wintergreen on her fainting couch. She opened her eyes for the first time, shook her head to rid herself of the cold cement of the dark cell. She said to Jake, who was leaning over her with concerned eyes, "Hand me my purple strapless, will you, sugar."

"Ricky, you can't go back down there. Not tonight."

"Since when have you called me Ricky?"

Jake stuttered, "I-I-I don't know, it just came...out."

"You never call me that. Even when we were first married. It was

Wintergreen. Not Ricky... Why tonight?"

"Because, you needed...me."

"I never lied, Jake. Remember? I never lied. Hand me the dress, will you. And see if I have any silver glitter left."

As she had gotten older, getting ready to go on stage, Wintergreen would layer her face with glitter to hide the bags under her eyes and to submerge her emerging jowls. Under the stage lights, the sheen from the silver, gold, or crimson sparkles seduced the audience, while she wooed them with the left-hand playing style of Earl Gardner, or occasionally blew them away with her sax or her whimsical scatting of "Foggy Day in London Town" and "Why Don't You Do Right."

"Jake! Did you hear me? Hand me my purple strapless."

"Now?" he asked, slumped in a chair opposite her.

"Indeed, yes!" she said, surprised that he would ask such a question. "It's more important than ever now. I'll be the only *lay-dee* in the place. Jake?"

Ricky, for the first time since Jake had brought her upstairs, took a good look at him. He was whiter than she'd ever seen him. She reached up and touched his cheek. "You're right, baby. I do need you."

He smiled slightly and came over to unzip her dress. After he handed her the purple dress and the silver glitter, he turned to go.

"Jake, sugar, help me with this necklace... Then too, I'll...I need you to carry me downstairs. I'll be at the piano when the twins finish."

Laphonya, who was now drunk, had taken the guitar right in the middle of the sisters-in-law's set and announced to the crowd, "I'm gonna play this box like it oughta be played." The twins were ho-hum tonight and the crowd didn't seem to mind when Laphonya interrupted them.

She'd been captivating the girls for fifteen minutes when the stage light came up abruptly, killing the downest, dirtiest blues this crowd had heard in a long time. The crowd booed and hissed—until they realized it was Wintergreen, upstage in a purple strapless, standing by the piano, smiling. The stage light carefully stopped at her waist.

Laphonya, who was as surprised as anyone, grabbed the mike. "Now that's hot!" The crowd whistled and stomped. Then Laphonya, thumping the guitar and keeping time with her right foot, began to sing—making it up as she went along.

"Now ain't that a pussy?
Da, da, da, da, da.
Now ain't that a pussy?
Da, da, da, da, da."

Wintergreen got into the mood of the thing and seated herself at the piano. Reaching to the side, she picked up the sax and began trading eights and singing in response:

"Now this is a pus-say!
Da, da, da, da, da.
Yep, this is a pus-say!
Da, da, da, da, da."

No one could believe it! There was Wintergreen—the hottest thing in the house—and Laphonya in a jam session. As the two women traded eights, the crowd joined in. The call and response between them went on for the better half of an hour.

Everyone forgot about the crawling, falling Wintergreen, except Wintergreen. The pain of that evening had marked the underside of her secret. For the other women there, it was one of those hot nights that they talked about for months afterwards; some would remember it for years.

THIRTEEN

Ruby Red heard the key in the lock and was out of her chair and into the foyer as Kali stepped through the door that Dee held open for her. It was a polite introduction. Dee was a little awkward. Preoccupied. That was unusual, she thought.

Thinking about what that meant, Ruby realized she was taken with the young girl. And could see why he was. The girl, on the other hand, seemed to be taking the rush of Dee in stride.

Ruby Red looked for signs in her. Not ones she could name. Just signs that could offer some answers. She searched the face for some small flirtations. Some unexplained lusts. Some well-kept addictions. There seemed to be none. Placing her palms together, moving her fingertips to her lips, and lowering her eyes, she welcomed Kali in a polite, low and musical tone.

Kali watched the black, black woman widen her eyes, which had already changed color from the first moments of the introduction and scattering of small talk. Her stride, as she led Kali, with Dee following behind, into the all-glass living room of the penthouse, was breathtaking. She moved across the room as smoothly and unhurriedly as her eyes moved: first over you, then settling around you–a comforting cloak with a live wire running through it. She was steady, gracious, and very, very polite.

Dee's voice broke into Kali's thoughts, "Ruby, tell Callie-girl I don't own a white coat. Was it cashmere, baby?" Kali nodded. Ruby Red, sliding gracefully into one of two chairs in the very large living room, narrowed her eyes, which now seemed green, and asked, "How do you spell that? Your name, I mean."

"Momma spelled it C-A-L-L-I-E. But I spell it K-A-L-I."

"Kalí is better. It fits you." Ruby Red repeated it softly with the accent on the last syllable. Turning to Dee, she said, "No, I don't remember sending a white coat to the cleaners."

"Come, Callie-girl, let me show you."

Kali looked down at Ruby Red as she passed her chair. She was sitting in a lotus position, head forward, eyes closed.

Dee had, in times past, arrived in the penthouse with women who seemed to be hiding secrets or at least wanting to. The latter found in Ruby Red a safe haven, an understanding, a "we are all in this together" feeling. The former held things that, obvious to even the most casual observer, were deep dark secrets to themselves. A few choice questions would send them into hours of confessions. And Ruby didn't mind. For whatever her role would be in getting them ready, these confidences made her job easier.

But underneath her own calm, still waters, she was, in fact, breaking up into little pieces. Pieces that seethed, others that flung themselves from her center, rupturing. The sudden explosions left her mouth filled with the taste of cotton and drew her eyes toward a flat terrain that exhausted them, day after day after day. It was carefully hidden, and most thought it to be a descending calm that enveloped her. Only Dee knew better, and she hated him for it.

He was father confessor to these women, the one understanding male in their lives. By the time they entered "the life," most of their lives had been peppered with abusive fathers working them over with indiscriminate dicks, masquerading brothers looking for any hole to put it in, or deranged second cousins just out for a little fun. But not this child. No father confessor needed here. Who then? What?

This girl would, in fact, find herself in his service, Ruby Red mused, like most of the others and very, very grateful. But over what road had she come? Was she traveling light? Or like most of them—traveling heavy—veteran performers bound up in the circus of their past? What was her need? For Dee had a knack for finding the devoted and the loyal, who remained that way regardless of what happened between them.

Dee led Kali into his bedroom. As he switched on the overhead light, a ceiling fan came on. She looked up, astonished. She had only seen them in Humphrey Bogart movies. Sure of her surprise, he never turned. Instead, he slid open an all-mirrored wall and said with his back toward her, "It was not me in Vanderbilt's apartment."

What had seemed like a wall to Kali was an entire closet. When Dee slid the mirror back the light came on. There were clothes on all three walls. Shoes were neatly racked at the bottom of the three sides—a matching pair for every suit and coat that hung.

"My coats are over here on this side. Oops! I was wrong. There *is* a white cashmere coat!"

Moving past him, she lifted the sleeve and examined the buttons—none loose and none missing. "Who taught you to speak like that, your mother or father?" The question surprised him. "What is 'oops'?" she asked.

"I heard it on television."

"Telephone," Ruby Red's voice drifted into the bedroom. Smooth and even.

Dee excused himself. Annoyed, he reached for the phone.

Kali went back into the living room where Ruby Red was still sitting, no longer in the lotus position. She looked at Kali and explained, "He doesn't like to be disturbed. He does one thing at a time. And only one." Ruby's voice faded into a drowsy monotone. Kali strained to hear what she had said; failing, she took a chair opposite her.

"You work for him." The statement should have been a question, and Ruby was a little irritated. It was a judgment call.

"You mean," her voice booming now, "do I sell my body to make him money?"

Kali was quiet; that was the question she was really asking.

"I never sell anything...that isn't for me. Melvin," her voice fading now, "thinks I do—or did." Recharging the sentence, she said, "Sex is an art form. Like dancing."

"That's what it is about you!"

Ruby Red was pleased and bowed her head. "I was the lead dancer for Katherine Dunham."

"Who?"

"Lena's scene in *Stormy Weather*, singing 'Stormy Weather'? The dance scene outside the window."

"The dance scene where?" Kali leaned in to hear her.

"In *Stormy Weather*. I danced it."

"And she was *good*. Drink?" Dee asked. He had come back into the living room and was headed toward the bar at the back. Kali had never seen so much glass in one place—with glasses hanging upside down from overhead racks attached to the ceiling. It occupied a well-stocked, well-lit world of its own. Unlike the sparsely furnished living room with two chairs and white and cream-colored cushions strewn about the room.

"We're having tea. Just like Miss Charlotte does," she said. It was her indirect acknowledgement to Ruby for having brought in the silver tea set while she and Dee had been in the bedroom.

"You girls make friends; I've still some telephoning to do."

Ruby smiled and proceeded to pour the tea.

"Three lumps, please."

"Three?"

Kali nodded. "Just what color are your eyes?"

"Any color you want them to be."

"What?"

"Watch."

Ruby, guiding the cup and saucer onto the glass tabletop, straightened her body as she wrapped her legs into the lotus position again and placed both of her hands, palms in, before her face. Removing them slowly, she asked, "What color?"

"Blue."

"That's because you are happy. Like a child. And need to see blue."

Then she placed her hands before her eyes again, breathing deeply and, slowly removing them, asked, "Now?"

"Green."

"That's because you are suddenly angry, because I guessed your feelings."

"How do you do that?"

"A parlor trick she learned in Haiti, while she was down there with Dunham," Dee interjected, coming through on his way into another room.

"Really?" Kali asked.

"Mother taught me. Melvin refused to learn."

"Funny, I never thought of you as greedy. Impatient, maybe. But never greedy." Ruby expected Dee to interrupt, but he didn't. "We're making more money than we ever have. So why?"

"Lilac is running counter to my plans. I need to replace her."

"Kalí is too young. And you haven't taken enough time…"

Dee jumped up. "Stop with this Cal*lee*-shit!" He was up in her face. Hands on her shoulders. "Don't make me have to threaten you, Ruby. Remember? You know I don't like being…"

"Unkind? You have a power jones, Melvin. One that could get you in trouble."

"From whom?" he said, moving back from her, startled.

She didn't answer. Waiting, she placed her palms together, brought her fingertips to her mouth and closed her eyes. Something shifted in her but it was unseen. A tremble started in her legs, and then she realized her teeth were chattering.

"Haven't I been good to you? Supplied you with…as much…" Suddenly he moved forward and slapped her hard across the face. Her head jerked to the side and back again but her eyes never opened. "Just run the numbers and be polite to the girls. Okay?" Then he repeated, "Get Callie-girl ready!"

There were spaces and places that Dee filled for Kali. None she could name, though. But *he* could—name each one she filled for him. His lists of the "best ever" were overflowing his mind. And he was not prepared. Oh, he was prepared for hurricane and drought, famine and flu. Or, like now, that his moneymaker wasn't making him any money. But not for Callie-girl. Positively, absolutely, no way, no how, was he ready. For she was the child he had never been. The playmate he'd never had; and the child he dared not father. He was unprepared.

Kali was Fay Wray to his King Kong. The mighty ape whose might snapped like a matchstick when she gave him "that look"—that all-embracing "come hither" stare that tumbled the mighty giant and made him easy prey for all the Bwanas lurking in the bush with elephant guns.

Dee had earned the name "Monkey" by a series of things that had happened in his life. In fact, he couldn't remember back to a time when he wasn't called Monkey. In that momentous moment when, as a toddler, he had first stood, his gaze riveted on a shiny toy just out of reach, his arms had all but dragged the ground; immediately he was crowned "the monkey." As he developed physically, other features reinforced the image.

His forehead had an alarming curvature that overarched small and beady eyes. Snarled body hair got caught in the crucifix he wore around his neck, and unusual amounts of it covered his entire body. He had wide cauliflower ears that stuck out from his head. He knew, though, that even this image could be transformed if he willed it.

He had built "the monkey" into alternating sets of images. Each image was carefully molded like hot wax and imprinted on the minds and, more importantly, the emotions of women. He could be lavish and cruel, exacting and forgiving. Helpless, helpful. Powerful and powerless. Cold and hot. Needy and giving.

All the women Dee worked with were imports—not from the neighborhood—bred exclusively for show, sex, and any and all fantasies. They were nourished on that all-important commodity: fear. They were charming, not all poor, but all had an inherent need, no matter how it appeared, to obey. Usually he met them at places larger than life: exclusive clubs, hotels, social events, the theater. Thinking they were dressed to the nines, they would arrive on the arm of some introverted banker, struggling lawyer, or corporate type. They would tell Dee later, "I knew you would understand."

His contempt for women could be measured in his attraction to men. But he remained cautious, limiting his involvement with them—fearful that his power might be challenged. Currently, Vanderbilt was his distraction and an exception because he was a throwaway. Unable to live in his own culture, Van was grateful for a home among people whose hatreds, in general, did not include the odd among them. But he was always the outsider.

Dee knew he could turn "the monkey" image into an asset on the strip, because the night people on John R. Street prized difference, and generally they could make it pay—or at the very least entertaining. And because his women were all imports, who rarely came out in the daytime, the day people of the neighborhood, concerned with survival, never felt needed by them.

Lilac he met in a bank line. Finishing her banking, she turned to go, and as she did, she dropped her beaded bag. Slowly he stooped to retrieve it. With his eyes, and with the bank teller watching, he deliberately followed the run in her stocking till it was out of sight but not out of his mind, her mind, or the bank teller's mind. Quickly, he gave his place in line away and effortlessly moved Lilac to the side of the large room.

"Don't be frightened," he pleaded.

"Should I?" In fact, she was. But his grotesqueness was layered in a three-hundred-dollar suit, a shirt with a Billy Eckstine collar, a twenty-five-dollar tie, and a quick smile. It aroused in her, as it generally did with women who had been abused all of their lives, a tenderness, not horror. His manner was reassuring and…

"Good…I enjoy a woman who…" Noticing her rather remarkable face and falling instantly in love, he whispered, "I find you incredibly lovely… Don't. Please don't turn away, even if I make you blush…I didn't mean to…"

"You didn't."

"No? I can't be sure…sometimes I'm so unsure."

"Really?"

"I'm almost too embarrassed to ask you this…do you believe in love at first sight?"

"No, not really."

"But, oh, my dear. Just take a look at yourself."

Gradually, the monkey image evaporated, and Dee was left standing tall, well-groomed, gracious, and smooth as glass.

Kali watched Dee remove the brace he needed to keep his back upright. The first time he meticulously peeled back layers of clothing meant to shock (first cashmere, virgin wool, silk, and finally, cotton) in a gesture deserving an Oscar for the "best melodramatic scene" from a B-movie, she remained quiet, seemingly unmoved. In his finale and with grandiose gestures, he unlatched the leather straps that held his brace, and his body slumped. Still, she was not alarmed. And he was not prepared.

Kali never flinched. Not at first. Not ever.

If Dee had not been so well-versed in his own dialogue and immersed in his own world of twilight and shadow, he might have understood. He failed to see that times were changing. Indulged and self-contained in a self-made world of money and power, he never understood that freaks come in all sizes and shapes—that beauty most often is a freak because it is superficial and seeks its own end. But his mask was complete—stuck—like those of the resident performers on John R. Street whose dance routines were jaded and overrehearsed. As it was, and as it turned out to be, the light he thought he saw in Kali's eyes wasn't love, not even admiration; it was malice. Something he had no way of expecting, because he only saw what she did look like. But for Kali it was what she *didn't* look like. Her spite sprung from a contorted root that grew from an arid place and from an earlier time and that she was looking for a way to vent.

Maybe it was the weather in Detroit, the promised wind currents from the South, or the bits of tumbleweed that blew up Woodward that spooked the old people who sat—dazed—in doorways or gazed stony-eyed from the windows of their rooms upstairs over the storefronts that lined Woodward Avenue. The tumbleweed skipped about, escaping the rush of white traffic gunning its way toward the suburbs. Whatever it was that beguiled Dee, he allowed those gray-green eyes to mean something. Not that Beauty was the most beautiful of all, but she embodied what he liked best in a woman: the part that is like a man.

Long before Beauty learned the power of gray-green eyes, she had cried for black ones. Early on, she had despised her milky white skin and viewed it as a shroud—a disgusting thing that separated her from blackness. At age seven, she had wickedly scratched both thighs with a safety pin, so badly that she had to be rushed to the hospital. It was her way of showing she didn't have white blood—that she wasn't a freak. Finally, she stopped expecting a place in a community where she was always going to be somebody's excuse for why the world was the way it was. And now she was ready to make someone else pay.

Dee was unaware that Beauty was a huntress—an entertainer of chaos. Nurtured on resentments, seething, eaten up by her own image, Kali, with that reckless spirit of hers, directed her life toward a series of high explosions just to hear the bombs go off. Few realized that disruption was what she chewed on; she grappled for the sheer excitement of the kill, the ecstatic final breath—no matter whose.

At breakfast Ruby asked, "When do I get Kali ready?"

"Next week," Dee replied. "While I'm in Idlewild."

But he didn't go. Instead, he took Kali shopping and lavished her with clothing. Unbeknownst to him, Ruby had been doing the same thing. Kali's closet was filled with African robes—a few made of Kinte cloth. Brass, ivory, and gold jewelry imported from Zaire filled her jewelry box.

Next week never came. Nor the next. Nor the next. Dee remained lost inside his "little boy." Even he wasn't clear who the little boy was anymore. All he knew was that she was never far from turning into the liquid-eyed little white boy who defied his parents one day and came over to play with him in the park, not far from Mistress' house (where his mother worked). The boy's mother, talking to a neighbor, hadn't seen them at first. When she did, she rushed over, yelling in a language that Dee didn't understand. The liquid-eyed little boy looked hurt, not by his mother who was dragging him away by the ear, but by the pain he saw in the dark face staring back at him. Dee's mother, unable to bear the disappointment on his face, had reminded him of his back and how tired he got while playing. That day Dee drowned in the liquid eyes of that little boy, and now he was drowning in Kali's as never before.

He bought his Beauty three dozen trousers like the chic ones Katharine Hepburn wore in those independent woman films she made in the forties. Raining them into the air then tearing the cellophane they were wrapped in, he spilled a collection of tailormade Hi-Lows all over Kali as she laughed that little boy laugh. Interested in picture perfect, he would tie the arms of sweaters around her neck and coax her to move her knees to her chest. Flash! The image would be developed in his mind, to be retrieved later for his own unsteady pleasure. With Kali sinking deeper and deeper into the plush velvet cushion of the lone photogenic chair in the rather stark all-white, in-white, on-white living room of his penthouse, he was moving farther and farther away from his own freak and towards hers. Oddly, it was in those clothes that her "womanness" came shining through, jolting him—sending him, predictably, to his "best ever" lists like a bee to honey.

Dee introduced Kali to all the "right" people at the right time and she disarmed them all: piercing their armament because she had that white-girl look, the smile, and the uncanny ability not to say anything remotely intelligent. From mayor to matron, from bank president to lawyer to doctor, Beauty enchanted them all. They connected with the little boy in her and bid him come out to play in whatever fantasy they imagined.

When they were together, she was the coquette and Dee the effeminate dandy. The game they played was great fun; Beauty thought herself in splendid company, and Dee knew himself to be.

It was clear that Dee's timing was off. He was not ready to release her. He hesitated. And during the wait, Kali refused to honor "the monkey." Dee began, for the first time in his life, to desperately want the Beauty to kiss the Beast so he could turn into a prince.

Mrs. Wintergreen had been busy with the pretty brown boy till Jake said, in passing, "Seems like you spend more time with him than you ought." Ought? Wintergreen was always surprised when a Black word slipped into Jake's vocabulary. He was usually so careful, but this time instead of teasing him, she thought about what he had said. Kali had been asking her more often to do this or have that done for her son. Wintergreen was spending more time on the phone to various stores. And it was true, she didn't spend any real time with Kali anymore. But she was grown. She worked a job. Besides, the boy had called her Momma. Her response was natural enough. She had called her own grandmother Momma. There was always somebody calling somebody else Momma. So what? But deep inside she knew she was hiding something from herself and that Jake saw it. She called Jake back into her office and demanded, "Tell me what you know about Kali and what you aren't saying?"

Waiting outside the Gotham, Kali was distracted by a former lady of the evening, now turned Militant Mother of the Church, who stood before a pair of long copper legs, encased in a short leather skirt split up to the crotch, emerging from a yellow cab.

As the woman stood up, the church mother pronounced, "Jesus saves, Sister!" shaking a tambourine in her face and handing her a pamphlet. "Don't let the devil make you do this."

"I make three hundred and fifty dollars a night. Remember? Go tell that to the women catching the trolley in the morning on their way to Grosse Pointe. Here's twenty dollars, Mother. God bless."

A few days earlier, Kali had put a card under Vanderbilt's door which read: "I forgive you! Come on out, you dirty rat!" And he had, amazed at how well she looked and how different. They dined together at the Alhambra, a restaurant complete with black "boys" in fezzes, short vests that exposed their stomachs, satin sashes, and turned-up slippers. Both Kali and Van avoided the unavoidable, each silently dropping Dee's name over everything they ate.

The avoidance of Dee was so loud between them that it jarred the people who dined at surrounding tables. They heard the drone of small talk and shifted in their chairs to better hear it, attracted by the queen and the boy.

It had something to do with Van's eyes and the series of cigarettes he wasn't smoking.

"I quit for the tenth time," he explained rather nervously in response to the question she hadn't asked.

She had seen eyes like that at one other time: outside the Gotham where he had stood waiting for Dee, dead eyes silhouetted against the shine from the polished brass of the entrance door.

Actually, Van knew. But he had made himself not know. Dee had been strangely absent from his life, his bedroom, and his shop. Thinking she might tell him what he really didn't want to hear, he didn't ask Kali about the shadow that had fallen across her otherwise bright eyes.

FOURTEEN

"Where's the baby?" The question jarred Kali as she moved down John R. Street on her way toward the Gotham. She looked up and realized she had just passed Brother and some woman. He wore a dashiki, and she flashed on how well it suited him. His well-kept conk was gone and in its place was a manicured Afro. She guessed he had given up the perpetual Donald Goines paperback he kept in his back pocket and was now reading the newspapers he was handing out as people passed.

"Brother!"

"Don't be runnin' game, Sunshine. You heard the question."

"Who's that?" Kali asked, hostilely, suddenly aware that she didn't like Brother with another woman.

"Diane, meet Sunshine," Brother half gestured. "Sunshine, meet Diane."

"Kali, my name is Kali, not Sunshine... He's with the babysitter, Brother..." she said, dropping her head and trying to move between them.

"Who? Wintergreen?" Brother asked, grabbing her arm. Kali looked at her arm and then at him. "You never learn, do you?"

"Yeah, who's got the baby, bitch?" Diane sneered.

"Cool it, Diane. This is *our* business," Brother said, turning from Diane, who had taken a stance against Kali.

Kali was distracted from responding by the appearance of Ruby Red gliding through the polished brass and clear glass entrance door of the Gotham and out from under the bold black-and-white stripes of the new awning. She wore a flaming red dress that reached toward her ankles, which were wrapped in gold straps from golden sandals that struck the sidewalk softly. Her ankles were sturdy and her feet turned out like those of a dancer. On her head were swirls of differently textured fabrics, red, yellow, black. She wore a braided gold belt that moved in the folds of her dress when she moved. It suddenly struck Kali that excursions in the daytime were rare for Ruby Red. Ruby was closely followed by a small and nervous little man whose orange and brown modified zoot suit was playing havoc with the bold and lively stripes protruding from the face of the Gotham. Hooked to his arm was a very large woman, whose manner and clothing got lost among the orange, brown, red and gold of her partners. The three formed an odd trio, like the misstep of a three-legged dog.

The man strolled over to where Kali, Diane and Brother were standing. And, without warning, he walloped his fist into Brother's balls, then nonchalantly turned and walked away to resume his stance with his two companions. The very large woman left Ruby's side, walked over to Kali, and touched her on the shoulder, as if to remind her of something. Kali moved to join the re-formed triangle, but turned back to Diane who was letting out a slew of mothafuckahs and damn yous as she tried to help Brother to his feet. With her attention on Brother, Kali hadn't noticed that the small and nervous little man had gotten into the driver's seat of a long black car which was parked in front of the hotel. It was clear he was having trouble seeing over the steering wheel. Ruby Red got in the back seat and signaled for Kali to get in beside her. The other woman closed the back door behind Kali, opened the front door for herself, and slid in. Next she made a sign with her forefinger pointing forward. The car jumped several times before it lurched into gear.

With her head forward and speaking in that detached way of hers, Ruby said, "Your friends are violent. Why do you have them?"

"Those aren't my friends; that's my husband and *his* friend." Kali mumbled and swiveled to get a look at them from the rear window of the car. "Where're we going?"

"To a party."

"A party? I'm not dressed. Why didn't you tell me over the phone?"

"I was about to," Ruby said matter-of-factly, her face a dark liquid, her irises bright black black marbles, floating in alabaster pools that opened wide then half closed. "But you hung up before I had a chance."

"Will M.D. be there?"

"Melvin is out of town," Ruby said too quickly.

Kali caught Ruby's tone but dismissed it in her reckless way. She did wonder briefly why they were heading toward the west side of Detroit; Dee wouldn't party there. But she easily dismissed the thought.

Actually, Kali's open door was swinging like a gate—and had been for some time now. The last time she and Dee had been together...well, he couldn't still be angry. He liked games as much as she did.

"Nothing better than a *good* party, I always say," the woman in the front seat said with a laugh, and winked at Red in the rearview mirror. Kali caught the wink, but again, she was careless and let it slide by.

Ruby Red pressed her mouth softly, then hard over the mouth of Kali, her tongue trying to force Kali's lips open. The bedroom door was shut, and the music from the living room had stopped. Kali, not wanting to appear frightened, struggled to move her head.

"Don't you like me? Not even a little?"

"Not here and not now," Kali said, surprised at the force Ruby Red had used.

"Relax, sugar. Lola won't be as nice, I can assure you." Kali tensed as Ruby dropped her arms and opened the door.

"Lola!" Lola moved toward the bedroom, stopping only to put her cigarette out in the ashtray and to remove rope from her bag.

Why are you doing this? The question registered on Kali's face, though it was not spoken. Her face opened, vulnerable for the first time, like a flower with its center exposed. The question began to wedge itself in between the layers of Red's consciousness. When she asked Kali, "Do you have any idea what *this* is?" she knew whatever threads she was hanging by were breaking one by one.

"No, but whatever it is..."

Lola interrupted, "Shut the door behind you, Red."

Each time Red heard Lola slap Kali across the face, she felt the next thread break. Slap. Snap. Slap. Snap. By the time she reached the kitchen where Ralph was, she was shaking. "How many have we broken, Ralph?... This place is a torture chamber."

"Get off it, Red. None of us got nothin' to complain about. By the time the monkey comes in and rescues them, their life takes off like a shot. Remember? They makes plen*tee* bread."

"Listen to you!" Ruby said, her voice beginning to crack. "Well, I'm sick of it!"

He looked up in earnest from the sports page and stared into her face. He was struck by the fact that he had never heard her raise her voice before.

"Sounds like a family affair to me. Maybe you best tell your brother that."

The apartment wasn't lavish but the rooms were large and the ceilings high. Much of the furniture was old but in good condition. And the lighting wasn't bad for an old apartment house on Detroit's west side. One bedroom, a study, and the kitchen flowed off the hallway. The other bedroom, where Kali was being kept, opened into the living room. That bedroom was in the front of the apartment. At the far end of the long, heavily carpeted hallway, there was a closed and locked door.

When Ruby stuck her key in the lock and slowly opened the door, she was met with: "Before you ask, it's at home in the top drawer of your dresser underneath your nylons." Dee was leaning into a warm and contented fire.

His tools were laid out, cleaned and recently sharpened. He had placed them on a meticulously clean white cloth which lay on the top of the mahogany coffee table that was in front of the camelback couch. There was an old-time radio in the corner that was playing classical music.

Wet snow was melting from his coat and hat which were hanging by the door. New snow had started falling that evening. Such an early snow had surprised even the most jaded of Detroiters who were never surprised by anything. Much of it had turned to slush by now, and Dee was irritated because his suede shoes were soaked through.

"I'll need you to sew this button on," he said, reaching into his pocket. "It came off in my hand when I took my coat off." Ruby's gaze fell on the white coat hanging limp on the wooden coat rack. When he dropped the button in her outstretched hand, she felt it like a hot coal. She snatched her hand away quickly, and the button hit the floor. Waves of sound like kettle drums filled the room, even though the floor was carpeted. Dee, realizing what was happening, shook his head. "Hang on, girl, your stuff is waiting."

"Thank God," she managed to whisper.

"Take some deep breaths and exhale slowly," he said while she closed her eyes and pressed her lips together, remembering at that moment why she hated him so. Slowly she opened her mouth and let out a small sound that grew louder and louder.

"Take it easy, girl," Dee said, reaching to touch her cheek. "We're almost there."

Grateful, she quieted down, but she was trembling. And her nose had begun to run. To steady herself, she unwrapped the swirls of fabric on her head and played with them in her lap. Pleating and repleating them, she managed to ask, "Why did you change your mind?"

"It's never been a question of changing my mind…" he said, bending to stoke the fire.

He had, in fact, changed his mind when Kali unexpectedly showed up at the front door of the big house on Chicago Boulevard. When he heard the persistent bell, he thought it was the workmen who were putting security bars on the basement and first floor windows. Determined to give them a piece of his mind—they had to know better than to lay on the bell—he snatched the large front door open only to find Kali standing there, grinning. He stood motionless, his mouth open.

"What the… Get the fuck away from here!"

Still amused, she just looked at him and chuckled. She knew that Dee was anything but agile so she pushed right past him, knocking him off balance, and went in. What new game is this? she thought as she sauntered down the darkened hallway. She could see that there were pictures on the walls and wondered, if he had taken the time to hang pictures on the wall, why hadn't he taken the time to put lights over them like they do in museums? To her right were two large oak doors. Sliding them open, she entered grandly, like the matron of the house, into a large and well-lit room. It was an airy one. The sheers at the window were softly blowing. The sudden light in the room was in direct contrast to the gloom in the hallway. It took her a few seconds to gain her eyesight. When she did, she was surprised and pleased with what she saw. This room wasn't sparse like the penthouse. It wasn't done in glass and metal, with only cushions and carpet for softness. It was filled with plants, sculpture, books, marble whatnots that filled the mantel and every other flat surface except for the one spot on the coffee table where a drink rested with ice cubes clinking in the glass.

Over the mantel hung a massive painting. The painter had painted a fox hiding in the thicket. The metal plate attached to the bottom of the frame read "A Call to the Hounds." While the stiff-backed male riders and stiffer ladies riding sidesaddle jumped the thicket, the hiding fox snickered. To complete the setting, there was a Persian cat asleep on the arm of one of several leather chairs that faced the fireplace.

The drink belonged to one of two white girls. They were seated on the Louis XIV sofa. And they were wearing identical white bucks, socks rolled tightly into doughnut rolls that revealed their ankles, green plaid jumpers and white starched blouses. *High school students!* Kali thought. One was seated rigidly in the corner of the sofa, her freckles and red hair enhanced by the green plaid of her jumper. Her right leg, crossed over her left, was nervously swinging. The other, the one the drink belonged to, was dark with long black hair and a noticeable mole just above the right corner of her lip. The mole was her signature piece. It added interest to her full mouth and gave her face, with its deep and caressing eyes, a subdued excitement that Kali felt, instantly. She watched, unabashedly, as the girl removed the drink from the table and slowly sipped it.

"I'm Kali, spelled K-A-L-I," Kali said, putting out her hand to the dark-haired one.

"I'm Kathy Cavanaugh, spelled K-A-T-H-Y and this is my best friend, P-A-M," Kathy laughed.

By now Dee stood in the doorway, entranced by the spelling bee, which was filling and refilling his best ever lists.

The girls were an odd pair, Kali thought. (But then Kali had never had a best friend.) Pam, it was clear to her, was only along for the ride and was oblivious to most of what was going on. It was obvious that Kathy kept Pam around to measure herself against. She, the pretty one, was sensual and aware of it. She knew the impact she made, and moved like all women who take their sexual cues from men. However, this repartee with Kali, this banter, was interesting and different and she wasn't quite sure why she was enjoying it.

Instead of giving her attention to Dee, Kali simply kept moving—keeping her chatter with Kathy up all the while. And she was surprised by her sudden and intuitive realization that Kathy's world was crueler, somehow less forgiving and more demanding than hers.

"I know your father, K-A-T-H-Y."

Suddenly the mood changed. "I hate him!" Kathy blurted out, then calmly asked, "Don't I, Pam?" Pam giggled nervously and gave some indiscernible reply.

No longer in trance, Dee moved toward Kali and ordered, "Don't bother to sit down."

Dee was following her like an out-of-shape boxer, trying to land just one punch on an agile and much younger opponent. Kathy was fascinated. Pam was confused.

Still talking and still eluding Dee, Kali said, "You look like your mother. Are you like her?"

"Yes, as a matter of fact, I do. And no, I would never...be married to..."

"Your father," Kali nodded, finishing the sentence for her.

Suddenly Dee lunged. Kali sidestepped. It was then that Monkey Dee, standing in the middle of his tastefully decorated living room, began to wobble on bowed legs and to rock off balance. The women laughed.

Whatever magic that Dee was capable of performing was lost forever on Kathy and Pam. It had been laughed away. Kathy had just been stolen from him by Kali and she, he thought, was going to pay for this—in a big way.

"Where do you know my father from?"

"Oh, places," Kali laughed and deliberately began to dance around Dee. He was afraid of grabbing her for fear of falling off the tightrope he was on.

"White girls?" Kali said, passing close by the unsteady Dee, who weakly grabbed at her. He fell. Kali left the house with the thunder of Kathy and Pam's laughter ringing in her ears.

Once out on the sidewalk, she stopped to look back. The house was carefully hidden behind a huge hedge that kept it in and the neighbors out. Once, these houses had first, second and third floor servants. Now they were being sold to anyone with money. "Even the Honorable Monkey Dee," Kali thought, clucking her tongue. She waved gaily at the workmen and walked away smiling, pleased with herself–thinking she was still playing with Dee, with no premonition that he had just stopped playing.

Suddenly the door opened. Dee and Ruby looked up. Lola leaned against the doorjamb with bloody scratches on her face and part of her cheekbone deeply imprinted with teeth marks.

Dee moved to go. But Ruby, the faster of the two and suddenly steady, said, "No, I'll go." Turning to Lola, she asked, "Is Ralph in there?"

All Lola could do was nod her head.

"Take a cab, Lola, you aren't needed anymore," Dee said. "I'll call you...soon."

Ruby threw open the door and yelled, "Stop! Ralph, get off of her!"

The room was in shambles. The curtains were torn off the windows, lamps were knocked over, and Kali was gagged and tied spread-eagle to the bedposts. She lay on her stomach. There were black and blue marks all over her naked body.

Ralph was straddling Kali like a dog in heat–getting ready for the final plunge. This one would set him loose–burst his nuts and rip her apart. He looked up, stopped for a minute, then moved to continue.

"Don't try it," Ruby hissed.

Ralph, raised in midair, looked back to see the glint of a straight-edge razor raised as Ruby, steady as a rock, stood there with shocking blue eyes, wide and ready, daring him to try it. He went limp.

Before she could do anything more, Dee pried the razor out of her hand and knocked her up against the door. Kali, making muffled sounds, was trying to rise from the bed.

"It's no longer funny, is it?... But I must admit, baby, you got what it takes," Dee said, moving towards the bed. With that Kali stopped struggling, half expecting that maybe he had come to stop this. Usually that's what he did do. But as she twisted her head around to try to see him, she saw his raised initials glowing from the tip of a red-hot poker coming toward her.

"Melvin! Don't!" Ruby screamed. Ralph knocked her into the living room. She fell against the table. Out cold. Dee pressed the branding iron hard against Kali's naked buttocks. She heard it sizzle and smelled burning flesh before she lost consciousness.

"Nobody gets away with the things you did, baby." Dee lifted her head by the kerchief keeping the gag in her mouth. He dropped her head; it was dead weight. He turned and, brandishing the still hot iron at Ralph, walked toward him. "Who gave you permission to strike my sister?"

When she regained consciousness, Kali lay quietly. She was aware that something terrible had happened, and she didn't want to remember it. Whatever it was that was hurting her was too terrible to remember. And, if she remembered, she was sure it would kill her. Ruby, she finally realized, was not so carefully bathing her with some herbal mixture. Through eyes constricted with pain, Kali could see Ruby's hands shaking as she held her stomach with one hand while she worked on Kali's burns. Kali could hear the chatter of Ruby's teeth, and feel her tears strike her body. For a moment after she gained consciousness, she felt numb all over. But Ruby's fingers began to awaken what she had forgotten. And in that unguarded moment she remembered what Dee had done to her. She screamed and screamed and screamed before she lost consciousness again.

While Kali lay unconscious and Red was out cold, Dee had cleared out of the apartment, taking Ralph with him. Whenever he found it necessary to brand his stock (and that wasn't too often), he told himself he disliked the whole bloody business. But inside it gave him a high, like no other. Actually, he couldn't wait to replay his best ever lists. This business with Kali had to be the best ever!

By the time the taxi pulled in front of Wintergreen's, it was early morning. Wintergreen saw it pull up. And yelled for Jake to go down. Red was in the back seat with Kali, who was lying on her stomach with her head in Ruby's lap. Ruby, on the way back to John R. Street, had been trying to comfort Kali, but was herself feverish, almost delirious. So Kali lay unattended except for an occasional thick "It'll be fine, Kalí" that intruded into her pain.

"We'll talk later, Red...when you can," Wintergreen said to Ruby, who stood before her, doubling up each time she was hit by a stomach cramp.

"No. We'll talk now!" Red managed to get out as she struggled to stand upright. "God give me strength, just this once," she whispered to herself. She repeatedly wiped her nose on the sleeve of her flaming red dress.

"He branded her, didn't he?" Wintergreen asked. Shifting her body in her chair and lighting a cigarette, she inhaled before she looked with deep concern at Red. "We can talk about this later."

"No, now," Red said weakly.

"I thought she knew better."

Still shaking badly, Red said, "How? *How* was she supposed to *know* better? Did you know better?... Did I?... I gotta get out of here....Fucking a boy and having a baby...what do you learn from that, Wintergreen?"

"How's Kali?" Wintergreen asked, turning to Jake who had just re-entered the room.

"I gave her morphine...till the doctor comes."

"She could've used some help, Wintergreen."

"Jake. Take Red..."

Shaking Jake's hand off her arm, Ruby yelled for the first time, "She's a *girl*, for Christ sakes!... A girl, Wintergreen...who thought she could play the game!"

"Why didn't you...?"

"I'm a goddamn junkie, lady. A junkie... Get her out of here. Out of this neighborhood. Off the strip. She won't survive a second time." Turning toward Jake, Red said, "Now you can take me home."

Wintergreen was dissatisfied that she had to wear her slippers across the street, but she had no street shoes she could wear. Charlotte was home. It was Saturday, and she would be cleaning. Charlotte cleaned every Saturday. Wintergreen knew because she had seen her shaking the mop sometimes. Sometimes beating the rugs. (And she knew, without ever being inside the old house, that Charlotte made a point of waxing her furniture to death.) Charlotte washed on Monday. Wintergreen knew. Starting in late April, she could see the tips of Monday's wash peeking from behind the house when the wind billowed them out, the whites so white they rivaled Mei Ling's. Late autumn found Charlotte's clothes rich in color, competing with the dropped leaves that fell from the few trees stuck in cement plots throughout the neighborhood. She had "watched" Charlotte for years hang clothes in summer, even though she couldn't see the clothesline in the back of the house. Charlotte's smooth body would burn in her mind and press against her closed eyelids while she sat marooned in her armchair.

She knew that Charlotte was still a country girl at heart. She rose early to get her work done before the heat of the day. How many times had Wintergreen imagined that ordered order of Charlotte's? Tuesday she would iron, and on and on and on.

Two canes would make it easier. But she discarded one. After all, she was Wintergreen! and she had conquered more than a cane or two. Next, she needed to decide how she was going to talk to Charlotte about Kali. That relationship was strained. Daughter-in-law had no use for mother-in-law. And Charlotte had her way of shutting down and closing off. What about the baby boy?

What to wear? At first, she wrapped her head in a scarf so that no one would recognize her. Put on a plain black dress, and an old sweater. Then she snatched all that off and thought, *after all these years...* So she put on a tight blouse and a tighter pair of pants, and slowly, painfully, walked the hundred miles across the street to Charlotte.

King Solomon answered the door and gestured with his head for her to go on into the parlor. Without a word he turned and went up the stairs, on his way to play checkers with a cousin on the third floor.

Charlotte looked up. Then stood up.

"Maybe you better sit back down, Charlotte."

"What's that woman doin' in here?" Brother asked King, meeting his father on the second floor.

"Leave it alone, boy. Do you think everythang is yo' business?"

"She took my wife and baby."

"Leave it alone, boy. Don't you know there are some things best left alone?"

"She got my baby."

"What you think you gon' do with a baby, boy?"

Brother tried to rush past his father. But the older man blocked his path. "Boy! Maybe we need to talk some. I see ya 'bout to git yo'self killed."

"Maybe you better sit down, Charlotte," Wintergreen repeated. "I see you've picked up some weight," she said, trying to seem detached.

"And ya still skinny as a rail."

"Where's your manners, aren't you going to invite me to sit down?"

Miss Charlotte said nothing. Wintergreen hobbled over to the nearest chair and, releasing her body from the security of the cane, fell into it.

Charlotte watched her, curious but restrained.

Both sat in silence. Wintergreen was the first to break it. "I remember you with more to say."

"The onlyest thang I remember 'bout ya is yo' leavin'. While the rest of us…"

"I was young. And it was Paris."

"What about me?"

"Charlotte, please…listen."

"No, ya listen. I waited…"

"I-I-I…"

"I, what?"

"Somehow, I imagined…All these years living across the street. Seeing you from the window. I thought it would be different."

"Different than what?… Life ain't no Shirley Temple movie, Ricky."

"No, I expect not. And it surely isn't forgiving," Wintergreen sighed.

"What did ya come here for, Ricky?"

"I thought…"

"…that ya could come waltzin' in here and make up fo' all those years? That we could be *friends?*"

"Waltzing in? Not hardly, Charlotte." For the first time, Charlotte's anger wavered.

Wintergreen attempted to get out of the chair, but failed. She sat for another moment catching her breath while Charlotte glared on. Still, Charlotte's expression was guarded, but she did ask, "What's wrong with yo' legs?"

"My feet. They...Bo Jangles stepped on them one too many times."

"What's wrong with yo' feet, Ricky?"

"They were broken in Berlin."

"Ya shoulda been more careful with all 'em blond dicks runnin' round."

"Ouch!" Wintergreen flinched and bit her lip so hard a tiny drop of blood erupted in the corner of her mouth. Charlotte saw the pinch of blood rise like a weighted pimple and watched Wintergreen move her tongue along the spot. Then she fixed her gaze on Charlotte, demanding that she listen. "By the time the war was over, I weighed seventy-eight pounds and lay in my own piss and shit because I couldn't get up. Like I can't seem to get up now..." With the tip of her cane she began tapping the floor. "I stayed alive because...I stayed alive for you, Charlotte," she blurted out, looking at Charlotte's unchanged expression. "I see I wasted my time." Once again she tried to pull her weight up out of the deep chair.

Charlotte's body, acting on a subconscious signal, shuddered—from forehead to toe. An overvoice, not hers, edged out from the small crack in the wall between them, gathered a life of its own, and muttered, "Oh, my God..." Charlotte's body, still acting without her consent, moved through that small crack in the wall to the chair opposite and knelt at Wintergreen's feet. Nervously, Charlotte fumbled with the black satin slippers. Wintergreen pulled back, hiding her eyes. Charlotte's fingers insisted. Through tiny cries Wintergreen begged, "Please, they're so ugly." Charlotte's fingers continued to remove the soft satin slippers and heavy white socks. And when the broken feet, folded almost double, lay exposed, Charlotte gasped. Greedily, her eyes took them in. Wintergreen protectively drew them up toward herself. Then finally she gave them over and burst into tears. Charlotte planted tiny kisses along the high and low places of the broken feet, washing them with great tears.

Her anguish was so felt in the old house that King, passing the parlor, peeked in to see what was the matter. For the first time, he saw that his wife was capable of deep feeling. And that discovery moved him in ways that he couldn't articulate then. Later, he realized he had seen a glimpse of Charlotte's soul. He saw it emerge, a fragile thing, as she kissed the feet of the other woman. And if he had any doubt over what he saw, it disappeared as he watched his wife's tears streak her face. The only thing he heard was the name "Ricky" repeated over and over again. He removed his head from the parlor door and shut it quietly.

Ricky untied Charlotte's scarf from her head as she knelt in front of her and let it fall about her shoulders. Her touch was tender. Charlotte's hair—like soft wool—filled her fingers. Then, laughing, she rubbed her face through it. "God, how I've missed the smell of it...of you, your hair, your body, my darling."

Charlotte, laughing and crying, took the ends of her scarf and wiped Ricky's tears one minute, then the taut skin stretched across the protruding bones of her feet, the next. Finally, with considerable effort, Ricky released the shame she felt over her damaged feet and allowed her passion to rise. Charlotte's groan moved to meet her passion as Ricky kneaded her breasts softly. Gently she brought Charlotte's head close and kissed her mouth. After the first lingering taste, Ricky pushed her tongue inside Charlotte's mouth and stayed.

FIFTEEN

The back third of the third floor knew there was no need to protest. When those two set their chairs and heads together on the second floor, nothin' and nobody on the first, second or third floor got any peace. If the truth be known, and it rarely was, the yowls from Lizzie and Laphonya rising against the floorboards, hitting against the ceiling, sending ripples through the pots of pinto, big lima, or great northern beans already standing in water on cold hot plates from last night, didn't bother everybody so much as not hearing the tale 'bout the niggah, the bear and the coon.

Even the rubber-soled shoes, laced with steel bits fresh from the day's romp inside Mr. Ford's factory, hushed–pretendin', as the uncles tended to the slicin' of salt pork, that they weren't straining to hear. That meat didn't need no real sharp knife cuttin' through it today, so wadn't no need to make all that noise scrapin' butcher knives up 'gainst the bricks outside the window. What was they tellin' 'bout Big John and ol' massah while massah was tendin' to everybody's business but his own?

Just about the time the beans made gravy, the aunts came in, passin' Lizzie and Laphonya with their chairs propped up against the wall, shellin' peas and talkin' dirty. While the aunts, mad as wet hens from the sass of the yellow streetcar and the double sass of their Miss Annes, needed to make hot water bread for the beans. Soon, as they started clanging spoons extra hard, Lizzie and Laphonya got louder.

"Don't see why 'em two don't go on back yondah," an aunt would say.

Then an uncle would say, "They got land down yondah; they don't got to git nowhere."

"Seem to me if they got all they say they got, they need to take to watchin' it."

"Hush up, woman. Somebody's watchin' it. Ya see that big yellah envelope come every month?... Well, it be stuffed fulla money."

All the aunts knew that going back home wasn't possible for them and going ahead felt foolish. They could go back in their memories...back where they planted baby okrie, beans and sweet potatoes; where they would hike their dress tails up, sit on the porch watching the fireflies make lanterns out of their bottoms, and spoon the day's hard work from themselves like taking sugar out of a bowl.

"Lizzie, let me tell 'bout the niggah, the Jew, and massah's wife." Everybody knew that Miss Charlotte would call up 'em stairs any minute to quiet 'em down. And everybody knew Laphonya would ignore her, but Lizzie wouldn't. And the storytelling would soon end.

"Lizzie, we got an invite to meet 'cross the street," Laphonya said after she'd finished the joke, while Lizzie was laughing so loud, she kept wiping tears from her eyes.

"Where?" Lizzie said, still unable to stop laughing. "Ain't nothin' cross the street, Laphonya."

"Bet there is. We gotta invite from Wintergreen."

"That devil woman?"

"The Lord works in mysterious ways."

"His wonders to perform," Lizzie added automatically, unmindful of how right she would be.

The first floor was quiet, as it can be sometimes; Charlotte was in the kitchen, King on his way in. But he had stopped in the doorway, propped his arms against the frame, and stood watching her. He was aware that underneath the apron and the housedress, she wore the daintiest of things, and he groaned inwardly with the thought of the motion and the locomotion of her hips. He could hold her naked in his mind for hours, long after she had fallen asleep and he was left dozing in the hardback rocker that sat in the hallway. With his eyes closed and his arms folded across his stomach, he could remember the feel of her—how her skin felt when he trailed his fingertips along the length of her hip. And he could taste, if he let himself, the pump of her nipple in his mouth. He had never, in all these years, got over his need to touch her bare skin. Sometimes, after everything was quiet and the house was left to settle in for the night, he would wish for her. After speaking her name softly in anticipation of her emergence from the parlor, he found himself always disappointed if she didn't come. And he would anxiously speak it again—louder this time, as if the sound of it would lure her into his room or into the hallway or kitchen. Sometimes it worked and he would feel triumphant. But other times it wouldn't, and his good mood would turn sullen and he would fall into bed alongside her sleeping body (if they hadn't had their monthly fight), indifferent to his touch.

Strange, he didn't desire her sexually so much, but he needed to touch her naked skin, somewhere, anywhere. She seemed to understand, and although they never talked about it, she would hike up her dressing gown (if she was wearing one), or he would slip his hand in the legs of her pajamas and lay it inside her thighs, or place it inside her opened pajama top seeking the feel of her breasts. Or if he was already asleep when she got in bed, he would, sleep-ridden, find a bare spot on her skin and rest his hand there. If they had had one of their famous fights, and he had ejected her from the bedroom, he couldn't sleep; while she, as far as he could tell, slept like a baby in her parlor.

Standing in the doorway, King once again found himself glad to have this woman. She had been the one so sure that coming North would be the right move, and it had been. The white folks at home treated him fair enough. He was, in their mind, a good ol' niggah, but Charlotte had reminded him more often than not, "Fair ain't enough, Solomon. Ya a man. And they ain't never gon' give ya that."

So he put his kin on the land to work it, took what money he had, and bought the old house on John R. Street. He received a yearly profit from the land, money from the Ford Motor Car Company, and a little rent from the kin that arrived and settled into the second and third floor rooms. But, more importantly, the land, since Gert's death, was his.

Then too, after the telegram came from Boston to say that Char-Lee had overdosed again, Charlotte had been the one to urge him to go see 'bout the boy one more time.

Char-Lee had played with Bird, Coltrane, and Dizzy. But "the Burn," as he was called in *Downbeat,* had in later years stopped cooking.

In Boston, King had found a scared, troubled, still-young but rapidly aging man who was strung out on heroin and sat in his room pushed up in a corner playing that same sad tune he had first played as a boy.

Once again, King stayed with him until he cold-turkeyed, got his lip back, and was talking in that strange way he did mostly when he was clean. But this time King heard something different, or felt something different, from Char-Lee. So he called home and told Charlotte to call his job and tell them once again somebody in the family had died. Next he pulled the boy to his bosom and held him till he cried himself to sleep. He knew what needed to be done.

King packed a confused Char-Lee on a plane, and both of them headed South. When the boy stepped foot on the back forty, he began to take one piece of his clothing off at a time: shoes, tie, shirt, pants. Then he started to run, leaving King far behind. By the time he reached the homestead he had nothing on but his jockey shorts. King arrived, much later, panting and puffing, with pieces of Char-Lee's clothing gathered in his arms.

King left "the Burn," some days later, rocking on the front porch of the old homestead getting to know all his "old" and new kin.

Miss Charlotte felt King watching her, but pretended she didn't. He asked, "Any coffee?"

"Huh?"

"Any coffee left?…What'd that woman want?"

"No."

"No?"

"What woman?"

King knew that Charlotte knew who he meant. "So Ricky ain't no man?"

Miss Charlotte, watering her plants on the window sill, turned away from the sink and looked at King.

"Ya didn't know ya been talkin' in yo' sleep all these years, did ya?"

"Solomon…"

"Ya think I'm pretty damn dumb, don't ya, Charlotte?"

"No. I nevah thought of ya as dumb…I guess I nevah thought of ya…much…Solomon…"

He flinched, but went on, "Let me finish. Why ain't ya nevah called me King? Do ya know I nevah knowed why till I looked into yo' parlor whilst that woman was there." He paused, waiting for Miss Charlotte to say something. She didn't. "It's cause I ain't never been no king or nothin' else to ya, Charlotte. Ain't it?"

"Solomon…"

"I loved ya from the first time I seen ya…pretendin' ya didn't care that ya had to leave New York. I knew that place held somethin' special for ya, Charlotte. Never knowed it was a woman, though. What do it mean?" he asked, choosing his words very carefully now. "If I catch ya with a man, I'll kill ya dead," he said finally.

Charlotte, still looking into King's face, her hands wet from the watering, saw confusion, pain, and felt, for the first time, his loneliness. She considered the manly statement he had just made. Rolled the meaning of the words over in her mind: *"If I catch ya with a man, I'll kill ya."* What else was he s'posed to say? she thought. Wiping her wet hands on her apron she announced, "Coffee'll take a minute. You get the cups whilst I make a pot."

All the women were there. Each had received a note on purple stationery with gold embossed lettering. A curious note that sent all the women backtracking in their minds to the last time they had seen Wintergreen anywhere else but on stage. Some remembered her buffet flats, but the time stated in the note was too early for that. Besides, she hadn't given one of those in years. Others, like Laphonya, sensed something more was about to happen because this time the invitation was addressed to Lizzie too.

The Ibo masks glared down from the wall of the apartment at the pretty brown boy playing alone in the playpen that stood next to Wintergreen's drum from Senegal.

The hanging masks, the smell of scented candles, and the drum gave the room a ritual effect. The boy, king of all he surveyed, received one and all. He looked up at every coo and attempted tug at his chin, giggled, and went back to his investigation of why the stuffed shaggy dog's eyes closed sometimes and opened others.

Most of the women here had been part of the first wave leaving the South. They had entered Detroit as young girls, and it had disrobed them with cold hands. But they had beat this city at its own game. They owned businesses, some were their own bosses and, each in her own way, took no shit from anybody. But they paid the price. They were haunted by a ripened sexuality buried beneath the eaves of wall-to-wall urban living. It demanded room and that was the one thing they didn't have. Instead, it remained curled up, closed—decaying—daring to surface at rent parties where they could shake their "thang" and prayer meetings where they could lift themselves up—out from the world. Even their children were born closed, crowded in cement buildings like tombs. And all the things that had been so natural about them were somehow not that way anymore.

Outside, they stifled that good feeling about being a woman and exchanged it for "respectability." But inside, it insisted—demanding a place. And when they could no longer hold it in, they rouged their cheeks, put their red dresses on, and their high heels, pompadoured their hair, and stepped out for the evening. But "out" didn't fit anymore, didn't fit well anymore in this frozen wasteland. They remained isolated in their respectability—languishing. Either bending their minds South to yesterday or turned toward this new northern wave—integration.

They were women born after slavery and before civil rights. Segregation was what they understood. And they were in danger of losing it. What were they supposed to make of these "rights"? They had followed the dream and come North believing that everythang was gon' be all right. At home they knew where they stood—nowhere, and they expected and accepted that. Here, white folks said one thing and did another. No rights, as far as they could see, was gonna change that.

So now here they were, collected together. What now? Wintergreen had called, and because she followed different rules and looked like she knew what she was doing, they came—to find out how she did it and looked so good doing it. Naturally, they were disturbed when she hobbled in from her bedroom in half-glasses and between two canes.

The conversation in the room was like the nip of biting flies. One would start, and before that one finished another bit. But underneath each nip were the same two questions, though never spoken: "What does Wintergreen want? And what happened to her?"

There was Mabel, owner of her own laundromat. Steady. Clear. Washed the big plate glass window, swept and mopped the big concrete floor twice a day. Put a shotgun to a niggah's head who sprinkled Tide all over the floor after her second mopping. He explained he was coverin' evil tracks with goober dust. He dared anybody big or small to mess with his mess. So she cocked the trigger back, and he swept the place clean.

There was Sam, the white woman, who had, Wintergreen suspected, more business on John R than an escort service. It was in her eyes. Patched and flecked with some secret war frozen behind the pain. She was bitter, all right. And Wintergreen knew a woman who was bitter was a good bet to get things done, as long as she wasn't bitter over a man. Black women hung up on a man get immobilized. Get drunk. Get mad. And finally get busy. Somebody's got to pay the rent. White women she wasn't so sure about. They were used to somebody else doing it for them. But Sam was a Jew and had her history in the blood—maybe she could hold her own and separate men out.

Maxine sat, crossing and recrossing her legs. She had chosen to dress, and closed early, obviously thinking the note meant something else. She ran a small beauty shop—a salon, she called it. She catered to the moneyed people in and around Woodward Avenue throughout the week, but made most of her money from the day people who came in on Friday and Saturday, getting ready for Saturday night and Sunday morning.

Silent, but noticed by everyone, was Charlotte's neighbor. Later everyone learned her name was Mei Ling.

Laphonya came, stepping in with Lizzie. Now how had she got her to come? Lizzie sat next to Ruby Red on one of the sofas, spoke but received no answer. Red had her palms pressed together, softly repeating a chant that drifted into silence while she dozed. Lizzie leaned over to Laphonya and whispered, "What's wrong with her?" Laphonya shrugged her shoulders. Lizzie turned up her nose, but after a few minutes questioned Laphonya again. "She ain't no devil woman too, is she?"

Laphonya beckoned for Lizzie to lean over, and whispered in her ear, "Why don't ya tell her 'bout *Jesus?*" Lizzie's eyes widened, and she snatched her skirt tighter—wrapped it around her thighs and crossed her legs, moving closer to Laphonya.

Cook's wife came. She catered all the big parties on John R. Street. She had married a black G.I. and had arrived from Japan to a country that made no sense. When Jimmy was killed in a knife fight, she married Cook, a Chinese man, finding in him more difference than Jimmy. He had come some years back to make money on Gold Mountain, leaving a family in China which he still sent money to.

Mildred had come, but Mrs. Wintergreen was uneasy. Mildred hated the Monkey too much. Mildred kept her lips permanently in a straight line. They were situated in a good-looking face that had aged before its time. Behind her back, folks called her "a mean, nappy-headed gal." It would take Wintergreen too long, she decided, to turn that personal anger into something she could use. Mildred would have to go.

Where was Charlotte? Wintergreen asked herself, forgetting for an instant that Charlotte never arrived anywhere on time. But before she would allow herself to linger on that, and on the life that had opened to her that night in Charlotte's parlor, she thought of Kali—the fiercely angry Kali and the reason why she had called this meeting.

Charlotte entered with a brilliant white scarf on her head—tied wonderfully, Wintergreen thought. Beneath her coat she wore a cool cotton dress to match. Wintergreen patted the peach leather chair next to her, and Charlotte seated herself.

Sappho and the Berry twins came in. The twins were playing the Paradise Theater up on Woodward Avenue. They stood near the boy's playpen and were, after cooing with him, engrossed in looking at the baby pictures that Sappho had pulled from her wallet.

Mrs. Wintergreen slowly began to stand, dropping one cane. She wobbled, and Charlotte reached to help her. She waved Charlotte away, and the women eased. They watched as she pulled an ivory holder from her pocket, placed a thin brown cigar in it, leaned down for Charlotte to light it, and slid the ivory between her teeth. This was the Wintergreen they knew.

"I've not let many people help me in my life," Wintergreen began, "but I'm starting tonight. Ladies, hear me out..."

Just then two young women, who were not invited, walked in. They were students who thought the world could be changed in a day by voting. Their hair was a mess, and they looked like they had slept in their clothes.

Damn students, Wintergreen thought. "Ladies, we are having a meeting. A private meeting."

"We want to help get rid of the exploiter of our people," the one who looked older, and should know better, said.

"Yeah, he's a pig," the other one said.

"Why don't ya comb yo' heads first?" Laphonya laughed, slapping her knee.

"This is an Afro." The younger woman turned toward her.

"No, that is a nap-o," Laphonya said, unable to help herself.

Wintergreen, sensing trouble, said, "I'm sure there are enough things going up on Wayne campus to keep you ladies busy."

"She invited us," the first one revealed, pointing to Charlotte. Charlotte smiled at them and turned to look up at Wintergreen who had stopped, changed the position of the cane and shifted her weight, waiting for an explanation.

"Maybe they can…" Miss Charlotte offered.

"It's not their business, Charlotte."

"But ya ain't *heard* what they got to say," Charlotte protested.

Just then Opal Henry arrived. Rich and dark; the color of plums. Her hands seemed wedded to the calabash she carried. She was sandwiched in between a day woman who had that just-scrubbed look. Her clothes were crisp, starched stiff; and she stood with her arms folded and sat down with them that way. On her other side was a woman who had circles faintly outlined on her cheeks. All three must have come through the bar (with Jake's permission) because they stood at the top of the back stairs, directly in the line of vision of the two students. Both young women slowly looked around. These women were an odd lot to them. And they only knew the one who had been at the Barthwell thing. She had asked some good questions, so when she had asked them to attend, they had jumped at the chance to go out and organize. But now they realized that none of these women had much education, except maybe the one limping on a cane. They were uncomfortable with uneducated women and didn't have a clue how to go about organizing them. They had come from homes where their own mothers had managed an education. And the women here were old. What could they expect from a generation that took all that shit offa white folks? they reasoned.

Miss Charlotte watched the young women's faces as their minds moved toward dismissing the other women in the room. She realized that it would take many more meetings with these students to get them to understand the real history of Negro people. That playin' the dumb niggah, or the crazy one, or the lazy one, wasn't always so easy, but each role played bought time for the next generation, hopefully, to move easier in the world. Now here was the next generation with their accusing eyes, asking, "Why didn't more of you stand up to white folks?" And she had asked the same questions of the generations before her. She now knew, unlike these young women, that there were no easy answers.

Charlotte spoke up. "I think maybe I made a mistake and we oughta do this some other day. But thank ya'll for comin'." The students, not knowing what else to do, moved through the women and went down the back stairs—glad to get out.

"Let me speak of what has recently happened in our community..."

Wintergreen continued. "And to that child's mother," pointing at the pretty brown boy, who looked up with the eyes of the shaggy dog now in his tiny palm. Seeing all the attention directed at him, he giggled and threw the dog's eyes out of the playpen. With that Wintergreen began...and in the finishing got what she wanted from the women. Reluctant Lizzie swore the services of Reverend Midas and Gidgeon Baptist Church.

Miss Charlotte reminded Lizzie and the group that she, although she sought the Lord in her own way, sent her dues just the same. And for three years running she had topped the dues list. So she was due something. After all, this was the mother of her grandchild! That got the women's attention and they sat for a moment, remembering that each could have a Kali somewhere in their family. They wanted to be moved by the tragedy of Kali, but in fact, were stuck around the question, "What did she expect if she messed with a pimp anyway?"

Kali's tale, like so many tales along the strip, had gone in one ear and out the other. Now their sins of omission had come home to roost. They were exposed. And nobody liked it. How did this child, who, on her own, had decided to turn tricks for a pimp, become a wart on their collective noses?

Wintergreen would call downtown. Sam would speak to the women who used her escort service, and they in turn could put a bug in their husbands' ears—who would hear it twice because all of them worked downtown. Maxine could reach the moneyed people along Woodward Avenue who came into her shop throughout the week. Mabel decided she would give Jesus a script, so he could make one of his impromptu sermons in her laundromat.

Laphonya, twisting in her seat, finally stood up. "Wait one damn minute! Ain't we movin' too fast here? Miss Thang done fell from sugar to shit. I cain't see that it's my fault. Everybody got somethin' goin' on in their life. But that don't mean they ho'. Far as I'm concerned she was asking fo' it," she said, spitting out her words. The room let out an aborted sigh.

"Watch it, Laphonya," Wintergreen shot back.

"Ya turned her out, Wintergreen."

"What!" Wintergreen exclaimed, dropping down in her chair and raising her cane like a sword, pointing it directly at Laphonya.

"Cut the 3-6-9," Laphonya said, stepping forward and moving the cane out of the way. "We all know that Kali was in the Chesterfield made up to look like ya. Wearin yo' clothes. Now how did she do that on her own?"

Wintergreen sat stunned into silence.

The day woman, nodding her head in agreement, folded and unfolded her arms. Miss Charlotte turned a false and overly sweet voice on Laphonya and asked, "What ya got 'gainst the chile, girl?"

"Child, my ass. What do I got 'gainst the chile? Tell us, Charlotte, when was the last time ya saw that child or *that* one?" Laphonya yelled, her voice changing octaves by the minute. She pointed to the baby who was responding to the loud voices in the room by rattling the bars of his playpen and throwing all of his toys out. "Remember when that *chile* streaked up yo' parlor with paint whilst ya sat on yo' fat ass?"

"Now, both ya stop," Lizzie demanded, bumping Ruby Red, who was looking over at Opal Henry with sad brown eyes filled with tears. Lizzie, shaking her head and leaning forward in her chair, continued in her Sunday-go-to-meeting voice, pronouncing a warning on both of them: "God don't like ugly!"

"Then He got trouble with you," Maxine said before she could stop herself. Lizzie was also the church secretary and worked closely with the very fair and rather young Reverend Midas. Which Maxine couldn't understand, considering that Lizzie was nobody's baby and ugly as sin. Lizzie lunged at Maxine, knocking over a chair.

Sam began to stir in her seat, while Mabel gathered her things. "Who needs this shit?" she asked to no one in particular.

"Cut it out, all of you!" Wintergreen shouted, rising from her seat with very little effort. "I asked you here to see what we could do *to-gether*. This shit stops now!"

Mei Ling sat amazed.

"I'll take care of it," Opal Henry said. Only the day woman, sitting with her arms still folded, heard her. Staring straight ahead, waiting for something else she could agree on, she turned to say something to the woman with the circles outlined on her cheeks. The woman was looking at her purple fingernails and trying to steady her unsteady leg.

"I'll take care of it," Opal Henry repeated—this time getting everyone's attention, including Wintergreen's.

"It's a joint effort, Opal. Or it will be no effort at all," Wintergreen finally said.

"I know what to do."

"That may be, but this is *our* responsibility."

"Can somebody shut her up?" Lizzie asked, announcing her request to the room.

Everyone thought she meant Opal Henry. But she meant Red, who was nodding out and humming to herself.

"No, *I'll* take care of it!" Kali stood in the doorway. "I'm past needing your help. I needed you when this happened." She ripped the loose-fitting gown over her head and stood there naked, slowly turning her body around so they could see the black and blue marks that lined her back and buttocks. Then she changed her stance—bending, she stuck her buttocks out at them and rotated her body so they could see the unmistakable initials, M.D., branded on the side of her buttocks.

The women reacted in various ways. Lizzie ran out of the room to the bathroom. Maxine shouted, "Good God!" Laphonya sat stunned. And Charlotte, much to everyone's surprise, broke down and cried like a baby. All looked except Red, who sat nodding out, intermittently wiping her nose.

"Not so fancy," Mildred blurted out and moved into the circle alongside Kali. Slowly she removed her own clothes as the women watched silent as stone. Laphonya caught her breath, as did Wintergreen and most of the other women when they looked in horror at the back side of Mildred's body all covered with small cuts made with curlicues at the ends—healed now into older scars. The letters M.D. were branded in several places down her sides and into her buttocks.

"God, Mildred!" Kali said as she reached over to feel the scars. Removing her hand from them, Kali looked over at the stunned women and said, "I hope all of you are satisfied. As for me, all of you can kiss my royal *yellah* ass." Still naked, Kali snatched up the baby, who had managed to rescue the eyeless shaggy dog he had thrown from his cage, and stormed out.

"Kali, hold up," Mildred shouted as she rushed—stepping into her panties and skirt—half running to catch up with her.

No one knew what to say.

"I said I can take care of this, Wintergreen." Opal Henry broke the silence, her long gray braid hanging down her back like a long twisting road. Her face, cast against the deep purple of her skin, was serious, but her eyes were red from the tears she had shed for the two women.

"No, Opal, we'll take care of it," Wintergreen repeated. "But you can tell us what we need do."

Opal Henry slowly began to rock her calabash and the swish, swish, swish sounds were enhanced by the deep beats made by Laphonya on the drum.

Charlotte began a deep hum and Wintergreen blended in her voice, and suddenly there was a wail. A large looking glass appeared in their midst. And, as they gazed into it, they could see a woman wearing yellow with a river threading through her hips. With her hands the woman reached into the river of herself and pulled out a curtain of stars and threw them over the women. Her mouth in a seductive oval, she said, "Look here!" Instead of their own reflections in the mirror, they saw the fiercely angry Kali. Felt what she felt. Hurt when she hurt. They saw the milky white skin covering her like a shroud. They saw her, afraid and confused, running from the darker-skinned girls in the neighborhood, who were laughing and jeering at her. They heard her mother and felt the terror in the child. All looked long and hard at her pink nipples and understood that those nipples had suckled a black baby, just like theirs had. They looked at her white-girl nose, her white-girl ass, her white-girl mouth and wondered why they had ever thought these were things to blame her for. They knew, at that moment, the pain in the scars she had inflicted on her thighs, trying desperately, at the time, to bleed black blood.

Alarmed, the women began to heave and swear, to call out to all the Kalis in the world. Sister, sister, look what you done to us. House niggahs, mulattoes, creoles, hi-yellahs. Sister, sister, look what you done done.

They glared at the mirror. And the Kali in the mirror turned suddenly and spat at them. A gesture they understood and forgave. Because each of them recognized the angry Kali in themselves.

From the vision that was flooding the room they knew that they had failed her. And Mildred, who they all knew and had seen for years, but had no idea of the pain surrounding her life.

But Kali had acted like a woman, instead of the girl they thought she was. She had erupted. She had fought them—allowing her anger to direct her. And they knew it was a good sign. She was healing because she now understood that her anger had been her anchor, as it had been theirs. It had saved them, and it would save her too.

"Sister, sister," the woman with the river threading through her hips shouted. "Look what you have done to each other!"

"Okay," Opal said, "but no outsiders. Those people downtown will finish us before they finish."

SIXTEEN

Brother knocked on the door of Kali's bedroom. When he heard Sunshine say, "Come in," he hesitated. When she opened the door, he felt something quietly give way inside himself. She looked so much older, tired—more weary than her years, he thought.

"Thought I'd come and see 'bout you."

Kali smiled a sad smile, leaned her head against the doorjamb, and said in a hoarse whisper, "Come in. It's good to see you again."

"You been taking care of yourself?"

Again he saw the hint of that sad smile and reflected that Sunshine had vanished and in her place was someone else.

"I know you've heard all about me, Brother, so let's be real."

"You need to come home so I can take care of ya."

"Do things seem that simple for you, Brother?"

"No, simple went out the window the day you left. I only want to be there for ya...whatever that is."

Kali looked for a long time at Brother, surprised at the harmony she felt.

"Come home?... You want me to come home? And be what?" Kali laughed. The sound of her sadness filled him with an ache he was sure he would never be free of.

"Well...we could get a place. I'm working head up. We could...could...ah...be a family again," he heard himself say.

And knew, as soon as it came out, that it was the wrong thing to say.

"What's the point?" Kali asked.

"Of family?" he asked, incredulously.

She smiled that same sad smile and reached up to touch his hair. "I like that," she said, taking both of her hands and feeling his Afro. "I wish my hair could do that."

"Baby, come home. We'll make it work...we'll be whatever you think we oughta be. But...come home...please...back to me and the baby."

"Brother, I feel a hundred years old. Do you know what I mean? Can you understand what I'm talking about?"

"I haven't exactly been standing still... Listen..."

"No, Brother, you listen. It isn't you. It's me. I can't go back. It's too late."

"I know. I know. But we could try..."

"Brother! For God's sake, leave it alone, will you?" Kali said with some of the spark of her old self. "I'm sorry. I truly am... But you've got to go now. I'm leaving."

"Leaving? Where?"

"I got a date I can't break."

He started to say something else but, instead, turned and left her room, with her sad smile indelibly stamped in his mind.

The evening light cast checkerboard patterns on the floor of the Gotham Hotel. Dee stopped briefly in the foyer to look at the late edition of the *Detroit Times*. He flipped to the editorial page and scanned an article entitled "Little Rock Revisited." He folded the newspaper, yawned, placed it under his arm, and entered the main lobby. It was empty. Not even Mildred was at her usual perch behind the desk ready to give him grief. He had been out all day taking care of business, and he had found himself unusually tired. He was ready for an early bed. He might go out later to check his traps, but for now...As he stood alone at the elevator pressing the penthouse button, he looked back into the lobby. Suddenly it was filled with people he didn't know. Except for Mildred, who was heard and not seen, giving some poor sucker a hard time. He turned and pressed the button to the elevator several times. The more he pressed, the more the events of the day surfaced. Starting with the dead bird, then the shoeshine boy, and ending...well, it hadn't ended yet. But God, he thought, I'm so tired. Finally the elevator came to a bouncing stop. He entered. It was empty. Where was Joe? The elevator boy? He couldn't remember when, if ever, he had been on this elevator without Joe. He started to step out and complain, but decided, no, taking on Mildred and all those people in the lobby…well, it was just too much. He closed the gate to the elevator with one hand and pushed the handle to the place marked "start." The elevator jumped. He stepped back, expecting that it would move, waiting. When nothing happened, he decided that he either needed to complain and get someone to drive this thing or figure out how to do it himself. He moved the handle back and forth. The elevator jumped—jerking him through all the floors until he reached his own. Finally, he stood in front of his apartment, but his key failed to open the contrary lock the first and second time. He wondered if Ruby had dared change the lock. This latest session with Callie had made Red…well, unlike he had ever seen her before.

This morning he had gone out for his usual cup of coffee when a bird, somehow caught in the wind currents of the city, had swooped down right past his ear and hit the window of the coffee shop just as he was going in. When he looked at the bird at his feet, he could see that its neck was broken. While sitting in his reserved booth in the coffee shop, he thought about the dead bird only briefly, because his attention was drawn to the music on the jukebox. It was blaring. It was so loud he asked the waitress if she would kindly turn it down. She smiled and went to the jukebox, but turned it up. He looked around to see why no one else was complaining. People were engaged in conversation, unaffected by the beat that was hammering out. He gulped his coffee down and headed for the door, forgetting to pay the waitress. When she confronted him on his way out the door, he found himself screaming at the top of his lungs—trying to be heard over the noise. All he remembered the waitress saying was, "No need to shout, mister. Just pay me two bits for the coffee."

Then he had stopped to have his shoes shined. When he reached into his pocket for some loose change to tip the shoeshine boy, who was really an older man, some twisted pieces of twine shaped into tiny little figures fell out. The shoeshine boy, out of concern for his customer and his tip, picked one up, then hurriedly threw it down, backing away.

"Mistah, somebody..." But his next customer, a white man, stepped on the twine, breaking its grip on the older Black man. The white man demanded, "Hurry up, Bow," flashing a five dollar bill. "Get these done in a hurry, and if I close my deal downtown today, tomorrow I'll double it."

"I'm glad, boss man, I don't make my living on the deals of white folks," Bow remarked, catching the white customer off guard.

"But you do," the white man said with a laugh. "If I don't make money, I don't get my shoes shined. If I don't get my shoes shined, you don't make the lavish tip I give you every time I come. If I don't come, and others like me, you don't make any money. See?"

Monkey Dee looked at the white man's shoes and knew that a few snaps of the rag and Bow had his money. The shoes only had dust on them. And he also knew that all these white boys got their kicks out of flashing big bucks. He stood there for a few moments watching Bow—then reached into his other pocket, walked over and handed Bow a twenty dollar bill, making sure the white man saw and heard him. "Keep the change, my man. That's for you whether I close my next deal or not."

Dee reached for the switch in the living room after switching the foyer light out. Decided no, the darkness felt good and moved through the apartment toward his bedroom with only the light of late evening settling into the room. As he hit the switches in his bedroom, the low bed lamp and the ceiling fan came slowly on. He tossed his keys and rings into the dish on the dresser and lay on the bed. He was exhausted. His eyes closed, and he folded one arm over them. After a short while he turned his head to one side, feeling the tenseness ease from his body. Then he felt a drop of something on his arm. He opened his eyes slowly. At first he didn't know what it was. Then he focused. Blood was splattered all over the walls! The doors to his mirrored closet were open and he could see blood on all his clothes and shoes. Before he dared uncover his eyes fully, he felt something splatter against his face and arm, something thicker. He held up his arm, inspecting it. But before he could decide what it was, something dropped again. He raised up on his elbows and looked up at the cathedral ceiling. Tied to the slowly rotating ceiling fan was a decapitated goat. Just as Dee realized, with horror, that he was the sacrificial lamb, the goat dropped.

Kali arrived sixteen hours later at the house on Chicago Boulevard, a shopping bag in her hand. It was late afternoon and shadows were beginning to form. She was glad the house was hidden behind a high hedge. Carefully she placed the bag before the door and stepped back because she heard thumping noises coming from the basement. She moved back to the sidewalk to see who or what was making them. It was Dee, down in his basement, running back and forth between the three basement windows that faced the front of the house. Suddenly he raised one and grabbed the bars. "Bitch! Motherfucking bitch!" he shouted, spittle running out of the side of his mouth. He shook the bars. Like he was rattling the bars to his cage. The goat business must have really gotten to him, Kali thought. She laughed and went back up on the porch to claim the shopping bag. Carefully she brought it back with her and reached into it. She removed a Coke bottle filled with gasoline. Horrified, Dee watched her light the rag that was stuffed in the top of the Coke bottle and throw it through the second floor window. The room went up in flames. On her way through the back yard, she stopped briefly at the garage and peeked in. Two shiny antique cars sat side by side. She tossed a gasoline bomb into each one of them. The garage went up just like the house. Hurriedly, she moved down the alley and into a blue car, its motor running. Mildred was at the wheel. Before Kali had the door closed, she was accelerating.

"You got the cars too!" Mildred said, her eyes wet from laughing and crying at the same time.

"Yeah, I got it all."

"Where to?" Mildred asked, wiping her eyes on her sleeve.

"You got some money?"

"I always got some money. Didn't your momma teach you that?"

"New York," Kali blurted out.

Mildred was sure she had just thought of it. "No, west…everybody goes west."

Kali leaned back. Mildred tossed her head back and laughed and laughed, shifted the car into fourth gear, and put the pedal to the floor.

"Turn the car around, Mildred."

"What? We're only at Toledo."

"Mildred, what's going to happen to Red?"

"Why should you care? She helped her brother do you in, didn't she?"

"Do you in, maybe…but not me. She stayed and cared for me."

"She felt guilty, that's all."

"No, Mildred, it wasn't like that. She stayed around to care for me. And she was in pretty bad shape. She still is. You saw her at the meeting…nodding out. I've got to go back and help her beat it. If I can."

"I don't get it," Mildred said, still gunning the car west. "I just don't get it. All those people–from your husband to your mother-in-law to your husband's aunts–they shit all over you. And you wanna go back?"

"I have to go back."

"What about Dee?"

"What about him? Since when did anybody investigate what Negroes do to each other?"

Mildred thought about that and nodded her head in agreement. "I remember too when you came into the Gotham, scared to death cause your mother-in-law threw you out."

"Mildred, my mother-in-law didn't put me out. I chose to leave. Like I chose all I did. My mother-in-law…well…is just trying to survive, you know? I guess I was somehow in the way." Kali looked out of the car window and muttered, "Like I must have been with my own mother." She looked over at Mildred.

"Spare me the sermon, please! I remember all the nights we set up at the Gotham, talking."

"But they had to have some guts to get through it all–you know that."

"Do you?"

"Well, yeah. I hope I do. But it wasn't me they were angry at…well…yes it was…but it wasn't… Mildred, turn the car around."

Mildred looked over at her and kept on driving. "If you expect this car to turn around, you gotta make more sense than you do now."

"It was…I don't know…like with the other girls in high school…I represented something to them; something they thought I had and they wanted…or didn't want…I don't know…"

Mildred rolled her eyes.

Kali was suddenly quiet, listening to the hum of the tires on the highway still heading west. But she felt it! She was sure she had felt it! The tug of the silken cord at her throat. This time she knew who it was. She thought about the time Miss Charlotte was brushing her hair and how good that had felt. And the concern she saw on her face the time when she was about to have the baby. And the things she had learned from her, in spite of herself. She looked over at Mildred again. "I mean, it was us that got branded, Mildred. They must have figured something out that we haven't. And it sure ain't Jesus. Cause he don't like no crazy-assed women," she laughed, poking Mildred in the side. Mildred couldn't help but laugh. And she was slowing the car down.

"It's kinda nice havin' a baby in the house again, ain't it, Laphonya?"

Just then Miss Charlotte reached the second floor landing and, walking toward them, said, "Ricky's downstairs, she wants to say goodnight to the boy."

Lizzie looked over at Laphonya, winked, and handed the boy over. As Miss Charlotte moved away, Laphonya asked, "Wondah what them two thank they gon' do with him?"

"Not much without me," Kali said, out of breath from running up the back stairs.

"The runaway girl is back," Laphonya said, looking up in surprise.

"Where's Mildred?" Lizzie asked, genuinely concerned.

"She dropped me off, turned the car around and kept going."

AFTERWORD

❧❧❧

Black Queer Memory in Cherry Muhanji's *Her*

I found my first copy of *Her* a year after it was published at the 1992 OutWrite Lesbian and Gay Writer's Conference in Boston, Massachusetts. I was living in a rural New England town where people pretended not to stare as I walked along, Black and butch and looking like I just stepped off a New York City subway. Queer literature of any kind was a rare treat and Black queer literature was a delicacy. News of *Her* had spread by word of mouth across a nationwide network of Black lesbian writers and readers. I eagerly scooped up a copy from the New Words Bookstore table at the conference. For me, the novel was an oasis in a New England desert. These nontraditionally gendered, sexually complicated characters, their lives, and their surroundings became a part of me: Sunshine's transition from wife and mother to Kali, a trash-talking queer "boy;" Wintergreen and Charlotte's smoldering love, separated for years by a single street; the dizzying ensemble of 1950s Black queer street life of Detroit. I let Muhanji's words wash over me until, finally, I was so overcome by the lyricism of the novel that I could not keep it all to myself and began reading it aloud to a friend. The story stayed with me long after I found my own living, breathing, Black queer community. Over a decade later, I began to teach the book in my college-level African American literature courses, and through teaching it, I increased my appreciation for the complexity of the novel's characters and my reverence for Muhanji's skill as a master storyteller.

Besides opening the door to representing unconventional Black characters, *Her* creates opportunities for different perspectives on African American migration. One of the most intriguing contributions of the novel is its insistence on the post-WWII midwest as a site of Black sexual and gender-transformative culture. This is significant for two reasons. First, most accounts of African American South-North migration concentrate on the period between 1915 and the 1930s, which is commonly referred to as the Great Migration. *Her* is a reminder of the distinctiveness and the import of other migration periods. Second, it unsettles the historical reliance on New York's Harlem Renaissance of the 1920s and 30s as *the* privileged time and place of African American queer history. As a result, the northern midwest comes into view as yet another historical space of queer emergence and suggests that there are many other overlooked sites of Black queer history. The sexual and gender fluidity in *Her*'s midwestern urban setting suggests that transformation is a fundamental part of the African American migration experience in general.

The transformation and transition of Black migrants does not stop once they have arrived in the North. Instead, the northern city is depicted as a place of continued migration and movement on a smaller scale. Characters migrate from one nation to another and from rural to urban regions, but their smaller movements, between houses, across streets, and up and down the block, are also treated as significant spatial shifts. There is an explicit centering on the small movements of *Her*'s female characters, which allows for the possibility of a feminist re-reading of migration that includes issues of mobility. The novel presents mobility as a practice of small movements between the public and the private, across social relations, and between individual and group identities. Mobility functions as a practice of physical ability and as a metaphor for emotional and social transitions.

Among Black women in the novel, the possibilities of movement and mobility include the hope of transforming centuries-old, intraracial skin color hierarchies and hostilities. Tensions based on skin shade permeate most of the women's interactions in the novel.

Charlotte dismisses Sunshine as another "hi-yellah" who "ain't worth much" (10). The dark-skinned women at the club direct their venom at Wintergreen, calling her a "[h]alf-white heifer" (88) as a way to release their rage and pain at racist and misogynist standards of beauty. Charlotte may have left her family farm behind to find a new destiny, but she cannot escape the legacy of the devaluation of dark skin. Even though it is Charlotte who has the "deep dark arms and full round breasts" and who "c[an] sing better than anybody," (100) it is Wintergreen's light skin that earns her a contract for a European tour. The two figures struggle to reconcile the public acknowledgement of light-skinned Black women's beauty and the relegation of dark-skinned women to the private and the dark. Wintergreen herself treats Charlotte this way, loving her privately, "in [a] dark, drowsy room" (50), and then leaving her the moment she has her chance at solo stardom. The women abandon their professional and personal relationship when Wintergreen does not insist that the other, darker-skinned members of the act come to Paris with her. The reclaiming of the lost passion between Charlotte and Wintergreen symbolizes a healing of the hurt between light and dark-skinned women.

The first act of reconciliation comes from Wintergreen, who struggles on broken feet to cross the street to meet Charlotte in her home, an example of characters moving a very short distance but traveling symbolic miles in emotional breadth. The two women's reunion sutures the expanse between light and dark, internal shame and external desire. One of the most erotically charged scenes in the novel centers around Wintergreen's crushed feet: Charlotte caresses them "[g]reedily," transforming them from "ugly" to part of Wintergreen's desired body (163). By finally allowing someone to touch her feet, Wintergreen crosses an erotic and emotional boundary. She "[gives] them over" (163), releasing the feelings of love and passion that she had cut out of her life since she was imprisoned in a Nazi prison camp. Charlotte's touch triggers an emotional waterfall for the two women. They need each other. Wintergreen suddenly realizes that her separation, especially from her darker-skinned lover and her colleagues from years before, has left a "seeping hole" of loneliness in her life (89). Charlotte and Wintergreen's reconnection lays the groundwork for the growing bond between the novel's other

Black women characters, who are initially divided along color lines. Their same-sex desire is depicted as a vehicle for the healing and transformation of racist and misogynist practices initiated in slavery that continue to poison dynamics between Black people.

The novel further comments on skin color divisions within African American communities and culture through its revision of traditional representations of the "tragic mulatta." As evidenced in *Her*, part of the Southern heritage that Black migrants brought with them to the North was a system of skin color hierarchy, culturally inscribed in the light-skinned Black female body. The mulatta figure is traditionally made "tragic" because she is represented as caught between a white world that will not accept her and a Black one to which she does not fully belong. African American women writers have often sought to unveil the absurdities of racial prejudice through the portrayal of a light-skinned woman who succeeds in fulfilling expectations of femininity in manner and presence, but is blocked from social mobility by prohibitions of race. Late nineteenth and early twentieth century novels such as Frances Ellen Watkins Harper's *Iola Leroy* (1892), Jessie Redmon Fauset's *Plum Bun* (1928), and Nella Larsen's *Passing* (1929) use the mulatta figure as a trope of middle-class respectability and femininity that could only be represented through the image of a light-skinned character. Sunshine's psychological splinter into Kali is a rejection of such portrayals of the middle-class, light-skinned Black heroines in these tales of passing.

In *Her*, the bitter implication of racial betrayal in the mulatta figure is resolved through Sunshine/Kali's identification with Blackness and Black vernacular culture. When the novel opens, Sunshine is a "proper" wife and mother who stoically takes the resentment and abuse from her husband's family with aplomb. She has been raised by a mother who wanted her to take advantage of her light skin and rise above what she calls "common Negroes" (23), however, the "black velvet star-studded" (44) nocturnal activity on John R. Street seduces Sunshine. Outside her domestic window is everything that her mother did not want her to see: "smooth-talking," "silk-suited" pimps and women with "red lips" and "plump, perfumed thighs" (44) who rule the night. *Her* presents the city as both a place of violence and exploitation and a place of play and pleasure, and the night life that unfolds outside Sunshine's window is a distinctly Black queer realm, a world she would never experience outside of a working-class Black setting. The issue of gender self-construction emerges in these spaces, and the assumption that biology determines gender recedes. Sunshine learns that the lines between "real" and "unreal," "men" and "women" can become blurred, and even irrelevant, as she is absorbed into the life of gender variant performers and patrons in the street's many clubs and bars.

The longing to be part of the street life leads Sunshine to tap into an alternate personality named Kali, a part of herself that she had partially created in childhood. Kali is proficient in Black vernacular culture and is able to be "clever," "sassy," and "outrageously funny" (23) in ways that Sunshine is not. This embrace of Blackness by a light-skinned literary protagonist inverts the traditional representation of light-skinned Black women as self-hating embodiments of white identification. Sunshine escapes tragedy in two ways: one, by conjuring an alter ego who is deft at negotiating and navigating Black cultural language, and two, by accepting mentorship from Wintergreen, who becomes her alternative light-skinned maternal figure. Wintergreen, a blues singer by profession, figuratively "sings the blues" for her lost career, for her relationship with Charlotte, for the hostility between light and dark-skinned women. By helping to transform Sunshine into Kali, Wintergreen is also resurrecting a lost part of herself. Wintergreen dresses Sunshine in her old clothes from the early part of her European tour. In her white satin trousers, "Kali turned slowly and said, 'I look like a boy,'" to which Wintergreen responds, "No, you look like me in Paris in '24" (98). Gazing at him/herself in the mirror, Kali speaks, announcing his/her gender ambiguity. The pronouncement that Kali is "like a boy" suggests that this is not a complete transition from female to male, but part of a nomadic expedition that does not have a definite ending—for instance, when placed in relation to masculine femininity, Kali is accepted at the gay male bars as one of their own. The title of the novel itself is a reference to the ambiguities and ambivalences at work in the story. *Her* is a reference to the central character, who has two personalities: Sunshine, the good housewife/mother, and Kali, the fast-talking street dweller and "boy." The title is an ironic play on Sunshine/Kali's gender ambiguity, specifically calling attention to how Sunshine/Kali functions as not entirely a woman in the text depending on her/his location.

In the story, Wintergreen's mentorship of Kali "into the life," specifically means into a blues ancestral line. One of the most crucial contributions of *Her* to literary history lies in its presentation of the blues as the ancestral house of African American queer iconography, not only in blues performance, but in the musical form itself, which incorporates multiple voices and yet allows for individual improvisation. The blues in *Her* epitomizes gender transgression and queer desire, as illustrated by Wintergreen's reconstruction of Kali into her own gender ambiguous blues performance style of "Paris '24." Throughout the novel, urban blues consumption and performance is central to Black queer cultural life. Black bars and clubs represent a safe space where one's gender can change once one crosses the threshold. Wintergreen's club is transformed once a year into the location of the "Bitches Bite" drag competition. However, on a more regular basis, Wintergreen's is a safe harbor for a variety of "blues women" who can relax in an atmosphere where their masculinity will not be attacked. Even though the "Bitches Bite" is not part of an official history of urban Detroit, the history of the women's community lives on in their memories of the evening: "For the…women there, it was one of those hot nights that they talked about for months afterwards; some would remember it for years" (138). In this way, the women's blues performances not only provide an affirming context and experience for the performers and audience, but also function as a vehicle for Black queer memory. The Black queer power of the blues is so strong in the novel that even Charlotte's sister Laphonya cannot resist the lure of Wintergreen's and eventually joins Wintergreen herself in a rousing blues duet of "Ain't That a Pussy" (138).

Laphonya's submission to the pull of Black queer cultural space does not come easily. Although Sunshine/Kali began slipping out into the night after only a few months of married life, Laphonya and her sister Lizzie's early lives were filled with duty and obligation. The sisters inherit the family farm (and a legacy of Black female sexual labor and agricultural toil), and their existence there, the novel's only description of rural life, de-romanticizes any nostalgia for the Black rural past. Laphonya recollects their Southern life as being primarily concerned with maintaining their land, which becomes synonymous with restoring a Black male line of succession. She recalls a grim tale of serial breeding, and of giving birth to thirteen male children who carry on their fathers' names. Her obligation to preserve their farm and the male line of kinship reduces Laphonya to the basic physical functioning of her anatomy and the gross mechanics of sexual inter-course. This narrative suggests that for Black women, the demands of familial duties often outweigh desire or sexual pleasure. Without other outlets or acknowledgement that they may have other desires besides fulfilling their obligations to family, the sisters' relationship takes a disturbing turn. The implied incest between the sisters illus-trates the destructive effects that the rural South had on Black women's sexuality.

Although urban life provides the sisters—and all of *Her*'s female characters—with a series of challenges, it also offers the possibility of some room for these Black women to acknowledge and express their own desires and to enter into a range of sexual possibilities that would otherwise be foreclosed, especially in this representation of Southern Black communities. Queer desire and sexuality are not the only sexual taboos that are represented in the novel. Both Wintergreen and Charlotte have clandestine relationships with white men. Wintergreen's husband, Jake, known to her patrons only as the bartender, is her silent partner, protector, and helpmate. Charlotte also enters into a sexual relationship with a white man, her boss, Sil Silverstein. Their unlikely relationship highlights the fact that the city places people who would otherwise not know each other into proximity, allowing for non-traditional and unexpected erotic attach-ments to develop.

By transforming urban space into an area of adult amusement, sexual recreation, gender play, and the breakdown of taboos, *Her* presents an expanded vision of Black female mobility, and its alter-native presentations of sexuality and gender create a political imper-ative to re-think African American urban migration history. *Her* is not alone as a Black lesbian text that challenges conventional per-spectives on Black history and culture. It joins a body of work pub-lished since the 1970s by African American women with explicitly lesbian themes, such as Ann Allen Shockley's *Loving Her* (1974) and

Say Jesus and Come to Me (1982); Gloria Naylor's *The Women of Brewster Place* (1982); Ntozake Shange's *Sassafrass, Cypress, & Indigo* (1982); Audre Lorde's *Zami, A New Spelling of My Name* (1982); and Jewelle Gomez's *The Gilda Stories* (1991). *The Serpent's Gift* by Helen Elaine Lee (1994); *Po Man's Child* (1999) by Marci Blackman; *Callaloo & Other Lesbian Love Tales* (1999) by LaShonda K. Barnett; and *The Bull-Jean Stories* (1998) and *love conjure/blues* (2004) by Sharon Bridgforth are only a few of such titles published in the U.S. after the publication of *Her*. Even though it stands in excellent company, as a novel, *Her* is unique in its confluence of style, language, setting, and characterization that establish it as not only a beautiful piece of writing, but also a novel which revises fixed sexual and gender categories, thereby disrupting definitions of Black identity and community.

Despite being enjoyed by readers, *Her* has yet to be thoroughly engaged by scholars. The newly-emerging field of Queer Studies is just beginning to practice the types of narrative interpretation employed in Ethnic Studies, and especially in African American cultural criticism. For me, teaching this novel (as well as those listed above) has provided me with an invitation to think about African American and African Diaspora literary studies in a new way. As Muhanji's novel is discovered by a new generation of readers, it hopefully will also be introduced to another generation of scholars who will keep making new insights about this rich and beautifully layered novel.

Mattie U. Richardson
University of Texas at Austin
Department of English
African and African American Studies
Women's and Gender Studies
August 2006

CHERRY MUHANJI

There is the rhythm of the mother, the suppressed poet, and the worker. There is the rhythm of the first-time college student at forty-six, the activist, and the budding prose writer. There is the dizzying rhythm toward the Master's in African American Studies; the rapid riffs necessary for an interdisciplinary Ph.D. in English, Anthropology, and African American Studies. There is the rhythm of the creative doctorate with a critical intro unique to the University Iowa[1] that culminated in a ho-hum novel that never wanted publishing.[2] But always, always there is the hum of the poet,[3] novelist,[4] and short story writer.[5] Threaded throughout this journey was the continuing bass line of travels to China, repeated trips to Cuba, a harrowing experience in Haiti, and an informative trip to Tijuana—where the rhythm of exploitation in the maquiladoras was palpable.

Suddenly, there was the "stopped time" of the professor/struggling to tutor sixth graders in Kansas City, for $65 a day.[6] But, always, always the working writer. Out from a sustained silence; a hush, the rhythm moved me through the Northwest where a creative/critical piece on jazz is published[7]—there the plot changed to the unsteady rhythm of a would-be playwright, with an effort entitled *miles and miles and miles of Miles* about Miles Davis, and a concert reader of plays—all this and an ongoing, despairing novel, *Detroit*, my hometown. I've come full circle.

—Strange rhythms these.

My life has been saved many times by writing.

---

[1] B.G.S., M.A., and Ph.D. (1985-1997)
[2] *Momma Played 1st Chair* (1997)
[3] "Testimony," *Bittersweet* (1985)
[4] *Her* (1990)
[5] *Tight Spaces* (1987), Before Columbus American Book Award
[6] Late 2000 till summer 2001
[7] "Soundtrack" (2003)

Aunt Lute Books is a multicultural women's press that has been committed to publishing high quality, culturally diverse literature since 1982. In 1990, the Aunt Lute Foundation was formed as a non-profit corporation to publish and distribute books that reflect the complex truths of women's lives and to present voices that are underrepresented in mainstream publishing. We seek work that explores the specificities of the very different histories from which we come, and the possibilities for personal and social change.

Please contact us if you would like a free catalog of our books or if you wish to be on our mailing list for news of future titles. You may buy books from our website, by phoning in a credit card order, or by mailing a check with the catalog order form.

Aunt Lute Books
P.O. Box 410687
San Francisco, CA 94141
415.826.1300
www.auntlute.com
books@auntlute.com

This book would not have been possible without the kind contributions of the Aunt Lute Founding Friends:

Anonymous Donor
Anonymous Donor
Rusty Barcelo
Marian Bremer
Marta Drury
Diane Goldstein

Diana Harris
Phoebe Robins Hunter
Diane Mosbacher, M.D., Ph.D.
Sara Paretsky
William Preston, Jr.
Elise Rymer Turner